QUENTIN DURWARD

QUENTIN DURWARD

by Walter Scott

ILLUSTRATED BY ERIC THOMAS
ABRIDGED BY MARYLYN ROBERTSON

General Editor: Grace Hogarth

COLLINS

William Collins Sons & Co Ltd
London · Glasgow · Sydney · Auckland
Toronto · Johannesburg · New York

Editor's note and illustrations
© 1972 Everyweek Educational Press Limited
First published by
William Collins Sons & Company Limited
1972
ISBN 0 00 184681 7

Made and printed in Great Britain by
William Collins Sons & Co. Ltd. Glasgow

Editor's Note

WALTER SCOTT (1771–1832) was a true Scotsman. He was descended from one of the Border clans that waged war—family against family—for generations. These wars were, of course, over by the time Scott lived but he loved the legends of Border warfare, and he had heard these told and retold round the fireside when he was a child. The stories stayed in his mind and he was so fascinated by them that, as a young man, he made many expeditions to the Border Country and studied its history at first hand. Eventually he became a lawyer in Edinburgh. Here, in a very literary society, it was natural that he should turn to writing them down, at first in narrative poems and then in novels, which were much better than the poetry. He became successful as a novelist, and famous in his own lifetime.

When we look at Scott's tremendous output during the years that he was writing, it is not surprising that the was a careless and rapid writer. Not only did he enjoy pouring out words, but circumstances finally forced him to do so. By 1826, he was involved in the ruin of a business in which he had become a partner. He had already put money into this enterprise and now he worked feverishly and heroically to pay off a tremendously heavy debt.

Quentin Durward was published in 1823, in three volumes, and it was the first novel he wrote which was not based on Scottish history. Perhaps by this time Scott had exhausted all the best subjects in his native country. At all events, he turned to France and to Louis XI for a new background. His hero was a young Scotsman who journeyed to Plessis les Tours to become a member of Louis' Scottish Archers of the Guard. Scott was obviously interested in the character of Louis XI and of his so different enemy, Charles the Bold of Burgundy, and used them to great advantage in the story. The book when first published was much crticized in Great Britain for its inaccuracy, and was not immediately popular. In France, however, its reception was most favourable and eventually, British readers came to accept it, too.

The novel *is* very inaccurate if judged as history. There is no doubt that Scott did take all manner of liberties with facts. As he acknowledged this in his introduction and made no pretence to historical accuracy, he deserves to be forgiven. Many of the incidents he describes actually happened but not at the time stated. He found it necessary to telescope and rearrange history in the interest of a first-rate story. He was not a historian but a novelist. He did try, as his letter show, to ascertain the details of background, but this was not always easy to do at the time that Scott lived. Even the castle of Plessis is wrongly set on a hill instead of in a valley. It was in vain that Scott, as his letters show, spent many hours with old geographical and statistical accounts, maps and gazetteers.

The success of *Quentin Durward* lies in the remarkable characterization of Louis XI, Charles, Duke of Burgundy, Galeotti, the Astrologer, and Phillipe a Comines, the Historian. While this characterization is not historically accurate, it is remarkably astute and gives motivation and colour to a fascinating story. The characters invented by Scott to round out the story are more lively than in many of his books, and they make *Quentin Durward* one of his most readable novels. As with all his romances, however, Scott has a tendency to be long-winded and to bury much of the story in pages of detailed description. This edition has been cut down to less than half its original length, but the author's words have not been changed, and every effort has been made to preserve the story quality.

G.H.

Contents

1. The Wanderer

IT was upon a summer morning some hundreds of years ago, that a youth, coming from Burgundy, approached the ford of a small river tributary to the Cher, near the royal Castle of Plessis-les-Tours, built two miles south of the fair town of that name, the capital of ancient Touraine, whose rich plain has been termed the Garden of France. The castle's dark battlements rose in the background over the extensive forest with which they were surrounded. On the bank of the brook opposite to that which the traveller was approaching, two men who appeared in deep conversation seemed to watch his motions. The age of the young traveller might be about nineteen, and his face and person, which were very prepossessing, did not, however, belong to the country in which he was now a sojourner. His short grey cloak and hose were rather of Flemish then of French fashion, while the smart blue bonnet, with a single sprig of holly and an eagle's feather, was already recognized as the Scottish headgear. He had at his back a satchel, which seemed to contain a few necessaries, a hawking

I

gauntlet on his left hand, though he carried no bird, and in his right a stout pole. Over his shoulder hung a small pouch of scarlet velvet, such as was then used by fowlers of distinction to carry their hawks' food. This was crossed by another shoulder-belt, to which was hung a hunting-knife.

Although his form had not yet attained its full strength, he was tall and active. His complexion was fair, in spite of a general shade of darker hue, with which the foreign sun, or perhaps constant exposure to the atmosphere in his own country, had, in some degree, embrowned it. His features, without being quite regular, were frank, open, and pleasing. A half smile, which seemed to arise from a happy exuberance of spirits, showed now and then; whilst his bright blue eyes, with a corresponding gaiety, had an appropriate glance for every object which they encountered, expressing good humour, lightness of heart, and determined resolution. He received and returned the salutation of the few travellers who frequented the road in those dangerous times, with the action which suited each; a fearless glance for the strolling spearman, half soldier, half brigand, a reverend greeting for the wandering pilgrim, or the begging friar, and with the dark-eyed peasant girl the interchange of a laughing good-morrow. In short, there was an attraction about his whole appearance not easily escaping attention, and which was derived from the combination of fearless frankness and good humour, with a handsome face and person.

The youth whom we have described had been long visible to the two persons who loitered on the opposite side of the small river which divided him from the park and the castle; but as he descended the rugged bank to the water's edge, the younger of the two said to the other, "It is our man—it is the Bohemian! If he attempts to cross the ford, he is a lost man—the water is up, and the ford impassable."

"Let him make that discovery himself, gossip," said the elder personage, "it may save a rope."

"I judge him by the blue cap," said the other, "for I cannot see

2

his face. Hark, sir—he halloos to know whether the water be deep."

"Nothing like experience in this world," answered the other, "let him try."

The young man in the meanwhile, receiving no hint to the contrary, entered the stream without further hesitation. The elder person, at the same moment, hallooed to him to beware, adding, in a lower tone, to his companion. "*Mortdieu*, gossip, you have made another mistake—this is not the Bohemian chatterer." But the intimation to the youth came too late. He either did not hear or could not profit by it, being already in the deep stream. To one less alert and practised in swimming, death had been certain for the brook was both deep and strong.

It was about the year 1468, when the feuds between France and Burgundy were at their highest though a dubious truce existed for the time between them, that the present narrative opens.

Now before the latter part of the fifteenth century France had to struggle for her very existence with the English, already possessed of her fairest provinces; while the utmost exertions of her King, and the gallantry of her people, could scarcely protect the remainder from a foreign yoke. Nor was this her sole danger. Her princes (in particular, the Duke of Burgundy) had no scruple in lifting the standard against their sovereign lord, the King of France, on the slightest pretence. When at peace, they reigned as absolute princes in their own provinces; and the House of Burgundy, possessed of the district so called, together with the richest part of Flanders, was itself so powerful as to yield nothing to the crown, either in splendour or strength.

Besides these evils, another, springing out of the long-continued wars between the French and English, added its misery to the kingdom. Numerous bands of soldiers, brave and successful adventurers, had been formed in various parts of France out of the refuse of other countries. These hireling combatants sold their swords for a time to the best bidder; and, when such service was not to be had, they made war on their own account, seizing castles and towers, making prisoners and ransoming them, and exacting tribute from the open villages around them. In the midst of the horrors arising from so distracted a state of public affairs, reckless expense distinguished the courts of the nobility; and their dependants, in imitation, expanded in magnificent display the wealth which they extorted from the people.

At this period, and as if to save the fair realm from the various miseries with which it was menaced, the throne was ascended by Louis XI, whose character, evil as it was in itself, combated, and in a great degree neutralized, the mischiefs of the time. Brave enough for every useful and political purpose, Louis had not a spark of that romantic valour generally associated with honour. Calm, crafty, and profoundly attentive to his own interest, he made every sacrifice of pride and passion which could interfere with it. He was careful in disguising his real sentiments and purposes, and frequently used the expression "that the king knew not how to reign, who knew not how to dissemble."

Yet there were contradictions in the character of this artful and able monarch. Himself the most insincere of mankind, some of the greatest errors of his life arose from too rash a confidence in the integrity of others. When these errors took place, they seem to have arisen from an over-refined system of policy, which induced Louis to assume the appearance of undoubting confidence in those whom it was his object to over-reach; for, in his general conduct, he was as suspicious as any tyrant who ever breathed. Two other points may be noticed, to complete the sketch of this formidable character; the first was Louis's excessive superstition, and the second a disposition to low pleasures and obscure debauchery. The wisest, or at least the most crafty sovereign of his time, he was fond of low life, and even mingled in the comic adventures of obscure intrigue with a freedom little consistent with the habitual and guarded jealousy of his character. Yet it was by means of this monarch's powerful and prudent, though most unamiable character that it pleased Providence to restore to the

4

great French nation the benefits of civil government, which, at the time of his accession, they had nearly lost.

Ere he succeeded to the crown, Louis had been an ungrateful and a rebellious son, levying open war against his father. For this offence, he was driven into exile, and forced to throw himself on the mercy, and most on the charity, of the Duke of Burgundy and his son, where he enjoyed hospitality, afterwards indifferently requited, until the death of his father in 1461. In the very outset of his reign, Louis was almost overpowered by a league formed against him by the great vassals of France, with the Duke of Burgundy and his son at its head. They levied a powerful army, blockaded Paris, fought a battle of doubtful issue under its very walls, and placed the French monarchy on the brink of actual destruction. Louis, who had shown great personal bravery during the battle of Montl'héry, now temporised and showed so much dexterity in sowing jealousies among the great powers that the enemy broke up their league and it was never again renewed in a manner so formidable. From this period, Louis, relieved of all danger from England by the Civil Wars of York and Lancaster, was engaged for several years, like an unfeeling but able physician, in curing the wounds of the body politic.

Still the King of France was surrounded by danger, especially from the increasing power of the Duke of Burgundy, one of the greatest Princes of Europe. Charles, surnamed the Bold, then wore the ducal coronet of Burgundy, which he burned to convert into an independent regal crown. The character of this Duke was in every respect the direct contrast to that of Louis XI. Duke Charles rushed on danger because he loved it, and on difficulties because he despised them. Notwithstanding the near relationship that existed between them, and the support which the Duke and his father had afforded to Louis in his exile when Dauphin, there was mutual contempt and hatred between them. The Duke of Burgundy despised the cautious policy of the King, and imputed to the faintness of his courage that he sought by leagues and other indirect means those advantages which, in his place, the Duke

5

would have snatched with an armed hand. He likewise hated the King because of the support which Louis afforded in secret to the discontented citizens of Ghent, Liège, and other great towns in Flanders. These turbulent cities, jealous of their privileges, and proud of their wealth, were frequently in a state of insurrection against their liege lord, the Duke of Burgundy, and never failed to find underhand countenance at the Court of Louis, who embraced every opportunity of fomenting disturbance within the dominions of his overgrown vassal.

The hatred of the Duke was retaliated by Louis with equal energy, though he used a thicker veil to conceal his sentiments. It was impossible for a man of his sagacity not to despise the Duke's headlong impetuosity. Yet the King feared Burgundy too. It was not alone the wealth of the Burgundian provinces, the discipline of the warlike inhabitants, and the mass of their crowded population, which the King dreaded, for the personal qualities of their leader had also much in them that was dangerous.

We left our soldier of fortune, the young Scot, swimming strongly against the current of the stream to the bank where the two men watched him. "By Saint Anne! but he is a proper youth," said the elder man, "Run, gossip, and help your blunder by giving him aid, if thou canst." He followed the younger man at a graver pace, saying to himself as he approached, "I knew water would never drown that young fellow.—By my halidome, he is ashore, and grasps his pole! If I make not the more haste, he will beat my gossip for the only charitable action which I ever saw him perform in the whole of his life."

There was some reason to augur such a conclusion of the adventure, for the Scot had already accosted the younger Samaritan: "Discourteous dog! why did you not answer when I called to know if the passage was fit to be attempted? May the foul fiend catch me, but I will teach you the respect due to strangers on the next occasion!" His opponent, seeing himself menaced, laid hand upon his sword; but his more considerate comrade, who came up, commanded him to forbear, and, turning to the young man, accused him in turn of intemperate violence in quarrelling with a young man who was hastening to his assistance. The young man, on hearing himself thus reproved by a man of advanced age and respectable appearance, immediately lowered his weapon, and said he would be sorry if he had done them injustice; but, in reality, it appeared to him as if they had suffered him to put his life in peril for want of a word of timely warning.

"Fair son," said the elder person, "you seem, from your accent, a stranger; and you should recollect your dialect is not so easily comprehended by us, as perhaps it may be uttered by you."

"Well, father," answered the youth, "I do not care much about the ducking I have had, and I will readily forgive your being partly the cause, provided you will direct me to some place where I can have my clothes dried; for it is my only suit, and I must keep it somewhat decent."

"For whom do you take us, fair son?" said the elder stranger, in answer to this question.

"For substantial burgesses, unquestionably," said the youth, "or, hold—you, master, may be a money-broker, or a corn-merchant; and this man a butcher."

"You have hit our capacities rarely," said the elder, smiling. "My business is indeed to trade in as much money as I can; and my gossip's dealings are somewhat of kin to the butcher's. As to your accommodation, we will try to serve you; but I must first know who you are, and whither you are going; for, in these times, the roads are filled with travellers who have anything in their head but honesty and the fear of God."

The young man cast a keen glance on him who spoke, and on his silent companion, as if doubtful whether they, on their part, merited the confidence they demanded; and the result of his observation was as follows. The eldest, and most remarkable of these men in dress and appearance, resembled the shopkeeper of the period. His jerkin, hose, and cloak were of a dark uniform colour, but worn so threadbare, that the acute young Scot con-

7

ceived that the wearer must be either very rich or very poor, probably the former. The expression of this man's countenance was partly attractive, partly forbidding. His strong features, sunk cheeks, and hollow eyes, had, nevertheless, an expression of shrewdness and humour congenial to the character of the young adventurer. But then, those same sunken eyes, from under the shroud of thick black eyebrows, had something in them that was at once commanding and sinister. Perhaps this effect was increased by the low fur cap, much depressed on the forehead, and adding to the shade from under which those eyes peered out; but it is certain that the young stranger had some difficulty to reconcile his looks with the meanness of his appearance in other respects. His cap, in particular, in which all men of any quality displayed either a brooch of gold or of silver, was ornamented with a paltry image, in lead. His comrade was a stout-formed, middle-sized man, more than ten years younger than his companion, with a down-looking visage and a very ominous smile. He was armed with a sword and dagger; and, underneath his plain habit, the Scotsman observed that he concealed a flexible shirt of linked mail, often worn by those who were called upon at that perilous period to be frequently abroad.

The young stranger, comprehending in one glance the result of this observation, answered after a moment's pause, "I am ignorant whom I may have the honour to address," making a slight reverence at the same time, "but I am indifferent who knows that I am a cadet of Scotland; and that I come to seek my fortune in France, or elsewhere, after the custom of my countrymen."

"*Pasques-dieu!* and a gallant custom it is," said the merchant, laughing. "But come, youngster, you are of a country I have a regard for, having traded in Scotland in my time; and, if you will come with us to the village, I will bestow on you a cup of burnt sack and a warm breakfast, to atone for your drenching.—But what do you with a hunting-glove on your hand? Know you not there is no hawking permitted in a royal chase?"

"I was taught that lesson," answered the youth, "by a rascally

8

forester of the Duke of Burgundy. I did but fly the falcon I had brought with me from Scotland at a heron near Peronne, and the rascal shot my bird with an arrow."

"What did you do?" said the merchant.

"Beat him," said the youngster, brandishing his staff.

"Know you," said the burgess, "that had you fallen into the Duke of Burgundy's hands, he would have hung you up like a chestnut?"

"Ay, I am told he is as prompt as the King of France for that sort of work. But, as this happened near Peronne, I made a leap over the frontiers, and laughed at him. If he had not been so hasty, I might perhaps have taken service with him."

The eldest man seemed like to choke with laughter at the lad's demeanour—his companion's hand stole to his sword-hilt, which the youth observing, dealt him a blow across the wrist, which made him incapable of grasping it; while his companion's mirth was only increased by the incident. "Hold," he cried, "most doughty Scot, for thine own dear country's sake; and you, gossip, forbear your menacing look. Let us be just traders, and set off the wetting against the knock on the wrist, which was given with so much grace and alacrity. And hark ye, my young friend," he said to the young man with a grave sternness, "no more violence. I am not fit object for it, and my gossip, as you may see, has had enough of it. Let me know your name."

"I can answer a civil question civilly," said the youth. "My name is Quentin Durward."

"Durward!" said the questioner, "is it a gentleman's name?"

"By fifteen descents in our family," said the young man, "and that makes me reluctant to follow any other trade than arms."

"A true Scot! Plenty of blood, plenty of pride, and great scarcity of ducats, I warrant thee.—Well, gossip," he said to his companion, "go before us, and tell them to have some breakfast ready at the Mulberry Grove. And for the Bohemian—hark in thy ear——" His comrade answered by a gloomy, but intelligent smile, and set forward at a round pace, while the elder man continued, addressing young Durward, "You and I will walk leisurely forward together, and we may take a mass at Saint Hubert's Chapel in our way through the forest; for it is not good to think of our fleshly before our spiritual wants."

Durward had nothing to object against this proposal, and they soon lost sight of their downward-looking companion, but continued to follow the same path which he had taken, until it led them into a wood of tall trees, through which were seen deer trotting in little herds in complete security. "You asked me if I were a good bowman," said the young Scot, "Give me a bow and a brace of shafts, and you shall have a piece of venison in a moment."

"*Pasques-dieu*! my young friend," said his companion, "take care of that; my gossip yonder hath the deer under his charge, and he is a strict keeper."

"He hath more the air of a butcher, than of a gay forester," answered Durward.

"Ah, my young friend," answered his companion, "my gossip hath somewhat an ugly favour to look upon at first; but those who become acquainted with him are never known to complain of him."

When mass was ended, they retired together from the chapel, and the elder said to his young comrade, "It is but a short walk from hence to the village—follow me." Proceeding along a path which seemed gradually to ascend, he recommended to his companion by no means to quit the track. Durward could not help asking the cause of this precaution. "You are now near the Court, young man," answered his guide; "and, *Pasques-dieu*! there is some difference betwixt walking in this region and on your own healthy hills. Every yard of this ground, excepting the path which we now occupy, is rendered dangerous by snares and traps armed with scythe-blades which shred off the unwary passenger's limb, and spikes that would pierce your foot through, and pit-falls deep enough to bury you in them for ever; for you are now within the royal precincts and we shall presently see the front of the Château."

"Were I the King of France," said the young man, "I would not take so much trouble with traps, but would try instead to govern so well that no man should dare to come near my dwelling with a bad intent."

His companion looked round affecting an alarmed gaze, and said, "Hush! I forgot to tell you that one great danger of these precincts is that the very leaves of the trees are like so many ears which carry all which is spoken to the King's own cabinet."

"I care little for that," answered Quentin Durward. "I bear a Scottish tongue in my head, bold enough to speak my mind to King Louis's face, God bless him."

While Durward and his new acquaintance thus spoke, they came in sight of the whole front of the Castle of Plessis-les-Tours, which, even in those dangerous times, when the great found themselves obliged to reside within places of fortified strength, was distinguished for the jealous care with which it was defended. There were three external walls, battlemented and turreted, around each of which, as the Frenchman informed his young companion, was sunk a ditch of about twenty feet in depth, supplied with water by a dam-head on the river. The verge of the outer and inner circuit of this triple moat was strongly fenced with palisades of iron, the top of each pale being divided into a cluster of sharp spikes. From within the innermost enclosure arose the Castle itself. The absence of any windows larger than shot-holes, irregularly disposed for defence, gave the spectator an unpleasant feeling, for the whole external front looked much more like that of a dark prison than a palace. This formidable place had but one entrance, with two strong towers, portcullis and drawbridge.

"And now tell me, young man," said Durward's companion, "did you ever see so strong a fortress, and do you think there are men bold enough to storm it?"

The young man looked long and fixedly on the place. "It is a strong castle, and strongly guarded; but there is no impossibility to brave men."

"Are there any in your country who could do such a feat?" said the elder, rather scornfully. "Perhaps you are yourself such a gallant?"

"I should sin if I were to boast where there is no danger," answered young Durward, "but my father has done as bold an act."

"Well," said his companion, smiling, "you might meet your match, and your kindred withal in the attempt; for the Scottish Archers of King Louis's Life-guards stand sentinels on yonder walls—three hundred gentlemen of the best blood in your country."

"And were I King Louis," said the youth, in reply, "I would trust my safety to the faith of the three hundred Scottish gentlemen, throw down my walls, call in my noble peers, and live as became me, amid breaking of lances in gallant tournaments, and feasting of days with nobles, and dancing of nights with ladies."

His companion again smiled, and turning his back on the Castle, led the way again into the wood. "This," he said, "leads us to the village of Plessis, where you will find reasonable accommodation."

"I thank you, kind master, for your information," said the Scot, "but my stay will be very short here."

"Nay," answered his companion, "I thought you had some friend to see in this quarter."

"And so I have—my mother's own brother," answered Durward.

"What is his name?" said the senior, "we will inquire him out for you."

"My uncle's name is Ludovic Lesly," said the young man.

"Of the three Leslys in the Scottish Guards," answered the merchant, "two are called Ludovic."

"They call my kinsman Ludovic with the Scar," said Quentin.

"The man you speak of," answered his companion, "we, I think, call *Le Balafré*, from that scar on his face—a good soldier.— And now, young man, answer me one question. I will wager you are desirous to take service with your uncle in the Scottish Guard. It is a great thing, if you propose so, especially as you are very

12

young, and some years' experience is necessary for the high office which you aim at."

"Perhaps I may have thought on some such thing," said Durward carelessly, "but if I did, the fancy is off."

"How so, young man?" said the Frenchman sternly.

"To speak plainly," said Quentin, "I should have liked the service of the French King full well; only I love the open air better than being shut up in a cage. Besides," he added, in a lower voice, "there grows a fair oak some flight-shot or so from yonder Castle—and on that oak hangs a man in a grey jerkin, such as this which I wear."

"That," said the man of France, "is the sign of our Sovereign's justice. If you live to be a loyal servant of your Prince, my good youth, you will know there is no perfume to match the scent of a dead traitor."

"Show me a living traitor," said the Scot, "and here are my hand and my weapon; but when life is out, hatred should not live longer.—But here, I fancy, we come upon the village; so, my good friend, to the hostelry, with all the speed you may. Yet, ere I accept your hospitality, let me know by what name to call you."

"Men call me Maitre Pierre," answered his companion.

In the meanwhile, they descended a narrow lane, at the bottom of which a gateway admitted them into the courtyard of an inn of unusual magnitude, for the accommodation of the nobles who had business at the neighbouring Castle, where very seldom, and only when such hospitality was altogether unavoidable, did Louis XI permit any of his Court to have apartments. A shield, bearing the *fleur-de-lys*, hung over the principal door of the large building; but there was about the yard none of the bustle which marked that business was alive, and custom plenty. It seemed as if the stern character of the royal mansion in the neighbourhood had communicated a portion of its gloom even to a place designed for merry society and good cheer.

2. Man-at-Arms

MAITRE PIERRE lifted the latch of a side door, and led the way into a large room, where a faggot was blazing on the hearth, and arrangements made for a substantial breakfast. He whistled, and the landlord entered and answered Maitre Pierre's *bon jour* with a reverence. "I expected a gentleman," said Maitre Pierre, "to order breakfast—Hath he done so?"

In answer, the landlord only bowed; and while he continued to bring and arrange upon the table the various articles of a comfortable meal, omitted to extol their merits by a single word. And yet the breakfast was admirable. There was a *paté de Perigord*, over which a gastronome would have wished to live and die, forgetful of kin, native country, and all social obligations whatever. Its vast walls of magnificent crust seemed raised like the bulwarks of some rich city, an emblem of the wealth which they are designed to protect. There was a delicate ragout, with just that spice of garlic which Gascons love, and Scotsmen do not hate. There was besides a delicate ham, and the most exquisite white bread, made into little round loaves of which the crust was so inviting, that, even with water alone, it would have been a delicacy. But the water was not alone, for there was a flask of exquisite *Vin de Beaulne.* So many good things might have created appetite under the ribs of death. What effect, then, must they have produced upon a youngster who had eaten little for the last two days? He threw himself upon the ragout, and the plate was presently vacant—he attacked the mighty pasty, marched deep into the bowels of the land, and, seasoning his enormous meal with an occasional cup of wine, returned to the charge, to the astonishment of mine host.

While thus engaged, Maitre Pierre's countenance expressed a kind of good-humour almost amounting to benevolence, which appeared remote from its ordinary severe character. And there was kindness too in the tone with which Quentin Durward reproached Maitre Pierre that he amused himself with laughing at his appetite, without eating anything himself.

"I am doing penance," said Maitre Pierre, "and may not eat anything before noon, save some comfiture and a cup of water.— Bid yonder lady," he added, turning to the innkeeper, "bring them hither to me." The innkeeper left the room, and Maitre Pierre proceeded, "Well, have I kept faith with you concerning the breakfast I promised you?"

"The best meal I have eaten," said the youth, "since I left Scotland."

"The Scottish Archers of the guard eat as good a one every day," said the old man. "They need not, like the Burgundians, choose a bare back that they may have a full belly—they dress like counts and feast like abbots."

"It is well for them," said Durward.

"And wherefore will you not take service here, young man? Your uncle might, I dare say, have you placed on the file when there should occur a vacancy. And, hark in your ear, I myself have some little interest, and might be of some use to you. You can ride, I presume, as well as draw the bow?"

"Our race are good horsemen, and I know not but I might accept of your kind offer. Yet, look you, food and raiment are needful things, but, in my case, men think of brave deeds of arms. Your King Louis—God bless him, for he is a friend and ally of Scotland—lies here in this castle, and gains cities and provinces by politic embassies, and not in fair fighting."

"Young man," said Maitre Pierre, "do not judge too rashly of the actions of sovereigns. Louis seeks to spare the blood of his subjects, and cares not for his own. He showed himself a man of courage at Montl'héry."

"Ay, but that was some dozen years ago," answered the youth. "I should like to follow a master that would keep his honour bright as his shield, and always venture foremost in the very throng of battle."

"Why did you not tarry at Brussels, then, with the Duke of Burgundy? He would put you in the way to have your bones broken every day; and, rather than fail, would do the job for you himself—especially if he heard that you had beaten his forester."

"Very true," said Quentin, "my unhappy chance has shut that door against me."

"Nay, there are plenty of dare-devils abroad, with whom mad youngsters may find service," said his adviser. "What think you of William de la Marck?"

"What!" exclaimed Durward, "serve the Wild Boar of Ardennes—a captain of pillagers and murderers, who slays priests and pilgrims? It would be a blot on my father's scutcheon for ever."

As he spoke, the door opened, and a girl rather above fifteen years old entered with a platter covered with damask on which was placed a small saucer of the dried plums which have always added to the reputation of Tours, and a cup of the curiously chased plate which the goldsmiths of that city were anciently famous for executing with great delicacy of workmanship. But the sight of the young person by whom this service was executed attracted Durward's attention far more; a quantity of long black

16

tresses, which, in the maiden fashion of his own country, were unadorned by any ornament, except a single chaplet lightly woven out of ivy leaves, formed a veil around her young and lovely countenance. Her dark eyes wore a pensive expression, though there was a faint glow on the cheek, and an intelligence on the lips and in the eye, which made it seem that gaiety was not foreign to a countenance so expressive, although it might not be its most habitual expression. Quentin's romantic imagination was pleased to infer, from what follows, that the fate of this beautiful vision was wrapped in silence and mystery.

"How now, Jacqueline!" said Maitre Pierre, when she entered the apartment. "Wherefore this? Did I not desire that Dame Perette should bring what I wanted—*Pasques-dieu!*—Does she think herself too good to serve me?"

"My kinswoman is ill at ease," answered Jacqueline, in a hurried yet a humble tone, "ill at ease, and keeps her chamber."

"She keeps it *alone*, I hope?" replied Maitre Pierre, with some emphasis.

Jacqueline turned pale at the answer of Maitre Pierre; for it must be owned, that his voice and looks had, when he expressed anger or suspicion, an effect both sinister and alarming. The chivalry of Quentin Durward was instantly awakened, and he hastened to approach Jacqueline, and relieve her of the burden she bore, and which she resigned to him, while, with a timid look, she watched the countenance of the angry burgess. Maitre Pierre proceeded, "I blame not thee, Jacqueline, and thou art too young to be—what it is pity to think thou must be one day—a false and treacherous thing, like the rest of thy giddy sex. No man ever lived to man's estate, but he had the opportunity to know you all. Here is a Scottish cavalier will tell you the same."

Jacqueline looked for an instant on the young stranger, as if to obey Maitre Pierre, but the glance, momentary as it was, appeared to Durward a pathetic appeal to him for support and sympathy; and he answered hastily, "That he would throw down his gage to any antagonist, of equal rank and age, who should presume to say such a countenance, as that which he now looked upon, could be animated by other than the purest and the truest mind."

The young woman grew deadly pale, and cast an apprehensive glance upon Maitre Pierre, in whom the bravado of the young gallant seemed only to excite scornful laughter: "You are a foolish young man," said Maitre Pierre, "and know as little of women as of princes—whose hearts," he said, crossing himself devoutly, "God keeps in His right hand."

"And who keeps those of the women, then?" said Quentin.

"I am afraid you must ask of them in another quarter," said Maitre Pierre composedly.

Quentin was again rebuffed. "Surely," he said to himself, "I do not pay this burgess of Tours all the deference which I yield him on account of the miserable obligation of a breakfast. But he is an extraordinary person; and that beautiful emanation that is even now vanishing—surely a thing so fair belongs not to this mean place, belongs not even to the money-gathering merchant himself, though he seems to exert authority over her, as doubtless he does over all whom chance brings within his little circle."

"This young man will serve me, Jacqueline—thou mayst withdraw. I will tell thy negligent kinswoman she does ill to expose thee to be gazed on unnecessarily," said Maitre Pierre.

"It was only to wait on you," said the maiden. "I trust you will not be displeased with my kinswoman, since——"

"*Pasques-dieu!*" said the merchant, interrupting her, but not harshly, "do you bandy words with me, or stay you to gaze upon the youngster here?—Begone—he is noble, and his services will suffice me." Jacqueline vanished. "That is a beautiful creature," said the old man, raising his head and looking steadily at Quentin, "a lovely girl to be the servant of an inn? She might grace the board of an honest burgess; but 'tis a vile education, a base origin."

Quentin was disconcerted, and was disposed to be angry—he himself knew not why—with this old man, for acquainting him that this beautiful creature was neither more nor less than what her occupation announced—the servant of the inn—an upper servant, indeed, and probably a niece of the landlord, or such like; but still a domestic, and obliged to comply with the humour of the customers, and particularly of Maitre Pierre, who probably had sufficiency of whims, and was rich enough to ensure their being attended to. The thought, the lingering thought, again returned on him, that he ought to make the old gentleman understand the difference between their conditions, and call on him to mark, that, how rich soever he might be, his wealth put him on no level with a Durward of Scotland. Yet, whenever he looked on Maitre Pierre's countenance with such a purpose, there was, notwithstanding the downcast look, pinched features, and mean and miserly dress, something which prevented the young man from asserting the superiority over the merchant which he conceived himself to possess. On the contrary, the oftener and more fixedly Quentin looked at him, the stronger became his curiosity to know who or what this man actually was; and he set him down internally for at least a Syndic or high magistrate of Tours, or one who was, in some way or other, in the full habit of exacting and receiving deference.

Meantime, the merchant signed to Quentin to give him the cup, adding, however, by way of question, as he presented it, "You are noble, you say?"

"I surely am," replied the Scot, "if fifteen descents can make me so. So I told you before. But do not constrain yourself on that account, Maitre Pierre—I have always been taught it is the duty of the young to assist the more aged."

"An excellent maxim," said the merchant, finishing his cup of water. He took a large purse from his bosom, made of the fur of the sea-otter, and streamed a shower of small silver pieces into the goblet, until the cup was more than half full. "Remain in this hostelry," said Maitre Pierre "until you see your kinsman, Le Balafré, who will be relieved from guard in the afternoon. I will cause him to be acquainted that he may find you here, for I have business in the Castle."

Quentin Durward would have said something to have excused

himself from accepting the profuse liberality of his new friend; but Maitre Pierre, bending his dark brows, and erecting his stooping figure into an attitude of more dignity than he had yet seen him assume, said, in a tone of authority, "No reply, young man, but do what you are commanded." With these words, he left the apartment, making a sign, as he departed, that Quentin must not follow him.

The young Scotsman stood astounded, and knew not what to think of the matter. He perhaps took the wisest resolution in the circumstances in resolving to be guided by the advice of his uncle; and, in the meantime, he put the money into his velvet hawking-pouch, and called for the landlord of the house, in order to restore the silver cup—resolving, at the same time, to ask him some questions about this liberal and authoritative merchant. The man of the house appeared presently but he positively declined to take back the beautiful silver cup. It was none of his, he said, but Maitre Pierre's, who had bestowed it on his guest.

"And pray, who is this Maitre Pierre," said Durward, "who confers such valuable gifts on strangers?"

"Who is Maitre Pierre?" said the host.

"Ay," said Durward, hastily and peremptorily. "And who is the butcherly-looking fellow whom he sent forward to order breakfast?"

"Why, fair sir, as to who Maitre Pierre is, you should have asked the question of himself; and for the gentleman who ordered breakfast to be made ready, may God keep us from his closer acquaintance!"

"This Maitre Pierre tells me he is a merchant," said the young Scot. "What commodities does he deal in?"

"Oh, many a fair matter of traffic," said the host, "and especially he has set up silk manufactories here. You might see the rows of mulberry-trees as you came thither, all planted by Maitre Pierre's commands, to feed the silk-worms."

"And that young person who brought in the confections, who is she, my good friend?" said the guest.

"My lodger, sir, with her guardian, some sort of aunt or kinswoman, I think," replied the innkeeper.

"And do you usually employ your guests in waiting on each other?" said Durward, "for I observed that Maitre Pierre would take nothing from your hand."

"Rich men may have their fancies, for they can pay for them," said the landlord. "This is not the first time that Maitre Pierre has found the true way to make gentlefolks serve at his beck." The young Scotsman felt somewhat offended at the insinuation; but, disguising his resentment, he asked whether he could be accommodated with an apartment. "Certainly," the innkeeper replied, "for whatever time he was pleased to command it."

"Could he be permitted," he asked, "to pay his respects to the ladies?"

The innkeeper was uncertain. "They went not abroad," he said, "and received no one at home."

"Carry to the ladies," Quentin said, "a flask of wine, with my humble duty; and say that Quentin Durward, a Scottish cavalier of honour, and now their fellow-lodger, desires the permission to dedicate his homage to them in a personal interview."

The messenger departed, and returned, almost instantly, with the thanks of the ladies, who declined the proffered refreshment, and with their acknowledgments to the Scottish cavalier, regretted that, residing there in privacy, they could not receive his visit.

Quentin bit his lip, took a cup of the rejected wine, which the host had placed on the table. "By the mass, but this is a strange country," said he to himself, "where merchants exercise the manners and munificence of nobles, and little travelling damsels keep their state like disguised princesses! I will see that black-browed maiden again, or it will go hard, however."

The landlord presently ushered him up a staircase, and from thence along a gallery into a turret-chamber. "I hope you will find your dwelling agreeable here, fair sir," said the landlord. "I am bound to pleasure every friend of Maitre Pierre."

"Oh, happy ducking!" exclaimed Quentin Durward, cutting a caper on the floor, so soon as his host had retired. "I have been fairly deluged by my good fortune."

As he spoke, he stepped towards the window, which commanded a pretty garden and a similar little window in another turret. The lattice was half open to admit the air, while the shutter was half closed to exclude the sun, or perhaps a too curious eye, and there hung on one side of the casement a lute, partly mantled by a light veil of seagreen silk. Our friend Quentin wished to learn a little more of his fair neighbour, the owner of the lute and veil, and he was interested to know whether she might not prove the same whom he had seen in humble attendance on Maitre Pierre. Durward peeped through the lattice and saw a white, round, beautiful arm take down the instrument. The maid of the little turret, of the veil, and of the lute, sang exactly such an air as we are accustomed to suppose flowed from the lips of the high-born dames of chivalry, when knights and troubadours listened and languished.

> Ah! County Guy, the hour is nigh,
>   The sun has left the lea,
> The orange flower perfumes the bower,
>   The breeze is on the sea.
> The lark, his lay who thrill'd all day,
>   Sits hush'd his partner nigh;
> Breeze, bird, and flower, confess the hour,
>   But where is County Guy?

This simple ditty had a powerful effect on Quentin, when married to heavenly airs, and sung by a sweet voice, the notes mingling with the gentle breezes which wafted perfumes from the garden, and the figure of the songstress being so partially visible, as threw a veil of mysterious fascination over the whole. At the close of the air, the listener could not help showing himself more boldly than he had yet done, in a rash attempt to see more than he had yet been able to discover. The music instantly ceased—the casement was closed, and a dark curtain, dropped on the inside, put a stop to all further observation on the part of the neighbour in the next turret. A moment later an attendant of the inn informed him that a cavalier desired to speak with him below.

The cavalier who awaited Quentin Durward's descent into the apartment where he had breakfasted, was one of those of whom Louis XI had long since said that they held in their hands the fortune of France, as to them was entrusted the protection of the royal person. Charles the Sixth had instituted this celebrated body, the Archers of the Scottish Body-Guard, with better reason than can generally be alleged for establishing round the throne a guard of foreign and mercenary troops. The divisions which tore from his side more than half of France, together with the wavering faith of the nobility who yet acknowledged his cause, rendered it impolitic to commit his personal safety to their keeping. The Scottish nation was the hereditary enemy of the English, and the ancient allies of France. They were poor, courageous and faithful and their high claims of descent, too, gave them a good title to approach the person of a monarch more closely than other troops, while the comparative smallness of their numbers prevented the possibility of their mutinying, and becoming masters where they ought to be servants.

The French monarchs made it their policy to conciliate the affections of this select band of foreigners, by allowing them honorary privileges and ample pay. They were sumptuously armed, equipped, and mounted; and each was entitled to allowance for a squire, a valet, a page, and two yeomen. With these followers, and a corresponding equipage, an Archer of the Scottish Guard was a person of importance; and vacancies being generally filled up by those who had been trained in the service as pages, the cadets of the best Scottish families were often sent to serve under some relation until a chance of preferment should occur.

Ludovic Lesly, or Le Balafré, as he was generally known in France, was upwards of six feet high, robust, strongly compacted in person, and hard-favoured in countenance, with a large and ghastly scar which, beginning on his forehead, and narrowly missing his right eye, had laid bare the cheek-bone. His dress and arms were splendid. He wore his national bonnet, crested with a tuft of feathers, and with a Virgin Mary of massive silver for a brooch. The Archer's mail-shirt was as clear and bright as the frostwork of a winter morning upon fern or brier. He wore a loose surcoat of rich blue velvet, with a large white St. Andrew's cross of embroidered silver. A broad strong poniard (called the *Mercy of God*) hung by his right side; he at present carried in his hand his two-handed sword which the rules of his service forbade him to lay aside. Quentin Durward thought he had never seen a more completely equipped and accomplished man-at-arms, yet he could not but shrink a little from the grim expression of his countenance, while he welcomed his nephew to France, and, in the same breath, asked what news from Scotland. "Little good tidings, dear uncle," replied young Durward "but I am glad that you know me so readily."

"Sit thee down—if there is sorrow to hear of, we will have wine to make us bear it." A flagon of champagne stood before them, of which the elder took a draught. "Come—unbuckle your Scottish mail-bag—give us the news of Glen-houlakin. How doth my sister?"

"Dead, fair uncle," answered Quentin sorrowfully.

"Dead!" echoed his uncle, with a tone rather marked by wonder than sympathy. "Why, she was five years younger than I, and I was never better in my life. And your father, fair nephew, hath he married again?"

"Alas! dear uncle, my mother was left a widow a year since, when Glen-houlakin was harried by the Ogilvies. My father, my two uncles, my two elder brothers, and seven of my kinsmen, the harper and some six more of our people, were killed in defending the castle; and there is not a burning hearth or a standing stone in all Glen-houlakin."

"Cross of Saint Andrew!" said Le Balafré, "that is what I call an onslaught! Ay, these Ogilvies were ever but sorry neighbours

to Glen-houlakin—an evil chance it was; but fate of war—fate of war."

"I fought it out among those who were older and stouter than I was, till we were all brought down," said Durward, "and I received a cruel wound, but they were tired at last, and my mother's entreaties procured mercy for me, when I was found to retain some spark of life; but although a learned monk, who chanced to be our guest at the fatal time, and narrowly escaped being killed in the fray, was permitted to bind my wounds, and finally to remove me to a place of safety, it was only on promise, given both by my mother and him, that I should become a monk."

"A monk!" exclaimed the uncle, "Holy Saint Andrew! that is what never befell me. So, fair nephew, you were to be a monk, then—and wherefore, I pray you?"

"That my father's house might be ended, either in the cloister or in the tomb," answered Quentin, with deep feeling.

"I see," answered his uncle. "Cunning rogues—very cunning!"

"I have little more to tell," said Durward, "except that, considering my poor mother to be in some degree a pledge for me, I was induced to take upon me the dress of a novice, and conformed to the cloister rules, and even learned to read and write."

"To read and write!" exclaimed Le Balafré. "I cannot believe it. Now, in Saint Louis's name, how did they teach it you?"

"It was troublesome at first," said Durward. "Then after several months' languishing, my good kind mother died, and as my health was now fully restored, I communicated to my benefactor, who was also Sub-Prior of the Convent, my reluctance to take the vows; and it was agreed between us, since my vocation lay not to the cloister, that I should be sent out into the world to seek my fortune, and that, to save the Sub-Prior from the anger of the Ogilvies, my departure should have the appearance of flight; and to colour it, I brought off the Abbot's hawk with me. But I was regularly dismissed, as will appear from the hand and seal of the Abbot himself."

"That is right—that is well," said his uncle. "Our King cares little what other theft thou mayst have made, but hath a horror at anything like a breach of the cloister. And, I warrant thee, thou hadst no great treasure to bear thy charges?"

"Only a few pieces of silver," said the youth, "for to you, fair uncle, I must make a free confession."

"Alas!" replied Le Balafré, "that is hard. But there is always wealth to be found, if a man has but the heart to seek it, at the risk of a little life or so, in the service of the good King of France."

"I understood," said Quentin, "that the Duke of Burgundy keeps a more noble state than the King of France, and that there is more honour to be won under his banners."

"You speak like a foolish boy, fair nephew," answered he with the Scar, "and yet when I came hither I was nearly as simple: I could never think of a King but what I supposed him feasting amid his Paladins with a great gold crown upon his head, or else charging at the head of his troops like Charlemagne. Hark in thine ear, man—it is all moonshine. Policy—policy does it all. It is an art this French King of ours has found out, to fight with other men's swords. Ah! it is the wisest Prince that ever put purple on his back—and yet he weareth not much of that neither—I see him often go plainer than I would think befitted me to do. But the Duke of Burgundy is a hot-brained, impetuous, pudding-headed, iron-ribbed dare-all."

"But is it true, as fame says, that this King keeps a meagre Court here at his Castle of Plessis? No nobles or courtiers in attendance, none of the high officers of the crown; secret councils, to which only low and obscure men are invited; all this resembles not the manners of his father, the noble Charles," said Quentin.

"You speak like a giddy child," said Le Balafré. "Look you: if the King employs Oliver Dain, his barber, to do what Oliver can do better than any peer of them all, is not the kingdom the gainer? If he bids his stout Provost-Marshal, Tristan, take off a turbulent noble, the deed is done and no more of it; when, were the commission given to a duke or peer of France, he might perchance send the King back a defiance in exchange. No, no, child, I tell thee Louis knows how to choose his confidants, and what to charge them with."

"But hark to the bell of Saint Martin's! I must hasten back to the Castle. Farewell—at eight tomorrow morning present yourself before the drawbridge, and ask the sentinel for me. You shall see the King, and learn to judge him for yourself—farewell." So saying, Balafré hastily departed, and Quentin resorted to a solitary walk along the banks of the rapid river Cher, reflecting on his interview with his uncle with a sense of disappointment. His hopes had been high; for a pilgrim, or a crippled soldier sometimes brought Lesly's name to Glen-houlakin, praising his undaunted courage. Quentin's imagination had filled up the sketch in his own way, and assimilated his successful and adventurous uncle (whose exploits probably lost nothing in the telling) to some of the champions of whom minstrels sang, and who won crowns and kings' daughters, by dint of sword and lance. He was now compelled to rank his kinsman greatly lower in the scale of chivalry, as an ordinary mercenary soldier, neither much worse nor greatly better than many of the same profession whose presence added to the distracted state of France.

Without being wantonly cruel, Le Balafré was, from habit, indifferent to human life and suffering; he was profoundly ignorant, greedy of booty, unscrupulous how he acquired it, and profuse in expending it on the gratification of his passions. Had his genius been of a more extended character he would probably have been promoted to some important command, for the King, who knew every soldier of his bodyguard personally, reposed much confidence in Balafré's courage and fidelity; but his capacity was too much limited to admit of his rising to higher rank, and though favoured by Louis on many occasions, Balafré continued a mere Lifeguardsman, or Scottish Archer.

Without seeing the full scope of his uncle's character, Quentin felt shocked at his indifference to the slaughter of his brother-in-law's whole family, and could not help being surprised, moreover, that so near a relative had not offered him the assistance of his purse, which, but for the generosity of Maitre Pierre, he would have been under the necessity of directly craving from him. (Not precisely needing money himself at that moment, it had not occurred to Balafré that his nephew might be in need.) Durward now regretted he had not had an opportunity to mention Maitre Pierre to Le Balafré, in the hope of obtaining some further account of that personage. "That old man," he thought to himself, "was crabbed in appearance, sharp and scornful in language, but generous in his actions; and such a stranger is worth a cold kinsman.—I will find out that man, which, methinks, should be no difficult task, since he is so wealthy as mine host bespeaks him. He will give me good advice for my governance, at least; and if he goes to strange countries, as many such do, I know not but his may be as adventurous a service as that of those Guards of Louis." As Quentin framed this thought, a whisper from the heart suggested that perchance the lady of the turret might share that adventurous journey.

On a slight eminence, rising above the beautiful river Cher, in the direct line of his path were two or three large chestnut trees, and beside them stood three or four peasants, motionless, with their eyes turned upwards, and fixed, apparently, upon some object amongst the branches of the tree next to them. Quentin hastened his pace, and ran lightly up the rising ground, time enough to witness the ghastly spectacle which attracted the notice of these gazers—which was nothing less than the body of a man, convulsed by the last agony, suspended on one of the branches.

"Why do you not cut him down?" said the young Scot, whose hand was as ready to assist affliction, as to maintain his own honour when he deemed it assailed. One of the peasants, turning on him a face as pale as clay, pointed to a mark cut upon the bark of the tree, having resemblance to a *fleur-de-lys*.

Neither understanding nor heeding this symbol, young Durward sprang lightly up into the tree, drew from his pouch the Highlander's trusty black knife, and, calling to those below to receive the body on their hands, cut the rope asunder in less than a minute. But his humanity was ill seconded by the bystanders. So far from rendering Durward any assistance, they seemed terrified at the audacity of his action, and took to flight with one consent. The body, unsupported from beneath, fell heavily to earth, the last sparks of life extinguished. Quentin gave not up his charitable purpose, however, without further efforts. He freed the wretched man's neck from the fatal noose, undid the doublet and threw water on the face.

While he was thus humanely engaged, a wild clamour of tongues, speaking a language which he knew not, arose around him; and he had scarcely time to observe that he was surrounded by several men and women of a singular and foreign appearance, when he found himself roughly seized by both arms, while a naked knife, at the same moment, was offered to his throat.

"Pale slave of Eblis!" said a man, in imperfect French, "are you robbing him you have murdered?" There were knives drawn on every side of him as these words were spoken, and the grim countenances which glared on him were like those of wolves rushing on their prey.

Still the young Scot's courage bore him out. "What mean ye, my masters?" he said; "if that be your friend's body, I have just now cut him down, in pure charity, and you will do better to try to recover his life, than to misuse an innocent stranger to whom he owes his chance of escape."

The women had by this time taken possession of the dead body, and seemed to abandon themselves to all the Oriental expressions of grief: wailing, and tearing their long black hair, while the men rent their garments and sprinkled dust upon their heads. Both male and female wore turbans and caps similar to his own bonnet and several of the men had curled black beards. One or two, who seemed their chiefs, had some tawdry ornaments of silver about their necks and in their ears, and wore showy scarfs of yellow or scarlet or light green; but their legs and arms were bare, and the whole troop seemed wretched and squalid in appearance. The disordered and yelling group were so different in appearance from any beings whom Quentin had yet seen that he was on the point of concluding them to be a party of Saracens, of those "heathen hounds," who were the opponents of gentle knights and Christian monarchs in all the romances which he had heard or read, when a galloping of horse was heard, and the supposed Saracens, who had raised by this time the body of their comrade upon their shoulders, were charged by a party of French soldiers.

This sudden apparition changed the measured wailing of the mourners into regular shrieks of terror. The body was thrown to the ground in an instant, and those who were around it showed the utmost activity in escaping from the point of the lances which were levelled at them, with exclamations of "Down with the accursed heathen thieves—take and kill!" Only two were struck down and made prisoners, one of whom was a young fellow with a sword who had previously offered some resistance. Quentin was at the same time seized by the soldiers, and his arms bound, those who apprehended him showing a readiness in the operation which proved them to be no novices in matters of police.

Looking anxiously to the leader of the horsemen, from whom he hoped to obtain liberty, Quentin recognized in him the silent companion of Maitre Pierre. "Trois-Eschelles and Petit-André," said the down-looking officer to two of his band, "these trees stand here quite convenient. I will teach these misbelieving, thieving sorcerers to interfere with the King's justice, when it has visited any of their accursed race. Dismount, my children, and do your office briskly." Trois-Eschelles and Petit-André were in an instant on foot, and Quentin observed that they had each, at the crupper and pommel of his saddle, a coil or two of ropes, which they hastily undid, and showed that, in fact, each coil formed a halter, with the noose adjusted, ready for execution. The blood ran cold in Quentin's veins when he saw three cords selected, and perceived that it was proposed to put one around his own neck. He called on the officer loudly, reminded him of their meeting that morning, claimed the right of a free-born Scotsman in an allied country, and denied any knowledge of the persons along with whom he was seized, or of their misdeeds. The officer whom Durward thus addressed took no notice whatever of his claim to prior acquaintance. He barely turned to one or two of the peasants who were now come forward, and said gruffly, "Was yonder young fellow with the vagabonds?"

"That he was, sir, and it please your noble Provostship," answered one of the clowns. "He was the first to cut down the rascal whom his Majesty's justice most deservedly hung up."

"It is enough that you have seen him meddle with the course of the King's justice by attempting to recover an executed traitor," said the officer, "Trois-Eschelles and Petit-André, despatch."

"Stay, signior officer!" exclaimed the youth, in mortal agony. "Hear me speak—my blood will be required of you by my countrymen in this world, and by Heaven's justice in that which is to follow."

"I will answer for my actions in both," said the Provost, coldly and made a sign with his left hand to the executioners; then, with a smile of triumphant malice, touched with his forefinger his right arm, which hung suspended in a scarf, disabled by the blow which Durward had dealt him that morning.

"Miserable, vindictive wretch!" answered Quentin, persuaded by that action that private revenge was the sole motive of this man's rigour, and that no mercy whatever was to be expected from him. The Provost rode on, followed by his guard, expecting two or three who were left to assist in the execution. The unhappy youth looked around him in agony, and was surprised, even in that moment, to see the stoical indifference of his fellow-prisoners, who were undaunted by the conduct of the executioners. Trois-Eschelles was a tall, thin man, with a peculiar gravity of visage, and a large rosary round his neck. Petit-André, on the contrary, was a round, active little fellow, who rolled about in execution of his duty as if it were the most diverting occupation in the world. I cannot tell why it was, but these two excellent persons, notwithstanding the variety of their talents, were more utterly detested than any other hangman in France, unless it were perhaps their master, Tristan l'Hermite, the renowned Provost-Marshal, or *his* master, Louis XI.

It must not be supposed that these reflections were of Quentin Durward's making. Life, death, time, and eternity were swimming before his eyes—an overwhelming prospect, from which human nature recoiled in its weakness, though human pride would fain have borne up. He addressed himself to the God of his fathers; and the executioners gently urged him forward to the fatal tree, bidding him be of good courage, for it would be over in a moment. The youth cast a distracted look around him. "Is there any good Christian who hears me," he said, "that will tell Ludovic Lesly of the Scottish Guard, called in this country Le Balafré, that his nephew is here basely murdered?"

The words were spoken in good time, for an Archer of the Scottish Guard, attracted by the preparations for the execution, was standing by to witness what was passing. "Take heed what you do," he said to the executioners "if this young man be of Scottish birth, I will not permit him to have foul play."

At these words of comfort, Quentin, exerting his strength, suddenly shook off both the finishers of the law, and, with his arms still bound, ran to the Scottish Archer. "Stand by me, countryman," he said in his own language, "for the love of Scotland and Saint Andrew! I am innocent—stand by me, as you shall answer at the last day!"

"By Saint Andrew! they shall make at you through me," said the Archer, and unsheathed his sword.

"Cut my bonds, countryman," said Quentin, "and I will detain them here, if I can.—Soldiers of the Provost's guard, stand to your arms."

Petit-André mounted his horse and left the field, and the other Marshals-men in attendance drew together so hastily at the command of Trois-Eschelles, that they suffered the other two prisoners to make their escape during the confusion. "We are strong enough to beat the proud Scots twice over, if it be your pleasure," said one of these soldiers to Trois-Eschelles.

33

But that cautious official made a sign to him to remain quiet, and addressed the Scottish Archer with great civility "Surely, sir, this is a great insult to the Provost-Marshal, that you should presume to interfere with the course of the King's justice."

"Tell me," said the Archer, "what has this young man done?"

"Interfered," answered Trois-Eschelles, with some earnestness, "to take down the dead body of a criminal, when the *fleur-de-lys* was marked on the tree where he hung with my own proper hand."

"How is this, young man?" said the Archer.

"As I desire your protection," answered Durward, "I will tell you the truth as if I were at confession. I saw a man struggling on the tree, and I went to cut him down out of mere humanity. I thought neither of *fleur-de-lys* nor of clove-gilliflower, and had no more idea of offending the King of France than our Father the Pope."

"What a murrain had you to do with the dead body, then?" said the Archer. "However, I will not quit a countryman's cause if I can help it.—Hark ye, Master Marshals-man, you see this is entirely a mistake. You should have some compassion on so young a traveller."

Petit-André returned at this moment. "Stand fast, Trois-Eschelles, for here comes the Provost-Marshal."

"And in good time," said the Archer, "here come some of my comrades." As the Provost Tristan rode up with his patrol on one side of the little hill, four or five Scottish Archers came as hastily up on the other, and at their head the Balafré himself. Upon this urgency, Lesly showed none of that indifference towards his nephew of which Quentin had in his heart accused him; for he no sooner saw his comrade and Durward standing upon their defence than he exclaimed, "Cunningham—gentlemen, lend me your aid. It is a young Scot—my nephew—draw, and strike in!"

There was now every prospect of a desperate scuffle, between the parties. But the Provost-Marshal made a sign to his followers to forbear from violence, while he demanded of Balafré, "What he, a cavalier of the King's Body Guard, purposed by opposing the execution of a criminal?"

"I deny that I do so," answered the Balafré. "Saint Martin! there is, I think, some difference between the execution of a criminal, and the slaughter of my own nephew?"

"Your nephew may be a criminal as well as another, Signior," said the Provost-Marshal; "and every stranger in France is amenable to the laws of France."

"Yes, but we have privileges, we Scottish Archers," said Balafré; "have we not, comrades?"

"Yes, yes," they all exclaimed together. "Privileges—privileges! Long live King Louis—long live the bold Balafré—long live the Scottish Guard—and death to all who would infringe our privileges!"

"But hear ye," said the Provost-Marshal, "this young fellow belongs not to you, and cannot share what you call your privileges."

"He is *my* nephew," said the Balafré, with a triumphant air.

"But no Archer of the Guard, I think," retorted Tristan l'Hermite. The Archers looked on each other in some uncertainty.

"Stand to it yet, comrade," whispered Cunningham to Balafré. "Say he is engaged with us."

"Saint Martin! You say well," answered Lesly; and, raising his voice, swore that he had that day enrolled his kinsman as one of his own retinue. This declaration was a decisive argument.

"It is well, gentlemen," said the Provost Tristan, who was aware of the King's nervous apprehension of disaffection creeping in among his Guards. "But I will report this matter for the King's own decision; and I would have you to be aware, that, in doing so, I act more mildly than perhaps my duty warrants me."

So saying, he put his troop into motion, while the Archers, remaining on the spot, held a hasty consultation what was next to be done. "We must report the matter to Lord Crawford, our Captain, in the first place, and have the young fellow's name put on the roll."

"But, gentlemen, and my worthy friends and preservers," said

Quentin, with some hesitation, "I have not yet determined whether to take service with you or no."

"Then settle in your own mind," said the uncle, "whether you choose to do so, or be hanged—for I promise you that I see no other chance of your 'scaping the gallows." This was an unanswerable argument, and reduced Quentin at once to acquiesce in what he might have otherwise considered as no very agreeable proposal; but the recent escape from the halter would probably have reconciled him to a worse alternative than was proposed. "He must go home with us to our barracks," said Balafré, "there is no safety for him out of our bounds whilst these man-hunters are prowling about. The Provost-Marshal smiled on us when we parted," continued he, addressing Cunningham, "and that is a sign his thoughts were dangerous."

"I care not for his danger," said Cunningham. "But I would have thee tell the whole to the Devil's Oliver, who is always a good friend to the Scottish Guard, and will see King Louis before the Provost can, for he is to shave him tomorrow."

"And now for the Chateau," said Balafré, "and my nephew shall tell us by the way how he brought the Provost-Marshal on his shoulders."

3. The Envoy

AN attendant upon the Archers having dismounted, Quentin Durward was accommodated with his horse, and, in company of his martial countrymen, rode towards the Castle of Plessis, about to become, although on his own part involuntarily, an inhabitant of that gloomy fortress, the outside of which had that morning struck him with so much surprise. At their approach the drawbridge fell. One by one they entered; but when Quentin appeared, the sentinels crossed their pikes, and commanded him to stand, while bows were bent, and harquebusses aimed at him from the walls—a rigour of vigilance used, notwithstanding that the young stranger came in company of a party of the garrison, nay, of the very body which furnished the sentinels who were then upon duty. Le Balafré, who had remained by his nephew's side on purpose, gave the necessary explanations, and, after some considerable delay, the youth was conveyed under a strong guard to the Lord Crawford's apartment.

This Scottish nobleman was one of the last relics of the gallant band of Scottish lords and knights who had so long and truly served Charles VI in those bloody wars which decided the independence of the French crown, and the expulsion of the English. He had fought, when a boy, abreast with Douglas, had ridden beneath the banner of the Maid of Arc, and now held high office in the household of Louis. His own frank and loyal character had gained a considerable ascendency over the King, who, though in general no ready believer in honour, trusted in that of Lord Crawford, and allowed him great influence. Balafré and Cunningham followed Durward and the guard to the apartment of their officer, by whose dignified appearance the young man was strongly impressed.

Lord Crawford was tall, and through advanced age had become gaunt, yet he was able to endure the weight of his armour during a march as well as the youngest man who rode in his band. He was hard-favoured, with a weather-beaten countenance, and an eye that had looked upon death as his playfellow in thirty pitched battles. He sat upon a couch covered with deer's hide, and with spectacles on his nose (then a recent invention), was reading a code of military and civil policy which Louis had compiled for his son the Dauphin.

Le Balafré, with great respect, stated at full length the circumstances in which his nephew was placed, and humbly requested his Lordship's protection. Lord Crawford listened attentively. "How often," he said, "must I tell you that the foreign soldier should bear himself modestly towards the people of the country, if you would not have the whole town at your heels? However, if you must have a fray, I would rather it were with that loon of a Provost than any one else; and it was but natural to help your young kinsman. Give me the roll of the company down from the shelf, and we will add his name to the troop, that he may enjoy the privileges.—There you stand, Quentin, in our honourable corps of Scottish Body-Guards, as esquire to your uncle, and serving under his lance. I trust you will do well—Ludovic, you will see that your kinsman follow his exercise diligently, for we will have spears breaking one of these days: the old banner will be soon dancing in the field again."

"I am glad of it, my Lord, and will drink a cup the deeper this evening to that very tune," said Balafré.

"I will send some wine to assist your carouse; but let it be over by sunset."

"Your Lordship shall be obeyed," said Ludovic, "and your health duly remembered."

"Perhaps," said Lord Crawford, "I may look in myself upon your mirth—just to see all is carried decently."

"Your Lordship shall be most welcome," said Ludovic; and the whole party retreated in high spirits to prepare for their military banquet, and invest the young recruit with the dress and appropriate arms of the Guard.

The banquet was joyous in the highest degree; Scottish songs were sung, old tales of Scottish heroes told and when their enthusiasm was at high flood, it received a new impulse from the arrival of Lord Crawford, who came to drink to the health of the gallant lad who had joined them this day. The pledge was filled, and answered with many a joyous shout, when the old leader proceeded to acquaint them that he had possessed Master Oliver of what had passed that day: "And as," he said, "the scraper of chins hath no great love for the stretcher of throats, he has joined me in obtaining from the King an order commanding the provost to suspend all proceedings against Quentin Durward; and to respect, on all occasions, the privileges of the Scottish Guard.

"Hark ye," said Lord Crawford, "ye are all true servants to the French crown, and wherefore should ye not know there is an envoy come from Duke Charles of Burgundy."

"I saw the Count of Crèvecoeur's horses and retinue," said another guest, "down at the inn yonder, the Mulberry Grove. They say the King will not admit him into the Castle."

"Now, Heaven send him an ungracious answer!" said Cunningham, "but what is it he complains of?"

39

"A world of grievances upon the frontier," said Lord Crawford. "And latterly, that the King hath received under his protection a lady of his land, a young Countess, who hath fled because, being a ward of the Duke, he would have her marry his favourite, Campo-basso."

"And hath she actually come hither alone, my lord?" said Cunningham.

"Nay, not altogether alone, but with the old Countess, her kinswoman."

"And will the King," said Cunningham, "interfere between the Duke and his ward?"

"The King will be ruled, as he is wont, by rules of policy; and you know," continued Crawford, "that he hath not publicly received these ladies, so, doubtless, he will be guided by circumstances."

"Well—Saint Andrew further the fray!" said Le Balafré. "I had it foretold me twenty years since that I was to make the fortune of my house by marriage!"

"For the lady, she is too wealthy to fall to a poor Scottish lord, or I would put in my own claim, fourscore years and all, or not very far from it. But here is her health, nevertheless, for they say she is a lamp of beauty," said Lord Crawford.

"I think I saw her," said another soldier, "when I was upon guard this morning, but she was more like a dark lantern than a lamp, for she and another were brought into the Chateau in close litters."

"But why should these litters contain this very same Countess Isabelle de Croye?" demanded Lord Crawford.

"Nay, my lord," replied the guard, "I know nothing of it save this, that my squire fell in with the muleteer who brought back the litters to the inn, for they belong to the fellow of the Mulberry Grove yonder—he of the Fleur-de-Lys, I mean—and he told him in secrecy, if it please your Lordship, that these two ladies whom he had conveyed up to the Castle in the close litters were great ladies, who had been living in secret at his master's house for some days, and that the King had visited them more than once privately, and had done them great honour; and that they had fled up to the Castle for fear of the Count de Crèvecoeur, the Duke of Burgundy's ambassador, whose approach was just announced by a courier."

"Then I will be sworn it was the Countess whose voice I heard singing to the lute, as I came even now through the inner court—such melody was there as no one ever heard before in the Castle of Plessis," said Cunningham.

"Hark! is not the Cathedral bell tolling to vespers?—One other draught to the weal of old Scotland, and then each man to his duty," said the commander. The parting-cup was emptied, and the guests dismissed.

Meanwhile, not a word that was spoken concerning the beautiful Countess Isabelle had escaped Durward, who, conducted into a small cabin, which he was to share with his uncle's page, made his lowly abode the scene of much high musing. At length the youth's reveries were broken in upon by the return of his uncle, who commanded Quentin to bed, that he might arise betimes in the morning, and attend him to his Majesty's antechamber.

The discipline of his father's tower, and of the convent of Aberbrothick, had taught Durward to start with the dawn; and he gaily put on the splendid dress and arms appertaining to his new situation amid the sounding of bugles and the clash of armour which announced the change of the vigilant guards on immediate attendance upon the person of Louis. His uncle looked with great accuracy and interest to see that he was completely fitted out in every respect: "Follow me to the presence-chamber," he said, and took up a partisan, large, weighty, and beautifully inlaid, and directing his nephew to assume a lighter weapon of a similar description, they proceeded to the inner-court of the palace, where their comrades were already drawn up, and under arms—the squires each standing behind their masters, to whom they thus formed a second rank. On a signal given, the Guards marched into the hall of audience, where the King was immediately expected.

With Lord Crawford, who was in attendance, dressed in the rich habit of his office, and holding a leading staff of silver in his hand, was the Count de Dunois, the son of the celebrated Dunois, known by the name of the Bastard of Orleans, who, fighting under the banner of Jeanne d'Arc, acted such a distinguished part in liberating France from the English yoke. Notwithstanding his connection with the royal family, and his hereditary popularity, both with the nobles and the people, Dunois had manifested such loyalty that he seemed to have escaped all suspicion, even on the part of Louis, who loved to see him near his person, and sometimes even called him to his councils.

Upon the arm of his relation Dunois, walking with a slow and melancholy step, came Louis Duke of Orleans, the first Prince of the blood royal (afterwards King, by the name of Louis XII). The jealously-watched object of Louis's suspicions, this Prince, who, failing the King's offspring, was heir to the kingdom, was not suffered to absent himself from Court. The dejection which his degraded and almost captive state naturally impressed on the unfortunate Prince, was at this moment greatly increased by his consciousness that the King meditated, with respect to him, one of the most unjust actions which a tyrant could commit, by compelling him to give his hand to the Princess Joan of France, the younger daughter of Louis, to whom he had been contracted in infancy, but whose deformed person rendered the insisting upon such an agreement an act of abominable rigour.

Very different was the bearing of the proud Cardinal, John of Balue, the favourite minister of Louis for the time, as he swept through the stately apartment in his crimson dress and rich cope to join the Prince and Dunois. "Is the King aware," said Dunois to the Cardinal, "that the Burgundian Envoy is peremptory in demanding an audience?"

"He is," answered the Cardinal, "and here comes the all-sufficient Oliver Dain to let us know the royal pleasure." As he spoke, a remarkable person, who then divided the favour of

Louis with the proud Cardinal himself, entered from the inner apartment, but without any of that consequential demeanour which marked the full-blown dignity of the churchman. On the contrary, this was a little, pale, meagre man, in a black silk jerkin and hose. He carried a silver basin in his hand, and a napkin flung over his arm indicated his menial capacity. His visage was penetrating and quick, although he endeavoured to banish such expression from his features by keeping his eyes fixed on the ground. But though modesty may easily obscure worth, it cannot hide court-favour. All attempts to steal unperceived through the presence-chamber were in vain, on the part of one known to have such possession of the King's ear as had been attained by his celebrated barber and groom of the chamber, Oliver le Dain, sometimes called Oliver le Diable from the unscrupulous cunning with which he assisted in the execution of his master's tortuous policy. At present he spoke earnestly for a few moments with Dunois, who instantly left the chamber. Ludovic Lesly, too, had the good fortune to be one of the individuals who, on the present occasion, were favoured by Oliver with a single word, to assure him that his matter was fortunately terminated.

Presently afterwards, he had another proof of the same agreeable tidings; for Quentin's old acquaintance, Tristan l'Hermite, the Provost-Marshal of the Royal Household, entered the apartment, and came straight to the place where Le Balafré was posted. This formidable officer's uniform, which was very rich, had only the effect of making his sinister countenance more strikingly remarkable. He regretted the mistake which had fallen between them on the preceding day, and observed it was owing to the Sieur Le Balafré's nephew not wearing the uniform of his corps, which had led him into the error for which he now asked forgiveness. Ludovic Lesly made the necessary reply, and as soon as Tristan had turned away, observed to his nephew that they had now the distinction of having a mortal enemy from henceforward in the person of this dreaded officer. "But a soldier," said he, "who does his duty, may laugh at the Provost-Marshal." Meanwhile Oliver again entered the inner apartment, the doors of which were thrown open, and King Louis entered the presence-chamber.

Quentin, like all others, turned his eyes upon him; and started so suddenly that he almost dropt his weapon when he recognized in the King of France that silk-merchant, Maitre Pierre, who had been the companion of his morning walk. Singular suspicions respecting the real rank of this person had at different times crossed his thoughts; but this, the proved reality, was wilder than his wildest conjecture.

The stern look of his uncle recalled him to himself; but not a little was he astonished when the King, whose quick eye had at once discovered him, walked straight to the place where he was posted, without taking notice of any one else. "So," he said, "young man, I am told you have been brawling on your first arrival in Touraine; but I pardon you, as it was chiefly the fault of a foolish old merchant, who thought your Scots blood required to be heated in the morning with *Vin de Beaulne*. If I can find him, I will make him an example to those who debauch my Guards. Balafré," he added to Lesly, "your kinsman is a fair youth, though fiery. We love to cherish such spirits, and mean to make more than ever we did of the brave men who are around us."

Le Balafré bowed to the ground. Quentin, in the meantime, recovered from his first surprise, studied the King's appearance more attentively. Louis, always a scorner of outward show, wore an old dark-blue hunting-dress, garnished with a huge rosary of ebony. But his eyes, now they were known to be those of an able and powerful monarch, seemed to have a piercing and majestic glance; and those wrinkles on the brow seemed now the furrows which sagacity had worn while toiling in meditation upon the fate of nations.

Presently after the King's appearance, the Princesses of France, with the ladies of their suite, entered the apartment. With the eldest, known in French history by the name of the Lady of Beaujeau, our story has but little to do. She was tall, and rather handsome, possessed eloquence, talent, and much of her father's

45

sagacity, who reposed great confidence in her, and loved her as well perhaps as he loved any one. The younger sister, the unfortunate Joan, the destined bride of the Duke of Orleans, advanced timidly by the side of her sister. She was pale, thin, sickly in her complexion, and very lame. Fine teeth, and eyes which were expressive of melancholy and resignation, with a quantity of light brown locks, were the only redeeming points which flattery itself could have dared to number to counteract the general homeliness of her face and figure.

The King (who loved her not) stepped hastily to her as she entered. "How now!" he said, "our world-condemning daughter. Are you robed for a hunting-party, or for the convent, this morning? Speak—answer."

"For which your highness pleases, sire," said the Princess, scarce raising her voice above her breath.

"No, fair daughter, I and another know your real mind better—Ha! fair cousin of Orleans, do we not? Approach, fair sir, and lead this devoted vestal of ours to her horse, and God's blessing and Saint Hubert's be on our morning sport!"

"I am, I fear, doomed to interrupt it, sire," said Dunois, "the Burgundian Envoy is before the gates of the Castle, and demands an audience."

"*Demands* an audience, Dunois?" replied the King. "Did you not answer him, as we sent you word by Oliver, that we were not at leisure to see him today?"

"This I said," answered Dunois; "but yet, sire——"

"*Pasques-dieu!* man, what is it that thus sticks in thy throat?" said the King.

"Your Grace," said Dunois, "I had more mind to have made him eat his own words, than to have brought them to your Majesty."

"Body of me, Dunois," said the King, "it is strange that thou, one of the most impatient fellows alive, shouldst have so little sympathy with the like infirmity in our blunt cousin, Charles of Burgundy."

46

"Know then, sire," replied Dunois, "that the Count of Crèvecoeur tarries below with his retinue, and says that since your Majesty refuses him the audience which his master has instructed him to demand upon matters of most pressing concern, he will remain there till midnight, and accost your Majesty at whatever hour you are pleased to issue from your Castle."

"He is a fool," said the King, with much composure. "Does the hot-head think it any penance for a man of sense to remain for twenty-four hours quiet within the walls of his Castle, when he hath the affairs of a kingdom to occupy him? Let the dogs be put up, and well looked to, gentle Dunois—we will hold council today, instead of hunting."

"My Liege," answered Dunois, "you will not thus rid yourself of Crèvecoeur; for his master's instructions are, that if he hath not this audience which he demands, he shall nail his gauntlet to the palisades before the Castle, in token of mortal defiance on the part of his master, shall renounce the Duke's fealty to France, and declare instant war."

"Ay," said Louis, frowning until his piercing dark eyes became almost invisible under his shaggy eyebrows, "is it even so?—will our ancient vassal prove so masterful? Nay then, Dunois, we must unfold the *Oriflamme*, and cry *Dennis Montjoye!*"

"Marry and amen, and in a most happy hour!" said the martial Dunois; and the guards in the hall, unable to resist the same impulse, stirred each upon his post, so as to produce a low but distinct sound of clashing arms. The King cast his eye proudly round, and, for a moment, thought and looked like his heroic father. But the excitement of the moment presently gave way to the host of political considerations which rendered an open breach with Burgundy perilous. Edward IV, a brave and victorious king, now established on the throne of England, was brother to the Duchess of Burgundy, and waited but a rupture between his near connection and Louis, to carry into France, through the gate of Calais, those arms which had been triumphant in the English civil wars. So that, after a pause, when Louis again spoke, it was with an altered spirit. "But God forbid," he said, "that aught less than necessity should make us cause the effusion of Christian blood, if anything short of dishonour may avert such a calamity. —Admit the Envoy of Burgundy to our presence."

A flourish of trumpets in the courtyard announced the arrival of the Count of Crèvecoeur, a renowned and undaunted warrior, who now entered the apartment.

"Approach, Seignior Count," said Louis. "What has Crèvecoeur to say in the words of Burgundy? Remember that in this presence Philip Crèvecoeur speaks to him who is his Sovereign's Sovereign."

Crèvecoeur bowed: "King of France, the mighty Duke of Burgundy once more sends you a written schedule of the wrongs committed on his frontiers by your Majesty's garrisons; the first point of inquiry is, whether it is your Majesty's purpose to make him amends for these injuries?"

The King, looking slightly at the memorial which the herald delivered to him upon his knee, said, "These matters have been already long before our Council. Many of the injuries complained of are affirmed without any proof. However we are not, as a Christian prince, averse to make satisfaction for wrongs actually sustained by our neighbour, though committed not only without our countenance, but against our express order."

"I will convey your Majesty's answer," said the ambassador, "to my most gracious master; yet, let me say, that, as it is in no degree different from the evasive replies which have already been returned to his just complaints, I cannot hope that it will afford the means of re-establishing peace and friendship between France and Burgundy."

"Be that at God's pleasure," said the King. "It is not for dread of thy Master's arms, but for the sake of peace only, that I return so temperate an answer to his injurious reproaches. Proceed with thine errand."

"My Master's next demand," said the ambassador, "is, that your Majesty will cease your underhand dealings with his towns of Ghent and Liege. He requests that your Majesty will recall the secret agents by whose means the discontents of his good citizens of Flanders are inflamed."

"Say to the Duke of Burgundy," replied the King, "that I know of no such indirect practices as those with which he charges me; that my subjects of France have frequent intercourse with the good cities of Flanders for the purpose of mutual benefit by free traffic, which it would be as much contrary to the Duke's interest as mine to interrupt. Proceed with your message."

"As formerly, Sire, with pain," replied the Count of Crèvecoeur; "the Duke of Burgundy further requires the King of France to send back to his dominions without delay Isabelle Countess of Croye, and her guardian the Countess Hameline. In respect the said Countess Isabelle being the ward of the said Duke of Burgundy, hath fled from his dominions, is here maintained in secret by the King of France, and by him fortified in her contumacy to the Duke, her natural lord and guardian, contrary to the laws of God and man, as they ever have been acknowledged in Europe."

"Count de Crèvecoeur," said Louis scornfully, "if it be your purpose to call me to account for the flight of every vassal whom your master's heady passion may have driven from his dominions, the bead-roll may last till sunset. Who can affirm that these ladies are in my dominions? Who can presume to say, if it be so, that I have received them with offers of protection?"

"Sire," said Crèvecoeur, "may it please your Majesty, I *was* provided with a witness on this subject—one who beheld these fugitive ladies in the inn called the Fleur-de-Lys, not far from this Castle—one who saw your Majesty in their company, though under the unworthy disguise of a burgess of Tours—one who received from them, in your royal presence, letters to their friends in Flanders—all which he conveyed to the Duke of Burgundy."

"Place the man before my face who dares maintain these palpable falsehoods," said the King.

"You speak in triumph, Sire; for you are well aware that this witness no longer exists. When he lived, he was called Zamet

Magraubin, by birth one of those Bohemian wanderers. He was yesterday executed by your Majesty's Provost-Marshal, to prevent, doubtless, his standing here to verify what he said of this matter to the Duke of Burgundy, in presence of his Council, and of me, Philip Crèvecoeur."

"We have had patience enough, and to spare," said the King, interrupting him, "and since thy sole errand here seems to be for the purpose of insult, we will send some one in our name to the Duke of Burgundy—convinced, in thus demeaning thyself towards us, thou hast exceeded thy commission."

"On the contrary," said Crèvecoeur, "I have not yet acquitted myself of it. Hearken, Louis of Valois, King of France—hearken, nobles and gentlemen—I, Philip Crèvecoeur, Count of the Empire, in the name of the most puissant Lord, Charles, by the Grace of God, Duke of Burgundy, Earl of Flanders, Count Palatine of Holland, do give you, Louis, King of France, openly to know, that you having refused to remedy the various offences wrought by you against the said Duke, he, by my mouth, renounces all allegiance to your crown—pronounces you false and faithless; and defies you as a Prince, and as a man. There lies my gage, in evidence of what I have said."

So saying, he plucked the gauntlet off his right hand, and flung it down on the floor of the hall. Until this climax of audacity, there was a deep silence in the royal apartment during the extraordinary scene; but at the clash of the gauntlet there was a general tumult: "Strike him down! Comes he here to insult the King of France in his own palace!" But the King appeased the tumult by exclaiming, in a voice like thunder: "Silence, my lieges! lay not a hand on the man, not a finger on the gage!—And you, Sir Count, of what is your life composed, or how is it warranted, that you thus place it on the cast of a die so perilous? Or is your Duke made of a different metal from other princes, since he thus asserts his pretended quarrel in a manner so unusual?"

"He is indeed framed of a different and more noble metal than the other princes of Europe," said the undaunted Count of

Crèvecoeur, "for, when not one of them dared to give shelter to you when you were yet only Dauphin, an exile from France, and pursued by the whole bitterness of your father's revenge, you were received like a brother by my noble master, whose generosity of disposition you have so grossly misused. Farewell, Sire, my mission is discharged." So saying, the Count de Crèvecoeur left the apartment abruptly, and without further leave-taking.

"After him—take up the gauntlet and after him!" said the King. "I mean not you, Dunois—My Lord Cardinal, it is your holy office to make peace among princes, do you lift the gauntlet, and remonstrate with Count Crèvecoeur on the sin he has committed in thus insulting a monarch in his own Court, and forcing us to bring the miseries of war upon his kingdom and that of his neighbour." Upon this appeal, Cardinal Balue proceeded to lift the gauntlet, with such precaution as one would touch an adder, and left the royal apartment to hasten after the challenger.

Louis paused and looked round the circle of his courtiers: "There is not one of you who knows not how precious every hour of peace is at this moment, when so necessary to heal the wounds of a distracted country; yet there is not one of you who would not rush into war on account of the tale of a wandering gipsy, or of some errant demosel, whose reputation, perhaps, is scarce higher. —Here comes the Cardinal, and we trust with more pacific tidings. How now, my Lord, have you brought the Count to reason?"

"Sire," said Balue, "my task hath been difficult——"

"But you prevailed with him to stay?" said the King.

"For twenty-four hours; and in the meanwhile to receive again his gage of defiance," said the Cardinal. "He has dismounted at the Fleur-de-Lys."

"See that he be nobly attended," said the King; "such a servant is a jewel in a prince's crown.—Twenty-four hours?" he added, muttering to himself, "'tis of the shortest. Yet twenty-four hours, skilfully employed, may be worth a year in the hand of incapable agents. Well—to the forest, my gallant lords!"

All the experience which the Cardinal had of his master's disposition, did not, upon the present occasion, prevent his falling into an error of policy: he could not help showing that he conceived himself to have rendered the King great and acceptable service. He pressed nearer to the King's person than he was wont to do, and endeavoured to engage him in conversation on the events of the morning. Now Louis was peculiarly averse to any one who seemed either to presume upon service rendered, or to pry into his secrets. Yet, hurried away by the self-satisfied humour of the moment, the Cardinal continued to ride on the King's right hand, turning the discourse whenever it was possible upon Crèvecoeur and his embassy; which, although it might be the matter at that moment most in the King's thoughts, was nevertheless precisely that which he was least willing to converse on.

And the King's horn rang merrily through the woods as he pushed forward on the chase, followed by two or three of his guards, amongst whom was our friend Quentin Durward. And here it was remarkable, that, even in the keen prosecution of his favourite sport, the King, in indulgence of his caustic disposition, found leisure to amuse himself by tormenting Cardinal Balue.

It was one of that able statesman's weaknesses that he affected great fondness for the martial amusement of the chase. Yet his gallant horse was totally insensible to the dignity of carrying a Cardinal, and paid no respect to him. The King knew this, and, by alternately exciting and checking his own horse, he brought that of the Cardinal, whom he kept close by his side, into such a state of mutiny against his rider that it became apparent they must soon part company; and then, in the midst of its lashing out, the royal tormentor rendered the rider miserable, by questioning him upon many affairs of importance, while each fresh rearing of his unmanageable horse placed Balue in a more precarious attitude, his robe flying loose in every direction.

Dunois laughed without restraint; while the King, enjoying his jest inwardly, mildly rebuked his minister on his eager passion for the chase which would not permit him to dedicate a few moments to business. "I will no longer be your hindrance to a course," continued he, addressing the terrified Cardinal, and giving his own horse the rein at the same time. Before Balue could utter a word by way of answer or apology, his horse, seizing the bit with his teeth, went forth at an uncontrollable gallop, soon leaving behind the King and Dunois, who followed at a more regulated pace, enjoying the statesman's distressed predicament. The horse galloped up a long green avenue, rode down the pack in hard pursuit of the boar, and carried the terrified Cardinal past the formidable animal itself. Balue, on beholding himself so near the boar, set up a dreadful cry for help and fell heavily to the ground.

The King, as he passed, said to Dunois, "Yonder lies his Eminence low enough—he is no great huntsman, though for a fisher (when a secret is to be caught) he may match Saint Peter himself. He has, however, for once, I think, met with his match." The Cardinal did not hear the words, but the scornful look with which they were spoken led him to suspect their general import. The momentary fright was over so soon as he had assured himself that his fall was harmless; but mortified vanity and resentment against his Sovereign had a much longer influence on his feelings.

After the chase had passed him, a single cavalier rode up with one or two attendants. To dismount and offer his assistance, to express surprise at the customs of the French Court, which thus permitted them to abandon in his needs their wisest statesman, were the natural modes of consolation which so strange a rencontre supplied to Crèvecoeur; for it was the Burgundian ambassador who came to the assistance of the fallen Cardinal. He found the minister in a lucky humour for essaying some of those practices on his fidelity, to which it is well known that Balue had the criminal weakness to listen. Already in the morning, more had passed betwixt them than the Cardinal durst have reported to his master, but it was not until this accident that, stung with wounded vanity, he resolved to show Louis that no enemy can be so dangerous as an offended friend. On the present occasion, he hastily requested Crèvecoeur to separate from him lest they should be observed, but appointed him a meeting for the evening in the Abbey of Saint Martin's at Tours, after vesper service.

In the meanwhile, Louis, who, though the most politic Prince of his time, upon this occasion had suffered his passions to interfere with his prudence, followed contentedly the chase of the wild boar, which was now come to an interesting point. It had so happened that a young boar had crossed the track of the proper object of the chase, and withdrawn in pursuit of him all the dogs (except two or three couple of old staunch hounds), and the greater part of the huntsmen. The King saw, with internal glee, Dunois, as well as others, follow upon this false scent, and enjoyed in secret the thought of triumphing over that accomplished knight. Louis was well mounted, and followed close on the hounds; so that, when the original boar turned to bay in a marshy piece of ground, there was no one near him but the King.

Louis showed all the bravery and expertise of an experienced huntsman; for, unheeding the danger, he rode up to the tremendous animal, which was defending itself with fury against the dogs, and struck him with his boar-spear; yet, as the horse shied from the boar, the blow was not so effectual as either to kill or disable him. No effort could prevail on the horse to charge a second time; so that the King, dismounting, advanced on foot against the furious animal, holding naked in his hand a short, straight sword. The boar instantly quitted the dogs to rush on his human enemy, while the King, taking his station, presented the sword with the purpose of aiming it at the boar's throat. But, owing to the wetness of the ground, the King's foot slipped, the point of the sword glanced off without making any impression, and Louis fell flat on the ground. Thus the animal missed his blow in his turn, and in passing only rent with his tusk the King's short hunting-cloak, instead of ripping up his thigh. But when the boar turned to repeat his attack, the life of Louis was in imminent danger.

At this critical moment, Quentin Durward, who had luckily distinguished and followed the blast of the King's horn, rode up, and transfixed the animal with his spear. The King, who had by

this time recovered his feet, came in turn to Durward's assistance, and cut the animal's throat with his sword. Before speaking a word to Quentin, he measured the huge creature by paces, wiped the blood from his hands, then took off his hunting-cap, hung it on a bush, and devoutly made his orisons to the little leaden images which it contained, and at length, looking upon Durward, said to him, "Is it thou, my young Scot? Thou hast begun thy woodcraft well, and Maitre Pierre owes thee as good entertainment as he gave thee at the Fleur-de-Lys yonder.—Why dost thou not speak? Thou hast lost thy forwardness and fire, methinks, at the Court, where others find both."

Quentin answered in few and well-chosen words that if he ventured to address his Majesty at all, it could be but to crave pardon for the rustic boldness with which he had conducted himself when ignorant of his high rank.

"Tush! man," said the King, "I forgive thy sauciness for thy spirit and shrewdness. Help me to my horse—I like thee, and will do thee good. Build on no man's favour but mine, and say nothing of thy timely aid in this matter of the boar."

The King then winded his horn which brought up Dunois and several attendants, whose compliments he received on the slaughter of such a noble animal without scrupling to appropriate a much greater share of merit than actually belonged to him.

"Now," said Louis, "who hath seen his Eminence my Lord Cardinal? Methinks it were but poor courtesy to Holy Church to leave him afoot here in the forest."

"May it please you, Sire," said Quentin, when he saw that all were silent, "I saw his Lordship the Cardinal accommodated with a horse, on which he left the forest—by the Ambassador of Burgundy, I think, and his people."

"Ha!" said Louis. "Well, be it so—France will match them yet." And the King, with his retinue, returned to the Castle.

4. The Politician

QUENTIN had hardly reached his little cabin in order to change, when his worthy relative required to know the particulars of all that had befallen him at the hunt. The youth took care in his reply to leave the King in full possession of the victory which he had seemed desirous to appropriate. Le Balafré's reply was a boast of how much better he himself would have behaved in the like circumstances, mixed with a gentle censure of his nephew's slackness. The youth had prudence to abstain from all further vindication of his own conduct. This discussion was scarcely ended when a low tap at the door announced a visitor and Oliver Dain entered the apartment. This able but most unprincipled man congratulated Lesly on the conduct of his young kinsman in the chase that day, which, he observed, had attracted the King's particular attention. He here paused for a reply and with his eyes fixed on the ground heard Balafré observe, "That his Majesty had been unlucky in not having himself by his side instead of his

A

nephew, as he would questionless have made in, and speared the brute, a matter which he understood Quentin had left upon his Majesty's royal hands, so far as he could learn the story."

"So, young man," said Master Oliver with an ambiguous smile, "is it the wont of Scotland to suffer Princes to be endangered for the lack of aid?"

"It is our custom," answered Quentin, determined to throw no further light on the subject, "not to encumber them with assistance in honourable pastimes, when they can aid themselves without it."

"Seignior Le Balafré," said Oliver, "you will be glad, doubtless, to learn that his Majesty is so far from being displeased with your nephew's conduct that he hath selected him to execute a piece of duty this afternoon."

"Selected *him*?" said Balafré, in great surprise. "Selected *me*, I suppose you mean?"

"I mean precisely as I speak," replied the barber, in a mild but decided tone, "the King hath a commission with which to entrust your nephew. Wherefore, young gentleman, get your weapons and follow me. Bring with you a harquebuss, for you are to mount sentinel."

"Sentinel!" said the uncle. "Are you sure you are right, Master Oliver? The inner guards of the Castle have ever been mounted by those only who have (like me) served twelve years in our honourable body."

"I am quite certain of his Majesty's pleasure," said Oliver, "and must no longer delay executing it."

"But," said Le Balafré, "my nephew is not even a free Archer, being only an Esquire, serving under my lance."

"Pardon me," answered Oliver, "the King sent for the register not half-an-hour since, and enrolled him among the Guard. Have the goodness to assist to put your nephew in order for the service."

Balafré, who had no ill-nature in his disposition, hastily set about giving him directions for his conduct under arms, but was unable to refrain from surprise at such luck chancing to fall upon the young man so early. "It had never taken place before in the Scottish Guard," he said, "not even in his own instance. But he was glad the lot had fallen on his fair nephew." Quick, and sharp of wit, Quentin could not but hug himself on having observed strict secrecy on the events of the chase, and formed a resolution that while he breathed the air of this mysterious Court, he would keep his tongue under the most careful regulation. His equipment was soon complete, and, with his harquebuss on his shoulder (for though they retained the name of Archers, the Scottish Guard very early substituted fire-arms for the long-bow, in the use of which their nation never excelled), he followed Master Oliver out of the barrack through a maze of stairs and vaults communicating with each other by secret doors into a spacious latticed gallery called Roland's Hall.

'You will keep good watch here," whispered Oliver. "Is your harquebuss loaded?"

"That," answered Quentin, "is soon done;" and proceeded to charge his weapon, and to light the slow-match (by which when necessary it was discharged) at the embers of a wood fire which was expiring in the huge hall chimney.

"Good watch!" thought the youthful soldier as his guide vanished through a side-door behind the arras. "Good watch! but upon whom, and against whom? Well, it is my duty, I suppose, and I must perform it." He tried to while away the time with some hymns he had learned in the convent in which he had found shelter after the death of his father. Presently, as if to convince himself he now belonged not to the cell but to the world, he chanted to himself some of the ancient ballads which the old family harper had taught him. This wore away a considerable space of time, but it was now more than two hours past noon, as Quentin was reminded by his appetite.

However, as the sentinel directed his solitary walk between the two entrances which formed the boundary of his duty, he was startled near one of those doors by a strain of music which was a combination of the same lute and voice by which he had been enchanted on the preceding day. He could not doubt, from the report of his uncle's comrades, and the scene which had passed in the presence-chamber that morning, that the siren who thus delighted his ears, was not, as he had profanely supposed, the daughter of an inn-keeper but the disguised Countess, for whose cause princes were now about to buckle on armour, and put lance in rest. A hundred wild dreams chased from his eyes the actual scene, and substituted their own bewildering delusions when at once, and rudely, they were banished by a rough grasp laid upon his weapon, and a harsh voice which exclaimed, "Ha! *Pasques-dieu*, Sir Squire, methinks you keep sleepy ward here!"

The voice was the impressive and ironical tone of Maitre Pierre, and Quentin, suddenly recalled to himself, saw, with shame and fear, that he had, in his reverie, permitted Louis himself to approach him so nearly as almost to master his weapon. The first impulse of his surprise was to free his harquebuss by a violent exertion, which made the King stagger. backward into the hall. His next to recover his harquebuss almost without knowing what he did, and, having again shouldered it, stand motionless before the Monarch, whom he had reason to conclude he had mortally offended. But Louis contented himself with saying, "Thy service of the morning hath already overpaid some negligence in so young a soldier. Hast thou dined?" Quentin, who rather looked to be sent to the Provost-Marshal than greeted with such a compliment, answered humbly in the negative. "Poor lad," said Louis in a softer tone than he usually spoke in, "hunger hath made him drowsy. I know thine appetite is a wolf," he continued, "and I will save thee from one wild beast as thou didst me from another; thou hast been prudent too in that matter, and I thank thee for it. Canst thou yet hold out an hour without food?"

"Four-and-twenty, Sire," replied Durward, "or I were no true Scot."

"I would not for another kingdom be the pasty which should encounter thee after such a vigil," said the King, "but the question now is, not of thy dinner, but of my own. I admit to my table this day, and in strict privacy, Cardinal Balue and this Burgundian— this Count de Crèvecoeur, and something may chance—the devil is most busy when foes meet on terms of truce. Thy duty must be to keep watch with thy loaded weapon and if there is treason, to shoot the traitor dead."

"Treason Sire! and in this guarded Castle!" exclaimed Durward.

"You think it impossible," said the King, not offended by his frankness. "Treason excluded by guards! Oh, thou silly boy!— who shall exclude the treason of those very warders?"

"Their Scottish honour," answered Durward boldly.

"True; most right—thou pleasest me," said the King cheerfully. "But treason! She sits at our feasts, she sparkles in our bowls, she wears the smiles of our courtiers—above all, she lies hid under the friendly air of a reconciled enemy. I will trust no one—no one. Hark ye; I will keep my eye on that insolent Count; ay, and on the Churchman too, whom I hold not too faithful. When I say, Forward Scotland, shoot Crèvecoeur dead on the spot."

"It is my duty," said Quentin, "your Majesty's life being endangered."

"Certainly—I mean it no otherwise," said the King. "I meditate no injury to these men—none. It would serve me nothing. They may not purpose equally fair by me. I rely on thy harquebuss."

"I shall be prompt at the signal," said Quentin, "but yet——"

"You hesitate," said the King. "Speak out—I give thee full leave."

"I would only presume to say," replied Quentin, "that your Majesty having occasion to distrust this Burgundian, I marvel that you suffer him to approach so near your person, and that in privacy."

"Oh, content you, Sir Squire," said the King. "When I walk boldly up to a surly mastiff and caress him, it is ten to one I soothe him to good temper; if I show fear of him, he flies on me and rends me. It concerns me nearly that this man returns not to his

61

headlong master in a resentful humour. I run my risk, therefore. I have never shunned to expose my life for the weal of my kingdom. Follow me." Louis led his young Life-guards-man, for whom he seemed to have taken a special favour, through the side-door by which he had himself entered into a small vaulted room, where a table was prepared for dinner with three covers. Behind a cupboard, and completely hidden by it, was the post which Louis assigned to Quentin Durward. "Remember the words, *Forward, Scotland*; and so soon as ever I utter these sounds, throw down the screen and be sure thou take good aim at Crèvecoeur. Oliver and I can deal with the Cardinal."

The King welcomed his visitors with such a degree of cordiality that Quentin was tempted to suppose either that the whole of his previous conversation with Louis had been a dream, or that the dutiful demeanour of the Cardinal, and the frank, open, and gallant bearing of the Burgundian noble, had entirely erased the King's suspicion. But whilst the guests, in obedience to the King, were in the act of placing themselves at the table, his Majesty darted one keen glance on them, and then instantly directed his look to Quentin's post. This was done in an instant; but the glance conveyed so much doubt and hatred towards his guests that no room was left for doubting that the apprehensions of Louis continued unabated. Yet appearing to have entirely forgotten the language which Crèvecoeur had held towards him in the face of his Court, the King conversed with him of old times, of events which had occurred during his own exile in the territories of Burgundy, and inquired respecting all the nobles with whom he had been then familiar, as if he retained towards all who had contributed to soften the terms of his exile, the kindest and most grateful sentiments.

"To an ambassador of another nation," he said, "I would have thrown something of state into our reception; but to an old friend who often shared my board, I wished to show myself, as I love best to live, old Louis of Valois, simple and plain. But I bid them have some care of our table. For our wine, you know, is the subject of an old emulation betwixt France and Burgundy, which we will presently reconcile; for I will drink to you in Burgundy, and you, Sir Count, shall pledge me in Champagne. Here, Count, I drink to the health of the noble Duke of Burgundy, our kind and loving cousin. Oliver, replenish yon golden cup and give it to the Count on your knee—he represents our loving brother. My Lord Cardinal, we will ourself fill your cup."

"You have already, Sire, even to overflowing," said the Cardinal.

"Because we know that your Eminence can carry it with a steady hand," said Louis. The Cardinal made a suitable answer, and Louis gave unrestrained way to the satirical gaiety of disposition which sometimes enlivened the darker shades of his character. In about an hour and a half the tables were drawn; and the King, taking courteous leave of his guests, gave the signal that it was his desire to be alone. So soon as all had retired, he called Quentin from his place of concealment. As he approached, he saw the light of assumed vivacity had left the King's eyes, and he exhibited all the fatigue of a celebrated actor when he has finished the exhausting representation of some favourite character upon the stage. "Thy watch is not yet over," said he to Quentin, "refresh thyself for an instant—yonder table affords the means. I will then instruct thee in thy further duty." He threw himself back on his seat, covered his brow with his hand, and was silent.

With patience, and not without a sense of amusement, the Monarch of France waited till his Life-guards-man had satisfied the keenness of a youthful appetite. "Take a cup of wine," said Louis. "And now wash speedily—forget not thy *bénédicité*, and follow me." Quentin obeyed, and followed Louis into the Hall of Roland. "Take notice," said the King imperatively, "thou hast never left this post—let that be thine answer to thy kinsman and comrades—and, hark thee, to bind the recollection on thy memory, I give thee this gold chain" (flinging on his arm one of considerable value). "And now attend. No man, save Oliver or I myself, enters here this evening. But ladies will come hither—

hearken to what they say. Thine ears, as well as thy hands, are mine. It will be best that thou pass for a Scottish recruit who hath come straight down from his mountains, and hath not yet acquired our language; this will lead them to converse without regard to your presence. You understand me. Farewell. Be wary, and thou hast a friend."

The King had scarce spoken these words ere he disappeared behind the arras, leaving Quentin to meditate on what he had seen and heard. The Lady of the Lute was certainly one of those to whom his attention was to be dedicated; and well in his mind did he promise to obey one part of the King's mandate, and listen with diligence to every word that might drop from her lips. But with as much sincerity did he swear to himself that no part of her discourse should be reported by him to the King which might affect the fair speaker otherwise than favourably.

At length a door opened, and a female figure entered. By her imperfect and unequal gait, Quentin at once recognized the Princess Joan, drew himself up in a fitting attitude of silent vigilance and lowered his weapon to her as she passed. She acknowledged the courtesy by a gracious inclination of her head as two ladies entered from the upper end of the apartment. One of these was the young person, who, upon Louis's summons, had served him with fruit while Quentin made his memorable breakfast at the Fleur-de-Lys. Invested now with all the dignity belonging to the heiress of a rich earldom, her beauty made ten times the impression upon him that it had done before. He now wondered what could ever have concealed from him her real character. Yet her dress was nearly as simple as before, being a suit of deep mourning, without any ornaments. Had death been the penalty, Durward must needs have rendered to this beauty and her companion the same homage which he had just paid to the royalty of the Princess. They received it as those who were accustomed to deference and returned it with courtesy.

The companion of the youthful Countess, dressed like herself simply, and in deep mourning, was at the age when women are apt to cling most closely to that reputation for beauty which has for years been diminishing, but it was evident from her manner that she had not relinquished the pretensions to future conquests. She was tall and graceful, though somewhat haughty in her deportment.

The Princess Joan had stood still in order to receive the stranger ladies; and as she was somewhat embarrassed in receiving and repaying their compliments, the elder stranger, ignorant of the rank of the party whom she addressed, was led to pay her salutation in a manner rather as if she conferred than received an honour through the interview. "I rejoice, madam," she said, "that we are at length permitted the society of such a respectable person of our own sex as you appear to be. I must say that my niece and I have had but little for which to thank the hospitality of King Louis. Nay, niece, never pluck my sleeve—I am sure I read in the looks of this young lady sympathy for our situation. Since we came hither, fair madam, we have been used little better than mere prisoners; and after a thousand invitations to throw our cause and our persons under the protection of France, the Most Christian King has afforded us at first but a base inn for our residence, and now a corner of this moth-eaten palace."

"I am sorry," said the Princess falteringly, "that we have been unable, hitherto, to receive you according to your deserts. Your niece, I trust, is better satisfied?"

"Much—much better than I can express," answered the youthful Countess. "I sought but safety, and I have found solitude and secrecy besides."

"Silence, my silly cousin," said the elder lady. "I must own there is nothing I have regretted more than taking this French journey. I looked for a splendid reception, and instead all has been seclusion and obscurity! The best society whom the King introduced to us was a Bohemian vagabond, by whose agency he directed us to correspond with our friends in Flanders. Perhaps," said the lady, "it is his politic intention to mew us up here until our lives' end, that he may seize on our estates after the extinction of the ancient house of Croye. The Duke of Burgundy was not so cruel; he offered my niece a husband, though he was a bad one."

"I should have thought the veil preferable to an evil husband," said the Princess, with difficulty finding opportunity to interpose a word.

"One would at least wish to have the choice, madam," replied the voluble dame. "It is, Heaven knows, on account of my niece that I speak; for myself, I have long laid aside thoughts of changing my condition. I see you smile, but, by my halidome, it is true— yet that is no excuse for the King, whose conduct, like his person, hath more resemblance to a money-changer of Ghent than to the successor of Charlemagne."

"Hold!" said the Princess, with some asperity in her tone. "Remember you speak of my father."

"Of your father!" replied the Burgundian lady in surprise.

"Of my father," repeated the Princess, with dignity. "I am Joan of France. But fear not, madam," she continued, in the gentle accent which was natural to her, "you designed no offence, and I have taken none. Command my influence to render your exile more supportable. Alas! it is but little I have in my power; but it is willingly offered."

Deep and submissive was the reverence with which Countess Hameline de Croye, so was the elder lady called, received the offer of the Princess's protection. She would have exhausted herself in expressing regret, had she not been put to silence by the Princess, who requested, in the most gentle manner, yet which, from a Daughter of France, had the weight of a command, that no more might be said in the way either of excuse or of explanation.

The Princess Joan then took her own chair with dignity and compelled the two strangers to sit, one on either hand. They spoke together, but in such a low tone that the sentinel could not over-hear their discourse. The conversation of the ladies had not lasted a quarter of an hour when the door at the lower end of the hall opened, and a man entered shrouded in a riding-cloak. Deter-mined not to be a second time caught slumbering, Quentin instantly moved towards the intruder, and, interposing between him and the ladies, requested him to retire instantly. "By whose command?" said the stranger, in a tone of contemptuous surprise.

"By that of the King," said Quentin firmly, "which I am placed here to enforce."

"Not against Louis of Orleans," said the Duke, dropping his cloak. The young man hesitated a moment; but how enforce his orders against the first Prince of the blood, about to be allied, as the report now generally went, with the King's own family?

"Your Highness," he said, "is too great that your pleasure should be withstood by me. I trust your Highness will bear me witness that I have done my duty, so far as your will permitted."

"You shall have no blame, young soldier," said Orleans; and passing forward, paid his compliments to the Princess, with that air of constraint which always marked his courtesy when addressing her. She hastened to present the Prince to the two ladies of Croye, who received him with the respect due to his eminent rank; and the Duke, taking a cushion from one of the settles, laid it at the feet of the beautiful young Countess of Croye and so seated himself, that, without appearing to neglect the Princess, he was enabled to bestow the greater share of his attention on her lovely neighbour. Soon his praises of Countess Isabelle's beauty flowed with such unrestrained freedom, owing perhaps to his having drunk a little more wine than usual, that at length he seemed almost impassioned, and the presence of the Princess appeared well-nigh forgotten. The younger Countess listened to the Duke's gallantries with embarrassment, and turned an entreating look towards the Princess, as if requesting her to come to her relief. But the wounded feelings, and the timidity of Joan of France, rendered her incapable of an effort to make the conversation more general. At length the Countess Isabelle made a determined effort to cut short what was becoming intolerably disagreeable to her, especially from the pain to which the conduct of the Duke was apparently subjecting the Princess. Just then the King himself entered the Gallery and sent a keen look on all around: "You here, my fair cousin of Orleans," he said, and turning to Quentin, added sternly, "Had you not charge?"

"Forgive the young man, Sire," said the Duke, "he did not neglect his duty; but I was informed that the Princess was in this gallery."

"And I warrant you would not be withstood when you came hither to pay your court," said the King, with detestable hypocrisy. "Lend Joan your arm to her apartment, while I will conduct these strange ladies to theirs." The King's tone made it a command, and Orleans accordingly made his exit with the Princess at one extremity of the gallery, while the King, ungloving his right hand, courteously handed the Countess Isabelle and her kinswoman to their apartment, which opened from the other. He bowed profoundly as they entered, then, with great composure, shut the door by which they had retired, and turning the huge key, took it from the lock and put it into his girdle. Louis now paced towards Quentin Durward. "Thou hast done wrong," said the King, "thou hast done foul wrong, and deservest to die. Speak not a word in defence! What hadst thou to do with Dukes or Princesses? What with *anything* but my order?"

"So please your Majesty," said the young soldier, "what could I do?"

"What is the use of that weapon on thy shoulder?" answered the King scornfully. "Thou shouldst have levelled thy piece, and if the presumptuous rebel did not retire on the instant, he should have died within this very hall. Go—send Oliver Dain to me— do thou begone to thy quarters."

Well pleased to escape so easily, yet with a soul which revolted at the cold-blooded cruelty which the King seemed to require from him in the execution of his duty, Durward hastened downstairs, and communicated the royal pleasure to Oliver. The wily barber bowed, and they parted, Quentin to his quarters, and Oliver to attend the King.

When the favourite attendant entered Roland's Gallery, Oliver found the King pensively seated upon the chair which his daughter had left some minutes before. The Monarch's first address was an unpleasant one: "So, Oliver, your fine schemes are melting like snow before the south wind! So much for thy fond romantic advice that I, of all men, should become a protector of distressed damsels! I tell thee, Burgundy is arming, and on the eve of closing an alliance with England. Singly, I might cajole or defy them; but united, united!—All thy fault, Oliver, who counselled me to receive the women, and to use the services of that damned Bohemian to carry messages to their vassals."

"My liege," said Oliver, "you know my reasons. The Countess's domains lie between the frontiers of Burgundy and Flanders —her castle is almost impregnable—her rights over neighbouring estates are such as, if well supported, cannot but give much annoyance to Burgundy, were the lady but wedded to one who should be friendly to France."

"It *is* a tempting bait," said the King, "and could we have concealed her being here, we might have arranged such a marriage for this rich heiress as would have highly profited France.—But that cursed Bohemian, how couldst thou recommend such a heathen hound for a commission which required trust? And these ladies—not only does Burgundy threaten us with war for harbouring them, but their presence is like to interfere with my projects in my own family. My simple cousin of Orleans hath barely seen this damsel, and I venture to prophesy that the sight of her is like to make him less pliable in the matter of his alliance with Joan."

"Your Majesty," said the counsellor, "may send the ladies of Croye back to Burgundy, and so make your peace with the Duke. Many might murmur at this as dishonourable; but if necessity demands the sacrifice——"

"If profit demanded the sacrifice, Oliver, the sacrifice should be made without hesitation," answered the King. "But I cannot relinquish the advantages which our scheme of marrying the maiden to a friend of our own house seems to hold out to us, planting a friend to ourselves, and an enemy to Burgundy in the very centre of his dominions, and so near to the discontented cities of Flanders."

"Your Majesty," said Oliver, "might confer her hand on some right trusty friend, who would take all blame on himself, and serve your Majesty secretly, while in public you might disown him."

"And where am I to find such a friend?" said Louis. "Were I to bestow her upon any one of our mutinous nobles, would it not be rendering him independent? And hath it not been my policy for years to prevent them from becoming so?—Dunois indeed—him, and him only I might trust. He would fight for the crown of France, whatever were his condition. But honours and wealth change men's natures. Even Dunois I will not trust."

"Your Majesty may find others," said Oliver, in his smoothest manner, "men dependent entirely on your own grace and favour, men who——"

"Men who resemble thyself, ha!" said King Louis. "No, Oliver, because I indulge thee with my confidence, dost thou think it makes thee fit to be a Count?—thee, I say, low-born and lower bred, whose wisdom is at best a sort of cunning, and whose courage is more than doubtful?"

"Your Majesty imputes to me a presumption of which I am not guilty, in supposing me to aspire so highly," said Oliver.

"I am glad to hear it, man," replied the King. "But methinks thy speech sounded strangely in that key. Well, to return, I dare not wed this beauty to one of my subjects. I dare not return her to Burgundy—I dare not transmit her to England, or to Germany, where she is likely to become the prize of someone more apt to unite with Burgundy than with France, and who would be more ready to discourage the honest malcontents in Ghent and Liege, than to yield them that wholesome countenance which might always find Charles the Hardy enough to exercise his valour on, without stirring from his own domains. The men of Liege, well supported, would find my fair cousin work for more than a twelvemonth, and backed by a warlike Count of Croye—Oh,

Oliver! Cannot thy fertile brain devise some scheme?"

Oliver paused for a long time, then at last replied, "What if a bridal could be accomplished betwixt Isabelle of Croye, and young Adolphus, the Duke of Gueldres?"

"What!" said the King, in astonishment, "sacrifice her to that furious wretch! No, Oliver, no—that were too unutterably cruel even for you and me. Besides, he is detested by the people of Ghent and Liege. No, no—think of some one else."

"My invention is exhausted, Sire," said the counsellor. "I can remember no one who, as husband to the Countess of Croye, would be likely to answer your Majesty's views. He must unite such various qualities—a friend to your Majesty—an enemy to Burgundy—of policy enough to conciliate the men of Ghent and Liege, and of valour sufficient to defend his little dominions against the power of Duke Charles. Of noble birth besides—that your Highness insists upon; and of virtuous character to boot!"

"Nay, Oliver," said the King, "I leaned not so much—that is, so *very* much, on character; but methinks Isabelle's bridegroom should be something less publicly and generally abhorred than Adolphus of Gueldres. For example, since I myself must suggest some one, why not William de la Marck?"

"Sire," said Oliver, "I cannot complain of your demanding too high a standard of moral excellence in the happy man, if the Wild Boar of Ardennes can serve your turn. De la Marck? Why, he is the most notorious robber and murderer on all the frontiers—excomminicated by the Pope for a thousand crimes."

"We will have him released from the sentence, friend Oliver—Holy Church is merciful."

"Almost an outlaw," continued Oliver, "and under the ban of the Empire."

"We will have the ban taken off, friend Oliver," said the King.

"And admitting him to be of noble birth," said Oliver, "he hath the manners, the face and the heart of a Flemish butcher. She will never accept of him."

"His mode of wooing, if I mistake him not," said Louis, "will render it difficult for her to make a choice."

"But how is he to meet with his bride?" said the counsellor, "Your Majesty knows he dare not stir far from his own Forest of Ardennes."

"In the first place," said the King, "the two ladies must be acquainted privately that they can be no longer maintained at this Court, except at the expense of a war between France and Burgundy, and that, unwilling to deliver them up to my fair cousin of Burgundy, I am desirous they should secretly depart from my dominions."

"They will demand to be conveyed to England," said Oliver, "and we shall have her return to Flanders with an island lord, having a round fair face, long brown hair, and three thousand archers at his back."

"No, no," replied the King, "to the safety of the Church alone we will venture to commit her; and the utmost we can do is to connive at the Ladies Hameline and Isabelle de Croye departing in disguise, and with a small retinue, to take refuge with the Bishop of Liege, who will place the fair Isabelle for the time under the safeguard of a convent."

"And if that convent protect her from William de la Marck, I have mistaken the man."

"Why, yes," answered the King, "thanks to our secret supplies of money, De la Marck hath together a handsome handful of outlawed soldiery, with which he contrives to maintain himself among the woods in such a condition as makes him formidable both to the Duke of Burgundy and the Bishop of Liege. He lacks nothing but some territory which he may call his own; and this being so fair an opportunity to establish himself by marriage, I think that, *Pasques-dieu*! he will find means to win and wed, without more than a hint on our part. I must determine the ladies of Croye to a speedy and secret flight, under sure guidance. This will be easily done—we have but to hint the alternative of surrendering them to Burgundy. Thou must find means to let

William de la Marck know of their motions, and let him choose his own time and place to push his suit. I know a fit person to travel with them."

"May I ask to whom your Majesty commits such an important charge?" asked the barber.

"To a foreigner, be sure," replied the King, "one who knows too little of the country, and its factions, to suspect more of my purpose than I choose to tell him—in a word, I design to employ the young Scot who sent you hither but now."

Oliver paused in a manner which seemed to imply a doubt of the prudence of the choice, and then added, "Your Majesty has reposed confidence in that stranger boy earlier than is your wont."

"I have my reasons," answered the King. "Thou knowest my devotion for the blessed Saint Julian. I had been saying my orisons to that holy Saint late in the night before last; mine eyes were no sooner closed than the blessed Saint Julian was visible to me, leading a young man whom he presented to me, saying that his fortune should be to escape the sword, the cord, the river, and to bring good fortune to the side which he should espouse, and to the adventures in which he should be engaged. I walked out on the succeeding morning, and I met this youth, whose image I had seen in my dream. In his own country he hath escaped the sword, amid the massacre of his whole family, and here, within two days, he hath been strangely rescued from drowning and from the gallows, and hath already been of the most material service to me. I receive him as sent hither by Saint Julian, to serve me in the most difficult, dangerous and desperate services. I have had his horoscope cast, besides, by Galeotti, and I have learned that this unfriended youth has his destiny under the same constellation with mine."

His favourite looked at him with an expression of sarcastic contempt which he scarce attempted to disguise, but whatever Oliver might think of the causes thus boldly assigned for the preference of an inexperienced stripling, he dared make no further objections. He therefore only replied that he trusted the young

Durward would prove faithful in the discharge of a task so delicate.

"We will take care he hath no opportunity to be otherwise," said Louis, "for he shall be privy to nothing save that he is sent to escort the Ladies of Croye to the residence of the Bishop of Liege. Of the probable interference of William de la Marck he shall know as little as they themselves. None shall know that secret but the guide; and Tristan must find one fit for our purpose."

"But in that case," said Oliver, "the young man is like to stand to his arms so soon as the Wild Boar comes on them, and may not come off so easily from the tusks as he did this morning."

"It skills as little that the messenger is slain after his duty is executed, as that the flask is broken when the wine is drunk out," said Louis composedly. "Meanwhile, we must expedite the ladies' departure, and then persuade Crèvecoeur that it has taken place without our connivance; we having been desirous to restore them to the custody of our fair cousin, which their sudden departure has unhappily prevented."

He parted with his counsellor and went to the apartment of the Ladies of Croye. Few persuasions would have been necessary to determine their retreat from the Court of France upon the first hint that they might not be eventually protected against the Duke of Burgundy; but it was not so easy to induce them to choose Liege for the place of their retreat. They requested to be transferred to Calais, where, under protection of the King of England, they might remain in safety until the Sovereign of Burgundy should relent in his rigorous purpose towards them. But this did not at all suit the plans of Louis, and he was at last successful in inducing them to adopt that which did coincide with them.

The power of the Bishop of Liege for their defence was not to be questioned, since his ecclesiastical dignity gave him the means of protecting the fugitives against all Christian princes. The difficulty was to reach the little Court of the Bishop in safety; but for this Louis promised to provide, by spreading a report that the Ladies of Croye had escaped from Tours by night, under fear of being delivered up to the Burgundian Envoy, and had taken their

flight towards Brittany. He also promised them the attendance of a small, but faithful retinue. The Ladies of Croye were so far from objecting to the hasty departure which Louis proposed that they even anticipated his project by entreating to be permitted to set forward that same night.

Adventure might be said to crowd upon the young Scot with the force of a springtide; for he was speedily summoned to the apartment of his Captain, Lord Crawford, where, to his astonishment, he again beheld the King. After a few words respecting the trust which was about to be reposed in him, Quentin was delighted with hearing that he was selected, with the assistance of four others under his command, one of whom was a guide, to escort the Ladies of Croye to the Court of their relative, the Bishop of Liege, in the most secret manner possible. A scroll was given him in which were set down directions for his guidance. He was to sustain the personage of the Steward of two English ladies of rank, who had been to Saint Martin of Tours, and were about to visit the holy city of Cologne, for the Ladies of Croye were to journey under the character of pilgrims. Quentin Durward's heart leapt for joy at the idea of approaching thus nearly the Beauty of the Turret, and in a situation which entitled him to her confidence, since her protection was in so great a degree entrusted to his conduct and courage. Louis, however, had not yet done with him. That cautious Monarch had to consult a counsellor of a different stamp from Oliver le Diable, and therefore led the way, followed by the impatient Quentin, to a separate tower of the Castle of Plessis, in which was installed in no small ease and splendour the celebrated astrologer and philosopher, Galeotti Martius.

The apartments of this courtly sage were far more splendidly furnished than any which Quentin had yet seen in the royal palace; and the magnificence displayed in the tapestries showed the elegant taste of the learned Italian. A rich Turkey carpet and a variety of mathematical and astrological instruments, all of the most rich materials and curious workmanship, were gifts of the

Emperor of Germany and the reigning Pope. The whole apartment formed a very impressive scene and the effect was increased by the manners and appearance of the individual himself, who, seated in a huge chair, was employed in curiously examining a specimen, just issued from the Frankfort press, of the newly invented art of printing. Galeotti Martius was a tall, bulky man, considerably past his prime, dressed in rich Genoa velvet lined with sables. He rose and bowed to the King.

"Tell me, Galeotti," said Louis, "hast thou proceeded further in the horoscope which I sent to thee? I have brought the party hither since the matter is pressing."

The bulky Sage arose from his seat, and, approaching the young soldier, fixed on him his keen large dark eyes, "Look up and be not afraid, but hold forth thy hand." When Galeotti had inspected his palm he led the King some steps aside. "My royal brother," he said, "all promises that this youth, though rash, will be brave and fortunate."

"And faithful?" said the King, "for valour and fortune square not with fidelity."

"And faithful also," said the Astrologer. "But yet——"

"But what?" said the King. "Father Galeotti, wherefore do you now pause? My youth was one of exile and suffering, and my ears are used to harsh counsel and take no offence at it."

"Then plainly, Sire," replied Galeotti, "if you have aught in your purposed commission, which—which, in short, may startle a scrupulous conscience—entrust it not to this youth."

"Be assured, good father, that whatever there may be in our commission, of the nature at which you have hinted, the execution shall not be entrusted to this youth, nor shall he be privy to such part of our purpose."

"In this," said the Astrologer, "you will walk wisely, Sire."

"Will this next midnight be a propitious hour in which to commence a perilous journey?" said the King.

"To him who *sends forth* the expedition," said the Astrologer, after a pause, "the stars do indeed promise success; but, methinks, that Saturn being combust, threatens violence and captivity to the party *sent*—the errand may be perilous, or even fatal, to those who are to journey."

The King paused, without giving any further indication how far this presaging speech (probably hazarded by the Astrologer from his conjecture that the commission related to some dangerous purpose) squared with his real object, which was to betray the Countess Isabelle of Croye into the hands of William de la Marck, a nobleman indeed of high birth, but degraded by his crimes into a leader of banditti, distinguished for his ferocious bravery.

The King then pulled forth a paper from his pocket and proceeded to read from it: "A person having on hand a weighty controversy is desirous, for the present, to seek accommodation by a personal interview with his antagonist. He desires to know what day will be propitious for the execution of such a purpose; also what is likely to be the success of such a negotiation, and whether his adversary will be moved to answer the confidence thus reposed in him with gratitude and kindness, or may rather be likely to abuse the opportunity which such meeting may afford him?"

"It is an important question," said Galeotti, "and requires that I should give it deep consideration."

"Let it be so, my good father in the sciences, and thou shalt know what it is to oblige a King of France. We are determined, if the constellations forbid not, to hazard something, even in our own person, to stop these anti-Christian wars."

"May the Saints forward your Majesty's pious intent," said the Astrologer, "and guard your sacred person!"

"Thanks, learned father. Here is something, the while, to enlarge your curious library." Louis, economical even in his superstitions, placed under one of the volumes a small purse of gold, and turned to address Durward. "Follow me," he said, "my bonny Scot, as one chosen by Destiny and a Monarch to accomplish a bold adventure."

Thus saying, the King left the apartment, followed by his young guardsman; and no sooner were they gone, than the Astrologer gave way to very different feelings from those which seemed to animate him during the royal presence. "The niggardly slave!" he said, weighing the purse in his hand. "But maybe there is some pearl of price concealed in this paltry case—I have heard he can be liberal when it suits his caprice or interest." He emptied the purse, which contained ten gold pieces. The indignation of the Astrologer was extreme. "Ten pieces! A pittance!—I will discover or contrive some remedy." So saying, the indignant Sage nevertheless plunged the contemned pieces of gold into a large pouch which he wore at his girdle: "Cardinal Balue is politic and liberal —this query shall to him, and it shall be his Eminence's own fault if the stars speak not as he would have them."

5. The Guide

AVOIDING all conversation with any one (for such was his charge), Quentin Durward proceeded hastily to array himself as might become an officer in a noble household. Oliver acquainted him that his uncle had been summoned to mount guard, purposely that he might make no inquiries. "Your excuse will be made to your kinsman," said Oliver, smiling. He added to his fair words a small purse of gold to defray necessary expenses on the road as a gratuity on the King's part. At a few minutes before midnight, Quentin, according to his directions, proceeded to the second courtyard, and found at this place of rendezvous the armed men appointed to compose the retinue, leading two mules loaded with baggage, and holding three palfreys for the two Countesses and Marthon, their waiting-woman; and a stately war-horse for himself, whose steel-plated saddle glanced in the pale moonlight. Not a word of recognition was spoken on either side. The men were only three in number; but one of them whispered to Quentin, in a strong Gascon accent, that their guide was to join them beyond Tours. At length a small door was unclosed, and three females came forth, attended by a man wrapped in a cloak. They mounted in silence the palfreys which stood prepared for them, while their attendant on foot led the way and gave the pass-words to the watchful guards whose posts they passed in succession. Thus they at length reached the exterior of these formidable barriers. Here the man on foot who had hitherto acted as their guide retreated through the barrier-gate, while Quentin thought, by the moon-glimpse, that he recognized in him the King himself.

When the riders were beyond the Castle, it was necessary for some time to ride with great precaution, in order to avoid pitfalls. The Gascon was, however, completely possessed of the clue to this labyrinth, and in a quarter of an hour's riding they found themselves beyond the limits of Plessis le Parc, and not far distant from the city of Tours. The moon shed a full sea of glorious light upon the landscape. Quentin saw with delight the princely Loire rolling through the richest plain in France between banks ornamented with towers and terraces, olives and vineyards. But he was recalled to the business of the moment by the voice of the elder lady demanding to speak with the leader of the band. Spurring his horse forward, Quentin respectfully presented himself to the ladies. "What was his name?" asked the Lady Hameline. He told it. "Was he perfectly acquainted with the road?"

"He could not," he replied, "pretend to much knowledge of the route, but he was furnished with full instructions, and he was, at their first resting-place, to be provided with a guide. Meanwhile, a horseman who had just joined them was to be their guide for the first stage."

"And wherefore were you selected for such a duty?" said the lady. "You seem young and inexperienced for such a charge."

"I am bound to obey the commands of the King, madam, but am not qualified to reason on them," answered the young soldier.

"And are you not," said the younger lady, addressing him in her turn, "the same whom I saw when I was called to wait upon the King at yonder inn?" Quentin answered in the affirmative. "Then, methinks, my cousin," said Lady Isabelle, addressing the Lady Hameline, "we must be safe under this young gentleman's guard; he looks not, at least, like one to whom the execution of a plan of treacherous cruelty upon two helpless women could be with safety entrusted."

"On my honour, madam," said Durward, "I could not, for France and Scotland rolled into one, be guilty of treachery or cruelty towards you!"

"You speak well, young man," said Lady Hameline, "but we are accustomed to hear fair speeches from the King of France and his agents. It was by these that we were induced to seek refuge in France. And in what did the promises of the King result? In an obscure and shameful concealing of us, under plebeian names, in yonder paltry hostelry."

"I would that had been the sorest evil, dear kinswoman," said Lady Isabelle. "I could gladly have dispensed with state—with all—for a safe and honourable retirement. God knows I never wished to occasion war betwixt France and my native Burgundy, or that lives should be lost for such as I am. I only implored permission to retire to a convent."

"You spoke then like a fool, my cousin," answered the elder lady, "and not like a daughter of my noble brother."

Quentin, with natural politeness, dreading lest his presence might be a restraint on their conversation, rode forward to join the guide. The moon had by this time long been down, and dawn was beginning to spread bright in the east. Quentin cast his eye on the person whom he rode beside, and, under the shadow of a slouched hat, he recognized the facetious features of Petit-André, whose fingers not long since had been so unpleasantly active about his throat. Impelled by almost superstitious horror, Durward instinctively spurred his horse from his hateful companion.

"Come, Seignior Archer," exclaimed Petit-André, "let there be no unkindness betwixt us! For my part, I always do my duty without malice, and with a light heart."

"Keep back, thou wretched object!" exclaimed Quentin, as the finisher of the law sought to approach him closer.

"Well," said the fellow, "be as churlish as you like—I never quarrel with my customers." And Petit-André drew off to the other side of the path. A strong desire had Quentin to have be-laboured him while the staff of his lance could hold together; but he was speedily aroused from such thoughts by the cry of both the ladies, "Look back! For the love of Heaven look to yourself, and us—we are pursued!" Quentin hastily looked back, and saw that two armed men were following them, riding at such a pace as must soon bring them up with their party.

"Do you, gracious ladies," said Durward, "ride forward."

Countess Isabelle looked to their guide, and then whispered to her aunt, who spoke to Quentin thus, "We have confidence in your care, fair Archer, and will rather abide the risk of whatever may chance in your company than we will go onward with that man, whose mien is, we think, of no good augury."

"Be it as you will, ladies," said the youth. "There are but two who come after us; and though they be knights, as their arms seem to show, they shall, if they have any evil purpose, learn how a Scottish gentleman can do his duty for your defence.—Which of you there," he continued, addressing the guards whom he com-manded, "is willing to break a lance with these gallants?"

Two of the men obviously faltered in resolution; but the third swore, "that he would try their mettle, for the honour of Gascony." While he spoke the two knights came up with the party. They were in excellent armour of polished steel, without any device by which they could be distinguished. One of them, as they ap-proached, called out to Quentin, "Sir Squire, we come to relieve you of a charge which is above your rank. You will do well to leave these ladies in our care, who are fitter to wait upon them, as we know that in yours they are little better than captives."

"Know that I am discharging the duty imposed upon me by my present Sovereign," said Durward, "and however unworthy I may be, the ladies desire to abide under my protection."

"Will you, a wandering beggar, put yourself on terms of resistance against belted knights?" exclaimed one of the champions.

"They are indeed terms of resistance," said Quentin, "since they oppose your insolent and unlawful aggression; and if there be difference of rank between us, which as yet I know not, your discourtesy has done it away. Draw your sword, or, if you will use the lance, take ground for your career."

While the knights rode back about a hundred and fifty yards, Quentin, looking to the ladies, bent low on his saddle-bow, as if desiring their favourable regard, and as they streamed towards him their kerchiefs, in token of encouragement, the two assailants gained the distance necessary for their charge. Calling to the Gascon to bear himself like a man, Durward put his steed into motion; and the four horsemen met in full career in the midst of the ground which at first separated them. The shock was fatal to the poor Gascon; for his adversary, aiming at his face, ran him through the eye into the brain, so that he fell dead from his horse. On the other hand, Quentin swayed himself in the saddle so dexterously that the hostile lance, slightly scratching his cheek, passed over his right shoulder; while his own spear, striking his antagonist fair upon the breast, hurled him to the ground. Quentin jumped off to unhelm his fallen opponent; but the other knight dismounted still more speedily, and bestriding his friend, who lay senseless, exclaimed, "In the name of Saint Martin, mount, good fellow, and get thee gone! You have caused mischief enough this morning."

"By your leave, Sir Knight," said Quentin, who could not brook the menacing tone in which this advice was given, "I will first learn who is to answer for the death of my comrade."

"That shalt thou never live to know or tell," answered the knight. "Nay, if thou *wilt* have it" (for Quentin now drew his sword, and advanced on him), "take it with a vengeance!" So saying, he dealt the Scot such a blow on the helmet as he had only read of in romance. Durward, stunned and beaten down on one knee, was for an instant at the mercy of the knight, had it pleased

84

him to second his blow. But compassion for Quentin's youth or admiration of his courage made him withhold from taking such advantage; while Durward, collecting himself, sprang up and attacked his antagonist with energy. It was in vain that this generous antagonist called aloud to Quentin, "that there now remained no cause of fight betwixt them, and that he was loath to be constrained to do him injury."

Durward continued to assail him with the rapidity of lightning and the duel was still at its hottest when a large party of horse rode up, crying, "Hold, in the King's name!" Both champions stepped back—and Quentin saw with surprise that his Captain, Lord Crawford, was at the head of the party who had thus interrupted their combat. There was also Tristan l'Hermite, with two or three of his followers; making, in all, perhaps twenty horse. The Knight, throwing off his helmet, hastily gave the old lord his sword, saying, "Crawford, I render myself. But hither— a word, for God's sake—save the Duke of Orleans!"

"The Duke of Orleans!" exclaimed the Scottish commander.

"Ask no questions," said Dunois—for it was no other than he— "it was all my fault. See, he stirs; let no man look upon him." So saying, he opened the visor of Orleans, and threw water on his face from the neighbouring lake. Quentin Durward, meanwhile, stood like one planet-struck. He had now, as the pale features of his first antagonist assured him, borne to the earth the first Prince of the blood in France, and had measured swords with her best champion, the celebrated Dunois; both of them achievements honourable in themselves, but whether they might be called good service to the King was a very different question.

The Duke had now recovered his breath, and was able to give attention to what passed between Dunois and Crawford, while the former pleaded eagerly that there was no occasion to mention in the matter the name of the most noble Orleans, while he was ready to take the whole blame on his own shoulders; and to avouch that the Duke had only come thither in friendship to him. Lord Crawford continued listening, with his eyes fixed on the ground, and from time to time he sighed and shook his head. At length he said, looking up, "Thou knowest, Dunois, that for thy father's sake, as for thine own, I would fain do thee a service."

"Noble Crawford," said Orleans, who had now entirely recovered from his swoon, "you are too like in character to your friend Dunois, not to do him justice. It was indeed I that dragged him hither, most unwillingly, upon an enterprise of hairbrained passion, rashly undertaken. Look on me all who will," he added, rising up and turning to the soldiery, "I am Louis of Orleans, willing to pay the penalty of my own folly. Meanwhile, as a child of France must not give up his sword to any one—not even to you, brave Crawford—fare thee well, good steel." So saying, he drew his sword from its scabbard, and flung it into the lake. It went through the air like a stream of lightning, and sank in the flashing waters, which speedily closed over it. All remained standing in astonishment, so high was the rank, and so much esteemed was the character, of the culprit; while, at the same time, all were conscious that the consequences of his rash enterprise were likely to end in his utter ruin. Dunois was the first who spoke, and it was in the chiding tone of an offended and distrusted friend: "So! your Highness hath judged it fit to cast away your best sword, in the same morning when it was your pleasure to fling away the King's favour, and to slight the friendship of Dunois?"

"My dearest kinsman," said the Duke, "how was it in my purpose to slight your friendship by telling the truth when it was due to your safety and my honour?"

"What had you to do with my safety, my most princely cousin, I would pray to know?" answered Dunois gruffly. "And then for your own honour—why, I think the honour would have been to have missed this morning's work, or kept it out of sight. Here has your Highness got yourself unhorsed by a wild Scottish boy."

"Never shame his Highness for that," said Lord Crawford. "It is not the first time a Scottish boy hath broke a good lance—I am glad the youth hath borne him well."

"I will say nothing to the contrary," said Dunois, "yet, had your Lordship come something later than you did, there might have been a vacancy in your band of Archers."

"Ay, ay," answered Lord Crawford; "I can read your handwriting in that cleft helmet.—Some one take it from the lad, and give him a bonnet with steel lining.—But, Dunois, I must now request the Duke of Orleans and you to take horse and accompany me, as I have power and commission to convey you to a place different from that which my goodwill might assign you." Then, addressing Quentin, he added, "You have done your duty. Go on to obey the charge with which you are entrusted."

"Under favour, my Lord," said Tristan, with his usual brutality of manner, "the youth must find another guide. I cannot do without Petit-André, when there is so like to be business on hand for him."

"The young man," said Petit-André, now coming forward, "has only to keep the path which lies straight before him, and it will conduct him to a place where he will find the man who is to act as his guide.—I would not for a thousand ducats be absent from my Chief this day!"

Lord Crawford turned his back upon the Provost Marshal, and requesting the Duke of Orleans and Dunios to ride one on either hand of him, he made a signal of adieu to the ladies, and said to Quentin, "God bless thee, my child; thou hast begun thy service valiantly, though in an unhappy cause."

He was about to go off—when Quentin could hear Dunois whisper to Crawford, "Do you carry us to Plessis?"

"No, my unhappy and rash friend," answered Crawford, with a sigh; "to Loches."

The name of a castle, or rather prison, yet more dreaded than Plessis itself, fell like a death-toll upon the ear of the young Scotchman. There were in this place of terror dungeons which were living graves, *cages*, in which the wretched prisoner could neither stand upright, nor stretch himself at length. It is no wonder that the name of this place of horrors, and the consciousness that he had been partly the means of despatching thither two such illustrious victims, struck sadness into the heart of the young Scot.

"Methinks, fair sir, you regret the victory which your gallantry has attained in our behalf?" said the Lady Hameline.

"I can regret nothing that is done in your service," Quentin answered; "but I had rather have fallen by the sword of so good a soldier as Dunois than have been the means of consigning that renowned knight and the Duke of Orleans to yonder dungeons."

"It *was*, then, the Duke of Orleans," said the elder lady, turning to her niece. "I thought so, even at the distance from which we beheld the fray. You see, kinswoman, what we might have been . . . This young gentleman did his duty bravely; but methinks 'tis pity that he did not succumb with honour, since his ill-advised gallantry has stood betwixt us and these princely rescuers."

"Madam," said Countess Isabelle firmly, "your speech is ungrateful to our brave defender. Had these gentlemen succeeded so far in their rash enterprise as to have defeated our escort, is it not evident that, on the arrival of the Royal Guard, we must have shared their captivity? For my own part, I give tears for the brave man who has fallen, and I trust" (she continued, more timidly) "that he who lives will accept my grateful thanks." As Quentin turned towards her to return fitting acknowledgments, she saw the blood which streamed down on one side of his face, and exclaimed, in a tone of deep feeling, "Holy Virgin, he is wounded! Dismount, sir, and let your wound be bound up."

In spite of all that Durward could say of the slightness of his hurt, he was compelled to dismount and unhelmet himself, while the ladies of Croye washed the wound and bound it with the kerchief of the younger Countess who felt for the patient, whom we have already said was eminently handsome, a thrill of pity and gratitude for his services. This incident seemed intended by Fate to complete the mysterious communication which, by many apparently accidental circumstances, had been established between two persons, who, though far different in rank and fortune, strongly resembled each other in youth, beauty, and the romantic tenderness of an affectionate disposition.

Meantime, they continued their pilgrimage, Quentin now riding abreast of the ladies, into whose society he seemed to be tacitly adopted. He did not speak much, however, being filled by the silent consciousness of happiness. Suddenly he heard the blast of a horn, and looking in the direction from which the sound came, beheld a singular horseman riding very fast towards them. His dress was a red turban secured by a clasp of silver, a green tunic tawdrily laced with gold and very wide white trousers gathered beneath the knee. In a crimson sash he wore a dagger on the right side, and on the left a short crooked Moorish sword; and over his shoulder hung the horn which announced his approach. He had a swarthy and sunburnt visage with a thin beard and piercing dark eyes.

"He also is a Bohemian!" said the ladies to each other. "Holy Mary, will the King again place confidence in these outcasts?"

"I will question the man, if it be your pleasure," said Quentin, "and assure myself of his fidelity as best I may—Art thou come hither to seek us?" was his first question. The stranger nodded. "And for what purpose?"

"To guide you to the palace of the Bishop of Liege."

"What token canst thou give me, that we should yield credence to thee?"

"Even the old rhyme, and no other," answered the Bohemian:
> The page slew the boar,
> The peer had the gloire.

"A true token," said Quentin; "lead on, good fellow—I will speak further with thee presently." Then falling back to the ladies, he said, "I am convinced this man is the guide we are to expect, for he hath brought me a pass-word, known, I think, but to the King and me."

While Quentin held this brief communication with the ladies, he noticed the stranger watching them attentively, and he rode up to the Bohemian: "What countryman are you?" he demanded.

"I am of no country," answered the guide. "I am a Zingaro, a Bohemian, an Egyptian, or whatever the Europeans, in their different languages, may choose to call our people; but I have no country."

"Are you a Christian?" asked the Scotchman. The Bohemian shook his head. "Are you a Pagan, then, or what are you?"

"I have no religion," answered the Bohemian. Durward started back, but recovered from his astonishment to ask his guide where he usually dwelt. "I have no home," replied the Bohemian.

"Yet you dress gaily, and ride gallantly," said Durward. "What are your means of subsistence?"

"I eat when I am hungry, drink when I am thirsty," replied the vagabond.

"Under whose laws do you live?"

"I acknowledge obedience to none, but as it suits my pleasure or my necessities," said the Bohemian.

"You have, then, may Heaven compassionate you, no country," said Durward, wondering, "and, may Heaven enlighten and forgive you, you have no God! What is it that remains to you?"

"I have liberty," said the Bohemian.

"But you are subject to instant execution, at the pleasure of the Judge, and to imprisonment also; where, then, is your boasted freedom?"

"In my thoughts," said the Bohemian, "which no chains can bind. I cannot extricate myself from prison, and fail of relief from my comrades, I can always die, and death is the most perfect freedom of all."

"What is thy name?" said Durward.

"My proper name is only known to my brethren—the men beyond our tents call me Hayraddin Maugrabin."

There was a pause, then the young Scot asked Hayraddin, "Will thou be faithful?"

"Wouldst thou believe me the more should I swear it?" answered Maugrabin, with a sneer.

"Thy life is in my hand," said the young Scot.

"Strike, and see whether I fear to die," answered the Bohemian.

"Will money render thee a trusty guide?" demanded Durward.

"If I be not such without it, No," replied the heathen.

"Then what will bind thee?" asked the Scot.

"To thee I am bound already," replied Hayraddin. "Remember the chestnut-trees on the banks of the Cher! The victim, whose body thou didst cut down, was my brother, Zamet Maugrabin."

"And yet," said Quentin, "I find you in correspondence with those very officers by whom your brother was done to death; for it was one of them who directed me where to meet you—the same, doubtless, who procured yonder ladies your services as a guide."

"What can we do?" answered Hayraddin gloomily. "These men deal with us as sheep-dogs do with the flock; they protect us for a while, drive us hither and thither at their pleasure, and always end by guiding us to the gallows of the Provost-Guard."

Durward fell back to the rest of the retinue very little satisfied with the character of Hayraddin. He proceeded to sound the other two men who had been assigned him, and he was concerned to find them stupid, and as unfit to assist him with counsel, as in their encounter they had shown themselves reluctant to use their weapons. "It is all the better," said Quentin to himself, his spirit rising with the apprehended difficulties of his situation. "That lovely young lady shall owe all to me. What one hand, ay, and one head can do, methinks I can boldly count upon."

Acting upon this resolution, Quentin let nothing interfere with the vigilant discharge of his duty. His favourite post was of course by the side of the ladies, who, sensible of his extreme attention to their safety, began to converse with him in almost the tone of familiar friendship, but he was as often riding with Hayraddin, questioning him about the road, to see whether he could discover anything like meditated treachery. As often again he was in the rear, endeavouring to secure the attachment of the two horsemen, by kind words and promises of additional recompense when their task should be accomplished. In this way they travelled for more than a week, by circuitous routes in order to avoid large towns.

Their resting-places were chiefly monasteries, which were

obliged to receive pilgrims with hospitality. One circumstance which gave Quentin trouble was the character of his guide, who, as a heathen, and addicted besides to occult arts (the badge of all his tribe), was often looked upon as a very improper guest. This was very embarrassing; for, on the one hand, it was necessary to keep in good humour a man who was possessed of the secret of their expedition; and on the other, Quentin deemed it indispensable to maintain a vigilant watch on Hayraddin's conduct. This of course was impossible if the Bohemian was lodged outside the precincts of the convent at which they stopped, and Durward could not help thinking that Hayraddin was desirous of bringing this about. Often it required all the authority, supported by threats, which Quentin could exert over him, to restrain his irreverent jocularity, and all the interest he could make with the Superiors, to prevent the heathen from being thrust out of doors.

But upon the twelfth day of their journey, after they had entered Flanders, and were approaching the town of Namur, all the efforts of Quentin became inadequate to suppress the consequences of the scandal given by his guide. The scene was a Franciscan convent and of a strict order. After rather more than the usual scruples had been surmounted, the Bohemian at length obtained quarters in an out-house inhabited by a lay brother, who acted as gardener. The ladies retired to their apartment, as usual, and the Prior invited Quentin to a slight monastic refection in his cell. Finding the Father a man of intelligence, Quentin did not neglect the opportunity of making himself acquainted with affairs in the neighbouring state of Liege, of which, during the last two days of their journey, he had heard such reports as made him apprehensive for the security of his charge during the remainder of their route. The replies of the Prior were not very consolatory. He said that "the people of Liege were wealthy burghers, that they had divers disputes with the Duke of Burgundy, their liege lord, and had repeatedly broken out into mutiny, whereat the Duke was so much incensed that he had sworn, by Saint George, on the next provocation, he would make the city of Liege like the desolation of Babylon. The good Bishop labours night and day to preserve peace. But —" here the Prior stopped, with a deep sigh. He then looked cautiously round, and lowered his voice, as if afraid of being overheard. "The people of Liege," he said, "are privily instigated to their frequent mutinies by men of Belial, who pretend, but, as I hope, falsely, to have commission to that effect from our most Christian King Louis; his name is freely used by those who inflame their discontents. There is, moreover, in the land, a nobleman of good descent and fame in warlike affairs, but otherwise a stumbling-block of offence to the countries of Burgundy and Flanders. His name is William de la Marck."

"Called the Wild Boar of Ardennes?" said the young Scot.

"And rightly so called, my son," said the Prior. "And he hath formed a band of more than a thousand men, holds himself independent of the Duke of Burgundy, and maintains himself and his followers by rapine and wrong. Even to our poor house did he send for gold as a ransom for our lives, and we were obliged to melt down the vessels of our altar to satisfy the rapacity of this cruel chief."

"I marvel," said Quentin, "that the Duke of Burgundy, who is so strong and powerful, doth not bait this boar to purpose."

"Alas! my son," said the Prior, "Duke Charles is now at Peronne, assembling his captains to make war against France. But it is in evil time that the Duke neglects the cure of these internal gangrenes; for this William de la Marck hath of late entertained open communication with Rouslaer and Pavillon, the chiefs of the discontented at Liege, and it is to be feared he will soon stir them up to some desperate enterprise."

"But the Bishop of Liege," said Quentin, "he hath still power enough to subdue this turbulent spirit—hath he not, good father?"

"The Bishop, my child," replied the Prior, "hath power as a secular prince, and he hath the protection of the mighty House of Burgundy; he hath also spiritual authority as a prelate, and he supports both with a reasonable force of soldiers. This William de la Marck was bred in his household, but he was expelled thence for a homicide. From thenceforward, being banished from the good Prelate's presence, he hath been his constant and unrelenting foe. However, a messenger who passed hither yesterday saith that the Duke of Burgundy hath despatched an hundred men-at-arms to the Bishop's assistance. This reinforcement is enough to deal with William de la Marck."

At this crisis their conversation was interrupted by the Sacristan, who, almost inarticulate with anger, accused the Bohemian of having added to the nightly meal cups of the younger brethren a heady and intoxicating cordial, under which several of the fraternity had succumbed. Moreover, the Bohemian had sung songs of worldly vanity and had derided Saint Francis and made jest of his miracles. Lastly he had foretold to a young monk that he was beloved by a beautiful lady, who should make him father to a thriving boy. The Father Prior listened to these complaints in silence, rose up, descended to the court of the convent, and ordered the lay brethren to beat Hayraddin out of the sacred precincts with their broom-staves and cart-whips. This sentence was executed accordingly, in the presence of Quentin Durward, who, however vexed at the occurrence, saw that his interference would be of no avail.

During this scene, a suspicion which Durward had formerly entertained recurred with additional strength. Hayraddin had, that very morning, promised him more discreet behaviour; yet he had broken his engagement. Something probably lurked under this; for the Bohemian lacked neither sense, nor, when he pleased, self-command; and might it not be probable that he wished to hold some communication with his own horde, from which he was debarred in the course of the day by the vigilance with which he was watched by Quentin, and had recourse to this stratagem in order to get himself turned out of the convent? Quentin resolved to follow his cudgelled guide, and observe (secretly if possible) how he disposed of himself. Accordingly, when the Bohemian fled, Quentin, hastily explaining to the Prior the necessity of keeping sight of his guide, followed in pursuit.

When Quentin sallied from the convent, he could see the Bohemian's dark figure in the far moonlight, flying with the speed of a flogged hound through the little village, and across the meadow that lay beyond. Being fortunately without his cloak and armour, the Scottish mountaineer was at liberty to put forth a speed unrivalled in his own glens; the Bohemian never even looked behind him, and consequently Durward was enabled to follow him unobserved. At length the Bohemian having attained the side of a stream, the banks of which were clothed with alders and willows, Quentin observed that he stood still, and blew a low note on his horn, which was answered by a whistle.

"A rendezvous," thought Quentin, "but how shall I come near enough to overhear what passes?—I will stalk them, by Saint Andrew, as if they were deer." Our friend descended with caution into the channel of the stream and crept along, concealed by the boughs overhanging the bank, his steps unheard amid the ripple of the water. In this manner, the Scot drew near unperceived, until he distinctly heard voices, though he could not distinguish the words. Being at this time under the drooping branches of a magnificent weeping willow, which almost swept the surface of the water, he caught hold of one of its boughs. Exerting much agility and strength he raised himself up into the body of the tree, and sat, secure from discovery, among the central branches.

From this situation he could discover that the person with whom Hayraddin was now conversing was one of his own tribe, and that their language was totally unknown to him. On a sudden, a whistle was again heard in the distance and presently afterwards a tall, stout, soldierly-looking man made his appearance. He wore a tight buff-jacket, the right sleeve of which displayed a silver boar's head, the crest of his Captain, and he held a lance in his hand. His whole equipment was that of one of the German adventurers who were known by the name of lanzknechts, in English, spearmen, a formidable part of the infantry of the period. These mercenaries were, of course, a fierce and rapacious soldiery. "Donner and blitz!" was his first salutation, in a sort of German-

French, which we can only imperfectly imitate, "Why have you kept me dancing in attendance dis dree nights?"

"I could not see you sooner, Meinheer," said Hayraddin, submissively, "there is a young Scot who suspects me already, and, should he find his suspicion confirmed, I were a dead man on the spot, and he would carry back the women into France again."

"Was henker!" said the lanzknecht, "we are three—we will attack them tomorrow, and carry the women off without going further. You said the two guards were cowards—you and your comrade may manage them, but I match your Scots wild-cat."

"You will find that foolhardy," said Hayraddin, "this spark hath matched himself with the best knight in France and come off with honour."

"Hagel and sturmwetter! It is but your cowardice that speaks," said the German soldier.

"I am no more a coward than yourself," said Hayraddin, "but my trade is not fighting. If you keep the appointment where it was laid, it is well—if not, I guide them safely to the Bishop's Palace, and William de la Marck may easily possess himself of them there, provided he is half as strong as he pretended a week since."

"We are as strong and stronger," said the soldier, "but we hear of five hundred lances of Burgundy; der Bischoff hath a goot force on footing."

"You must then hold to the ambuscade at the Cross of the Three Kings, or give up the adventure," said the Bohemian.

"Geb up—geb up the adventure of the rich bride for our noble captain—Teufel! I will charge through hell first."

"The ambuscade at the Cross of the Three Kings then still holds?" said the Bohemian.

"Mein Got, ay—you will swear to bring them there; and when they are down from their horses and on their knees before the cross, we will make in on them, and they are ours."

"Ay: but I promised this piece of necessary villainy only on one condition," said Hayraddin. "I will not have a hair of the young man's head touched. Swear this to me, by your Three dead Men of Cologne."

"Du bist ein comische man," said the lanzknecht, "I swear. But were it not making sure work to have riders on the other road, by the left bank, to trap them if they go that way?"

The Bohemian considered a moment, and then answered, "No—they shall travel on the right bank of the Maes, for I can guide them which way I will. Fare thee well, and keep the appointment."

Quentin Durward watched until they were out of sight, and then descended from his place of concealment, his heart throbbing at the narrow escape which he and his fair charge had made—if, indeed, it could yet be achieved—from a deep-laid plot of villainy. On his return to the monastery, he communed earnestly with himself concerning the safest plan to be pursued. The violence of Duke Charles in the one country was scarcely more to be feared than the cold policy of King Louis in the other. After deep thought, Durward could form no better plan for the security of the Countesses than that, evading the ambuscade, they should take the road to Liege by the left hand of the Maes, and throw themselves, as the ladies originally designed, upon the protection of the excellent Bishop. That Prelate's will to protect them could not be doubted, and, if reinforced by this Burgundian party of men-at-arms, he might be considered as having the power.

Quentin imagined that the death or captivity to which King Louis had, in cold blood, consigned him, set him at liberty from his engagements to the Crown of France; which, therefore, it was his determined purpose to renounce. The Bishop of Liege was likely, he concluded, to need soldiers, and he thought that, by the interposition of his fair friends, he might get some command, and perhaps might have the charge of conducting the Ladies of Croye to some place more safe than the neighbourhood of Liege.

97

6. The City and the Castle

BY peep of day Quentin Durward had forsaken his little cell, had roused the sleepy grooms, and, with more than his wonted care, seen that everything was prepared and that the horses were fit for a long day's journey, or, if that should be necessary, for a hasty flight. Quentin then betook himself to his own chamber, armed himself with unusual care, and belted on his sword with the feeling of approaching danger.

He let the Ladies of Croye understand that it would be necessary that they should prepare for their journey this morning rather earlier than usual; and, accordingly, they left the convent immediately after a morning repast, and the little cavalcade was not an hundred yards from the monastery before Maugrabin joined it. Quentin at once fell back to his accustomed post beside the ladies. A considerable degree of familiarity had begun to establish itself between them. The Ladies of Croye had been highly pleased and interested by the grace of his general behaviour and the mixture of shrewd intelligence which naturally belonged to him with the simplicity arising from his secluded education and distant country. The elder Countess treated him (being once well assured of the nobility of his birth) like a favoured equal; and though her niece showed her regard to their protector less freely, yet Quentin thought he could plainly perceive that his company and conversation were not by any means indifferent to her. But on this anxious morning, he rode beside the ladies of Croye without any of his usual attempts to amuse them.

"Gentle ladies," said Durward at length, "— I am compelled to ask—can you trust me?"

"Trust you?" answered Countess Hameline. "Certainly. But why the question? You know of some pressing danger?"

"I have read it in his eye this hour past!" exclaimed Lady Isabelle, clasping her hands.

"Gentle lady," replied Durward, "my object is to alter our route, by proceeding directly by the left bank of the Maes to Liege, instead of crossing at Namur. This differs from the order assigned by King Louis, but I heard news in the monastery of marauders on the right bank of the Maes, and of the march of Burgundian soldiers to suppress them. Both circumstances alarm me for your safety. Have I your permission so far to deviate from the route of your journey?"

"My ample and full permission," answered the younger lady.

"Now, may God bless you for that word, lady," said Quentin joyously. So saying, he spurred his horse, and rejoined the Bohemian. "We will try for once," thought the Scot, "whether we cannot foil a traitor at his own weapons.—Honest Hayraddin," he said, "thou hast travelled with us for ten days, yet hast never shown us a specimen of your skill in fortune-telling; which you are, nevertheless, so fond of practising, that you must needs display your gifts in every convent at which we stop. Give me then present proof of your skill." And Quentin, ungloving his hand, held it out to the Zingaro.

"This line from the hill of Venus," said the Bohemian, "accompanying the line of life argues a large fortune by marriage, whereby the party shall be raised among the noble by the influence of successful love."

"Such promises you make to all who ask your advice," said Quentin.

"What I tell you is as certain," said Hayraddin, "as that you shall in a brief space be menaced with mighty danger."

"The seers of my land," said Quentin, "excel your boasted knowledge, and I will give thee proof of it. Hayraddin, the danger which threatens me lies on the right bank of the river—and I will avoid it by travelling to Liege on the left bank."

The guide listened with an apathy, which, knowing the circumstances in which Maugrabin stood, Quentin could not comprehend. "If you accomplish your purpose," was the Bohemian's reply, "the dangerous crisis will be transferred from your lot to mine, for it requires little knowledge of Louis of Valois to presage that he will hang your guide."

"The attaining with safety the purpose of the journey," said Quentin, "must atone for a deviation from the exact line of the prescribed route."

"Ay," replied the Bohemian, "if you are sure that the King had in his own eye the same termination of the pilgrimage which he insinuated to you. But as you will, seignior, I am, for my part, equally ready to guide you down the left as down the right side of the Maes. Your excuse to your master you must make out for yourself."

Quentin, although rather surprised, was at the same time pleased with the ready acquiescence of Hayraddin, for he needed his assistance as a guide. Abandoning, therefore, all thoughts of their original route, the little party followed that by the left bank of the broad Maes, so speedily and successfully that the next day early brought them to the purposed end of their journey.

They found that the Bishop of Liege, perhaps to avoid being surprised by the mutinous population of the city, had established his residence in his beautiful Castle of Schonwaldt, about a mile outside Liege. Just as they approached the Castle, they saw the Prelate returning in procession from the city, in which he had been officiating at High Mass. But when the party came more near, they found that circumstances around the Castle argued a sense of insecurity which contradicted that display of pomp and power which they had just witnessed. Strong guards of the Bishop's soldiers were maintained all around the mansion which seemed to argue a sense of danger in the reverend Prelate, who found it necessary thus to surround himself with all the defensive precautions of war. But the ladies of Croye, when announced by Quentin, were reverently ushered into the great hall, where they met with the most cordial reception from the Bishop.

Louis of Bourbon, the reigning Bishop of Liege, was in truth a generous and kind-hearted prince, loved as a noble ecclesiastic, generous and magnificent in his ordinary mode of life. The Bishop was so fast an ally of the Duke of Burgundy that the latter claimed almost a joint sovereignty in his bishopric.

The Prelate assured the Ladies of Croye of his intercession for them at the Court of Burgundy. He promised them also such protection as it was in his power to afford. "At every event, my dearest daughters," said the Bishop, "be assured I will care for your safety as for my own; and should matters become yet more distracted here, we will provide for your safe conduct to Germany; for not even the will of our brother and protector, Charles of Burgundy, shall prevail with us to dispose of you in any respect contrary to your own inclinations. We cannot comply with your request of sending you to a convent; for, alas! we know no retreat to which our authority extends, beyond the bounds of our own castle. But here you all are most welcome. For yourselves, you shall reside here with my sister Isabelle, a Canoness of Triers, with whom you may dwell in all honour."

Separated from Lady Isabelle, whose looks had been for so many days his load-star, Quentin felt a strange chillness of the heart. The shock of the separation was not the more welcome than it seemed unavoidable, and the proud heart of Quentin swelled at finding he was parted with like an ordinary escort whose duty is discharged. He made a manly, but, at first, vain effort, to throw off this dejection; and yielding to the feelings he could not suppress, he sat down in a recess in the great Gothic hall of Schonwaldt, and there mused upon his hard fortune which had not assigned him rank or wealth sufficient to prosecute his daring suit to the young Countess. Quentin tried to dispel the sadness which overhung him by despatching letters to the court of Louis, announcing the arrival of the Ladies of Croye at Liege.

He was interrupted by a touch on the shoulder, and, looking up, beheld the Bohemian standing by him. "Well, what dost thou want? Speak, and begone!" said Quentin sternly.

"I want my due; my ten crowns of gold for guiding the ladies hither," said Hayraddin.

"With what face darest thou ask any guerdon beyond my sparing thy worthless life?" said Durward fiercely. "Thou knowest that it was thy purpose to have betrayed them on the road."

"But I did *not* betray them," said Hayraddin. "The party that I have served is the party who must pay me."

"Thy guerdon perish with thee, then, traitor!" said Quentin, telling out the money. "Get thee to the Boar of Ardennes, or to the devil! but keep hereafter out of my sight, lest I send thee thither before thy time."

"Know, Quentin Durward, that you have foiled me to the marring of thine own fortune," said Hayraddin. "Yet I mean still to surprise you with my gratitude for yonder matter on the banks of the Cher. And now farewell, but not for a long space—I go to bid adieu to the Ladies of Croye."

"Thou?" said Quentin in astonishment, "*thou* be admitted to the presence of the ladies, where they are in a manner recluses under the protection of the Bishop's sister, a noble canoness? It is impossible."

"Their maid, Marthon, however, waits to conduct me to their presence," said the Zingaro, with a sneer.

Ere Durward could reply, the Bohemian had left the hall. Quentin instantly followed him as he descended a small staircase to a door opening into the garden. Crossing the garden to another part of the building, where a postern-door opened behind a massive buttress, Hayraddin looked back, and waved his hand in signal of an exulting farewell to his follower, who saw that the door was opened by Marthon, and that the vile Bohemian was admitted into the apartment of the Countesses of Croye. Quentin bit his lips with indignation, and blamed himself severely that he had not made the ladies sensible of the infamy of Hayraddin's character. "But it is all a deception," he said. "He has procured access to these ladies upon some false pretence, and with some mischievous intention. It is well I have learned where they lodge. I will watch Marthon, and solicit an interview with them, were it but to place them on their guard."

While the young lover was thus meditating, an aged gentleman of the Bishop's household approached and made him aware, though with the greatest civility of manner, that the garden was private, and reserved only for the use of the Bishop, and guests of the very highest distinction. Quentin bowed and hurried out of the garden, finding no better way of escape than pretending a desire of visiting the neighbouring city, and setting off thither at a round pace. Quentin was soon within the walls of the city of Liege, then one of the richest in Flanders, and in the world. In a few minutes, his attention was engrossed by the busy streets, the lofty houses, the splendid display of the richest goods and most gorgeous armour in the warehouses and shops around—all these combined to form a picture of wealth, bustle, and splendour, to which Quentin had been hitherto a stranger. He admired also the various canals communicating with the Maes, and he failed not to hear a mass in the venerable Church of Saint Lambert.

It was upon leaving this place of worship that Quentin began to observe that he was himself the object of attention to several groups of substantial-looking burghers, amongst whom arose a buzz which spread from one party to another, while the number of gazers continued to augment rapidly. At length he formed the centre of a considerable crowd. Quentin looked around him, and fixing upon a jolly, stout-made man, whom, by his velvet cloak and gold chain, he concluded to be a burgher of eminence, and perhaps a magistrate, he asked him, "Whether he saw anything particular in his appearance, to attract public attention?"

..."Surely not, seignior," answered the burgher. "The Liegeois do not find that there is anything in your dress or appearance, saving that which is most welcome to this city."

"This sounds very polite, worthy sir," said Quentin, "but by the Cross of Saint Andrew, I cannot even guess at your meaning."

"Your oath, sir," answered the merchant of Liege, "as well as your accent, convinces me that we are right in our conjecture. And though it is surely not for us to see that which you, worthy seignior, deem it proper to conceal—my name is Pavillon."

"And what is my business with that, Seignior Pavillon?" said Quentin.

"Nay, nothing—only methinks it might satisfy you that I am trustworthy. Here is my colleague Rouslaer, too."

Rouslaer advanced, a corpulent dignitary, whispering caution to his neighbour: "The place is too open—the seignior will retire to your house or mine, and drink a glass of Rhenish, and then we shall hear more of our good friend and ally."

"I will drink no Rhenish," said Quentin impatiently, "and I have no news for you."

"Nay, then, sir," said Rouslaer, "let me ask you roundly, wherefore wear you the badge of your company if you would remain unknown in Liege?"

"What badge?" said Quentin.

"Why," said the other burgher, "who wear bonnets with the Saint Andrew's cross and *fleur-de-lys*, save the Scottish Archers of King Louis's Guards?"

"And supposing I am an Archer of the Scottish Guard, why should you make a wonder of my wearing the badge of my company?" said Quentin.

"He has avowed it!" said Rouslaer and Pavillon, turning to the assembled burghers. "He hath avowed himself an Archer of Louis's Guard—of Louis, the guardian of the liberties of Liege!" A general shout now arose from the multitude, in which were mingled the various sounds of "Long live Louis of France! Long live the Scottish Guard! Long live the valiant Archer! Our liberties, our privileges, or death! No taxes! Long live the valiant Boar of Ardennes! Down with Charles of Burgundy!"

Half-stunned by the noise, Quentin had yet time to form a conjecture concerning the meaning of the tumult. He had forgotten that after his skirmish with Orleans and Dunois, one of his comrades had, at Lord Crawford's command, replaced his cloven helmet with one of the steel-lined bonnets which formed a part of the well-known equipment of the Scotch Guards. That an individual of this body, which was always kept very close to Louis's person, should have appeared in the streets of a city whose civil discontents had been aggravated by the agents of that King, was interpreted by the burghers of Liege as a determination on the part of Louis openly to assist their cause. To remove a conviction so generally adopted, Quentin saw was impossible. He therefore hastily resolved to temporise, and to get free the best way he could. But artisans of every calling thronged forward to join the procession to the Stadthouse and escape seemed impossible.

In this dilemma, Quentin appealed to Rouslaer, who held one arm, and to Pavillon, who had secured the other. He intimated that "if just now conducted to the Stadthouse, he might unhappily feel himself under the necessity of communicating to the assembled notables certain matters which he was directed by the King to reserve for the private ears of his excellent gossips, Meinheers Rouslaer and Pavillon of Liege." This last hint operated like magic on the two citizens, who hastily agreed that Quentin should leave the town for the time, return by night to Liege, and converse with them privately in the house of Rouslaer, near the gate opposite to Schonwaldt. Quentin hesitated before telling them that he was at present residing in the Bishop's palace under pretence of bearing

H

despatches from the French Court, although his real errand was, as they had well conjectured, designed to the citizens of Liege; and this tortuous mode of conducting a communication was so consonant to the character of Louis as to excite no surprise.

Just then the progress of the multitude brought them opposite to the door of Pavillon's house, in one of the principal streets, but which communicated from behind with the Maes, by means of a garden. It was natural that Pavillon should desire to do the honours of his dwelling to the supposed envoy of Louis, and a halt before his house excited no surprise on the part of the multitude. Meinheer Pavillon ushered in his distinguished guest and Quentin speedily laid aside his remarkable bonnet for the cap of a felt-maker, and flung a cloak over his other apparel. Pavillon then furnished him with a passport to pass the gates of the city, and to return by night or day, and committed him to the charge of his daughter, a fair and smiling Flemish lass, while he himself hastened back to his colleague to amuse their friends at the Stadthouse with the best excuses which they could invent for the disappearance of King Louis's envoy.

The worthy burgess was no sooner gone than his pretty daughter, Trudchen, escorted the handsome stranger down to the water-side, and there saw him embarked in a boat. While this was rowed by two stout Flemings up the sluggish waters of the Maes, Quentin had time enough to reflect what account to give of his adventures in Liege when he returned to the Bishop's palace. He resolved to confine himself to so general an account as might put the Bishop upon his guard, while it should point out no individual to his vengeance. He was landed from the boat, rewarded his rowers with a guilder, and entered the castle by the principal gate. The castle bell had tolled and he found everyone assembled for dinner in the great hall and already placed at table. A seat at the upper end of the board had, however, been reserved beside the Bishop's domestic chaplain who welcomed the late-comer. In vindicating himself from the suspicion of ill-breeding, Quentin briefly described the tumult which had been occasioned in the city,

and endeavoured to give a ludicrous turn to the narrative by saying he had been with difficulty extricated by a fat burgher of Liege and his pretty daughter. But the company were too much interested in the story to taste the jest; there was a solemn pause which was only broken by the Major-Domo saying, "I would to God that we saw those hundred lances of Burgundy!"

"Why should you think so deeply on it?" said Quentin. "You have many soldiers here, whose trade is arms; and your antagonists are only the rabble of a disorderly city."

"You do not know the men of Liege," said the Chaplain. "Twice has the Duke of Burgundy chastised them for their repeated revolts against the Bishop, and the last time he defeated them Liege lost nearly six thousand men. And yet the sight of an Archer's bonnet is sufficient again to stir them to uproar."

When the tables were drawn, the Chaplain proposed to Quentin to go down into the garden and take a view of the curious foreign shrubs with which the Bishop had enriched it. Quentin excused himself, as unwilling to intrude, and communicated the check which he had received in the morning. The Chaplain smiled, and said, "That there was indeed some ancient prohibition respecting the Bishop's private garden. But of late years this has fallen entirely out of observance, and remains but as the superstition which lingers in the brain of a superannuated gentleman-usher." Nothing could have been more agreeable to Quentin than the prospect of a free entrance into the garden, though the young lover heard with total neglect, if indeed he heard at all, the enumeration of plants, herbs, and shrubs, which his conductor pointed out to him. He was relieved at length by the striking of a clock, which summoned the Chaplain to some official duty. The reverend man made many unnecessary apologies for leaving his new friend, and concluded by giving him the agreeable assurance that he might walk in the garden till supper without much risk of being disturbed.

At length left to himself, Quentin inspected every window which looked into the garden near the small door by which he had seen Marthon admit Hayraddin to the apartment of the Countesses. But nothing stirred which could either confute or confirm the tale which the Bohemian had told until it was becoming dusky; and Quentin began to be sensible that his sauntering so long in the garden might be subject of suspicion. Just as he had resolved to depart, he heard above him a slight and cautious sound. As he looked up, a casement opened and a female hand was seen to drop a letter. To snatch up this billet and hie to a place of secrecy was the work of a single minute. Then he opened the precious scroll:

What your eyes have too boldly said, mine have perhaps too rashly understood. But if you dare do aught for one that hazards much, you need but pass into this garden at prime tomorrow, wearing in your cap a blue-and-white feather. Farewell—and doubt not thy fortune.

Within this letter was enclosed a ring with a table diamond, on which were cut the arms of the House of Croye.

The first feeling of Quentin upon this occasion was unmingled ecstasy. Retiring to the interior of the castle and lighting his lamp, he betook himself to his chamber to read again and again the precious billet. But a thought pressed upon him, though he repelled it as ungrateful—that the frankness of her confession implied less delicacy than was consistent with the romantic feeling of adoration with which he had hitherto worshipped the Lady Isabelle. Yet did not her very dignity of birth reverse, in her case, the usual rules which impose silence on the lady until her lover shall have first spoken? This scruple was succeeded by another doubt, harder of digestion. The traitor Hayraddin had been in the apartments of the ladies; was this train not of his laying—perhaps to seduce Isabelle out of the protection of the worthy Bishop? Quentin's couch was sleepless that night.

At the hour of prime—ay, and an hour before it, he was in the castle-garden with a feather of the assigned colour in his cap. No notice was taken of his appearance for nearly two hours; at length he heard a few notes of the lute, the lattice opened above the postern-door and Isabelle appeared at the opening, greeted him half-kindly, half-shyly, coloured extremely at the deep and significant reverence with which he returned her courtesy—shut the casement, and disappeared. The authenticity of the billet was ascertained! The fair writer had given him no hint what was to follow; but no immediate danger impended. The Countess was in a strong castle, under the protection of a Prince, and it was sufficient if the exulting Squire kept himself prompt to execute her commands whenever they should be communicated to him. But Fate purposed to call him into action sooner than he was aware of.

It was the fourth night after his arrival at Schonwaldt, when Quentin awoke to sounds of tumult. He sprang from bed, and understood from the shouts which reached his ears that the outside of the castle was assaulted by a numerous and determined enemy. Just as Quentin had hastily put on his dress and arms, the Bohemian, Hayraddin Maugrabin, entered the apartment with a lamp.

"Caitiff and traitor!" said Quentin, without further greeting.

"I never betrayed any one but to gain by it," answered Maugrabin. "Hearken for a moment: the Liegeois are up—William de la Marck with his band leads them. If you would save the Countess follow me, in the name of her who sent you a table-diamond, with three leopards engraved on it!"

"Lead the way," said Quentin hastily, "in that name, I dare every danger!"

"As I shall manage it," said the Bohemian, "there is no danger. Follow me, and my debt of thankfulness is paid, and you have a Countess for your spouse."

The Bohemian, seeing that Quentin was now fully armed, ran down the stairs into the little garden. Quentin could hear the various war-cries of "Liege! Liege! Sanglier! Sanglier!" shouted by the assailants, and the feebler cry of "Our Lady for the Prince Bishop!" but the interest of the fight was indifferent to him in comparison with the fate of Isabelle of Croye, which, he had reason to fear would be dreadful, unless she were rescued from the cruel freebooter who was now bursting the castle gates.

Quentin followed the Bohemian across the garden, with the intention of being guided by him until he should discover symptoms of treachery, and then striking his head from his body. Hayraddin seemed himself conscious that his safety turned on a feather-weight. At the door which led to the ladies' apartments, upon a signal made by Hayraddin, appeared two women, muffled in the black silk veils worn by the women in the Netherlands. Quentin offered his arm to one of them, who clung to it with trembling eagerness. The Bohemian, who conducted the other female, made straight for the postern which opened upon the moat where a little skiff was drawn up. "On, on—with all the haste you can make," said Hayraddin. "Horses wait us in yonder thicket of willows. You two must ride for Tongres ere the way becomes unsafe—Marthon will abide with the women of our horde, with whom she is an old acquaintance."

"Marthon!" exclaimed the Countess, "is not this my kinswoman?"

"Excuse me that little piece of deceit," said Hayraddin, "I dared not carry off *both* the Ladies of Croye from the Wild Boar of Ardennes."

"Wretch!" said Quentin, emphatically, "I will back to rescue Lady Hameline."

"Hameline," whispered the lady, in a disturbed voice, "hangs on thy arm, to thank thee for her rescue."

"What!" said Quentin. "Is Lady Isabelle then left behind! Farewell—farewell." And the Scot shot back to the castle with the speed of the wind. Hayraddin turned to Countess Hameline who had sunk down on the ground, between shame, fear, and disappointment. "Here has been a mistake," he said, "up, lady, and come with me—I will provide you, ere morning comes, a gallanter husband than this smock-faced boy."

"Monster! you said the stars had decreed our union, and caused me to write—Oh wretch that I was!" cried the unhappy lady.

"And so they *had* decreed your union," said Hayraddin, "had both parties been willing.—Up, and follow me."

"I will not stir a foot," said the Countess obstinately.

"By the bright welkin, but you shall, though!" exclaimed Hayraddin.

"Nay," said Marthon, "she shall not be misused. She is a kind woman, though a fool.—And you, madam, rise and follow us."

"Believe me, I will care for you honestly, and the stars shall keep their word, and find you a good husband," said Hayraddin.

Like some wild animal, subdued by terror and fatigue, the Countess Hameline yielded herself up to the conduct of her guides. "How could I dream," said Hayraddin to Marthon in their own language, "that he would have made scruples about a few years, when the advantages of the match were so evident? And thou knowest, there would have been no moving yonder coy wench to be so frank as this coming Countess here. I loved the lad too, and would have done him a kindness: to wed him to this old woman was to make his fortune: to unite him to Isabelle were to have brought on him De la Marck, Burgundy, France—every one that challenges an interest in disposing of her hand. And this silly woman's wealth being chiefly in gold and jewels, we should have had our share. But away with her—we will bring her to William with the Beard. By the time he has gorged himself with wassail he will not know an old Countess from a young one. Away—bright Aldeboran still influences the destinies of the Children of the Desert!"

7. The Sack, and Flight

IN the surprised and affrighted Castle of Schonwaldt one individual endeavoured to force his way into the scene of tumult and horror as if he sought that death from which all others were flying. Approaching Schonwaldt, Quentin Durward threw himself into the moat. Swimming to the drawbridge, he caught hold of one of the chains which was hanging down, and swayed himself out of the water. As he struggled to make good his footing, a lanzk-necht, with his bloody sword in his hand, made towards him, and raised his weapon for a blow which must have been fatal.

"How now, fellow!" said Quentin, in a tone of authority. "Is that the way in which you assist a comrade? Give me your hand."

The soldier in silence, and not without hesitation, helped him upon the platform. Without allowing him time for reflection, the Scot continued in the same tone of command, "To the western tower, if you would be rich, the Priest's treasury is in the western tower." These words were echoed on every hand and carried off one body of the assailants, and another was summoned together, by war-cry and trumpet-sound, to assist in repelling a desperate sally, attempted by the defenders of the Keep.

Quentin, therefore, crossed the garden, bearing himself as if he were one, not of the conquered, but of the victors, but ere he reached the turret, three men rushed on him with levelled lances, crying, "Liege!" Putting himself in defence, but without striking, he replied, "France, friend to Liege!" "Vivat France!" cried the burghers of Liege, and passed on. The same signal proved a talisman to avert the weapons of five of La Marck's followers, whom he found straggling in the garden, and who set upon him, crying, "Sanglier!" In a word, Quentin began to hope that his character as an emissary of King Louis, the private instigator of the insurgents of Liege, and the secret supporter of William de la Marck, might possibly bear him through the horrors of the night.

On reaching the turret, he shuddered when he found the side-door now blockaded with bodies. Finding two of them dead he had dragged them hastily aside, when the third laid hand on his cloak, and entreated him to assist him to rise: "I am stifled here, in mine own armour! I am the Syndic Pavillon of Liege! Do not leave me to die like a smothered pig!" In the midst of this scene of blood and confusion, the presence of mind of Quentin suggested to him that this dignitary might have the means of protecting their retreat. He raised him on his feet, and asked him if he was wounded. "Not wounded," answered the burgher, "but much out of wind. For whom are you?"

"For France," answered Quentin.

"What! my young Archer?" said the Syndic. "Nay, if it has been my fate to find a friend in this fearful night, I will not quit him, I promise you. Go where you will, I follow.—Oh, it is a fearful night!"

At the top of the stair was an anteroom; a dead man lay across the hearth. Quentin sprang through into the bedroom of the Ladies of Croye and called Lady Isabelle's name, but no answer was returned. At length, a feeble glimmer of light announced some recess behind the arras. Quentin forced the concealed door into a small oratory, where a female figure was kneeling in agonizing supplication before the holy image. He hastily raised her from the ground, and, joy of joys! it was she whom he sought to save—Countess Isabelle. He pressed her to his bosom and entreated her to be of good cheer for that she was now under the protection of one who had hand and heart to defend her.

"Durward!" she said, "is it indeed you?—then there is some hope left. I thought all living and mortal friends had left me to my fate. Do not again abandon me!"

"Never!" said Durward. "Whatever shall happen—whatever danger shall approach!"

"Very touching, truly," said a rough, asthmatic voice behind. "A love affair, I see; and, from my soul, I pity the tender creature, as if she were my own Trudchen."

"You must do more than pity us," said Quentin, turning towards the speaker, "you must assist in protecting us, Meinheer Pavillon. Be assured this lady was put under my especial charge by your ally the King of France; and, if you aid me not to shelter her from violence, your city will lose the favour of Louis of Valois. Above all, she must be guarded from the hands of William de la Marck."

"That will be difficult," said Pavillon, "for these lanzknechts are very devils at rummaging out wenches; but I'll do my best. We will to the other apartment, and there I will look from the window and get together some of my brisk boys." And he began to halloo from the window, "Liege, Liege, for the gallant skinners' guild of curriers!" His immediate followers collected at the summons, and established a guard under the window from which their leader was bawling, and before the postern-door.

As all opposition had now ceased, and the great bell was tolled, communicating to Liege the triumphant possession of Schonwaldt by the insurgents, Pavillon despatched a messenger to command his lieutenant, Peterkin Geislaer, to attend him directly. Peterkin came at length, to his great relief. He was a stout, squat figure, with a square face, and broad black eyebrows—an advice-giving countenance, so to speak.

"Peterkin," said his commander, "this has been a glorious night. I trust thou art pleased for once?"

"I am well enough pleased that you are so," said the doughty lieutenant. But I tell you, Master Pavillon, that this Boar is like to make his own den of Schonwaldt, and 'tis probable to turn out as bad a neighbour to our town as ever was the old Bishop, and worse. Here has he taken the whole conquest in his own hand, and it is a shame to see how they have mishandled the old man among them."

"I will not permit it, Peterkin," said Pavillon, bustling up. "I disliked the mitre, but not the head that wore it. We are ten to one in the field, Peterkin, and will not permit these courses."

"Ay, ten to one in the field, but only man to man in the castle; besides, all the rabble take part with De la Marck, partly because he has broached all the ale-tubs and wine-casks, and partly for old envy towards us, who are craftsmen, and have privileges."

"Peter," said Pavillon, "we will go to the city. I will stay no longer in Schonwaldt."

"But the bridges of this castle are up, master," said Geislaer, "the gates locked, and guarded by these lanzknechts."

"But why has he secured the gates?" said the alarmed burgher, "or what business hath he to make honest men prisoners?"

"I cannot tell," said Peter. "Some noise there is about the Ladies of Croye, who have escaped during the storm of the Castle. That first put the Man with the Beard beside himself with anger, and now he's beside himself with drink also."

The Burgomaster seemed at a loss; Durward saw their only safety depended on sustaining the courage of Pavillon. "Meinheer," said Quentin, "go boldly to William de la Marck, and demand free leave to quit the castle, you, your lieutenant, your squire, and your daughter. He can have no pretence for keeping you prisoner."

"But who is my squire?" asked Pavillon.

"I am, for the present," replied the Scot.

"You!" said the embarrassed burgess, "but are you not the envoy of King Louis?"

"True, but my message is to the magistrates of Liege—and only in Liege will I deliver it. You must get me secretly out of the Castle in the capacity of your squire."

"Good—my squire. But you spoke of my daughter. My daughter is, I trust, safe in my house in Liege."

"This lady," said Durward, "will call you father while we are in this place."

"And for my whole life afterwards," said the Countess, throwing herself at the citizen's feet. "Oh, be not hard-hearted! Think your own daughter may kneel to a stranger, to ask him for life and honour—think of this, and give *me* the protection you would wish *her* to receive!"

"In troth," said the good citizen, much moved with her appeal, "I think, Peter, this pretty maiden hath a touch of our Trudchen's sweet look—I thought so from the first. She *shall* be my daughter, then, well wrapped up in her black silk veil; and if there are not enough true-hearted skinners to protect her, being the daughter of their Syndic, it were pity they should ever tug leather more."

"Admirably spoken," said Quentin: "only be bold, noble Mainheer Pavillon.—Here, sweet lady, wrap yourself close in this veil. Be but confident, and a few minutes will place you in freedom and safety."

"Hold a minute," said Pavillon. "This De la Marck is a fury; what if the young lady be one of those of Croye?"

"And if I were one of those unfortunate women," said Isabelle, "could you for that reject me in this moment of despair?"

"Well, say you *be* a countess, I will protect you nevertheless, having once passed my word," said the Syndic.

They resolved, therefore, to repair boldly to the great hall of the castle, where the Wild Boar of Ardennes held his feast, and demand free egress for the Syndic of Liege and his company. Quentin supported Isabelle through the scene of horrors as they crossed the courts, still strewed with the dying and dead and they entered the fearful hall, preceded by Pavillon and his Lieutenant, and followed by a dozen of the skinner's trade.

In the castle-hall there now reigned a scene of wild and roaring debauchery. At the head of the table, in the Bishop's throne, sat the redoubted Boar of Ardennes himself, well deserving that dreaded name. Evil practices had reddened his eyes and given the whole face a hideous likeness to the monster which it was the terrible Baron's pleasure to resemble. The soldiers sat around the table, intermixed with the men of Liege, some of them of the very lowest description; among whom Nikkel Blok the butcher, placed near De la Marck himself, was distinguished by his tucked-up sleeves which displayed arms smeared to the elbows with blood, as was the cleaver which was uplifted before him. The better class of burghers who were associated with William de la Marck's soldiers in this fearful revel showed that they feared their companions; while some of lower education, or nature more brutal, saw only in the excess of the soldier a gallant bearing, which they would willingly imitate by swallowing immense draughts of wine and beer.

When the Syndic Pavillon was announced in this tumultuous meeting, he endeavoured to maintain his dignity as well as he could, in a short address, in which he complimented the company upon the great victory gained by the soldiers of De la Marck and the good citizens of Liege.

"Ay," answered De la Marck sarcastically, "we have brought down the game at last, quoth my lady's bitch to the wolf-hound. But ho! Sir Burgomaster, who is this fair one? Unveil—no woman calls her beauty her own tonight."

"It is my daughter, noble leader," answered Pavillon, "I am to pray your forgiveness for her wearing a veil; she has a vow for that effect to the Three Blessed Kings."

"I will absolve her of it," said De la Marck, "for here, with one stroke of a cleaver, will I consecrate myself Bishop of Liege. Yes!— Bring in our predecessor in the holy seat!"

A bustle took place in the hall, while Pavillon placed himself near the bottom of the table, his followers keeping close behind him. Near the spot sat a handsome lad, a natural son of the ferocious De la Marck, towards whom he sometimes showed affection. Quentin, who had learned this point of the leader's character from the chaplain, planted himself as close as he could to the youth in question, determined to make him a hostage should other means of safety fail them. As he did so, the Bishop of Liege was dragged into the hall of his own palace by the brutal soldiery. His dishevelled state bore witness to the ill-treatment he had already received.

The scene which followed was short and fearful. The unhappy Prelate showed in this extremity a dignity well becoming the high race from which he was descended. His look was undismayed— De la Marck himself was staggered by the firm demeanour of his ° prisoner. It was not until he had emptied a large goblet of wine, that, resuming his haughty insolence of manner, he thus addressed his unfortunate captive: "Louis of Bourbon, I sought your friendship, and you rejected mine. What terms wilt thou now offer to escape this dangerous hour?—Nikkel, be ready."

The butcher rose, seized his weapon and stood with it uplifted in his bare and sinewy arms. The Bishop cast an unshaken look upon the tyrant, and then said with firmness, "Hear me, good men all, if there be any here who deserve that name, hear the only terms I can offer this ruffian. William de la Marck, thou hast stirred up to sedition an imperial city, hast assaulted and taken the palace of a Prince of the Holy German Empire and slain his people, and for this thou hast deserved to be declared outlawed and fugitive. Thou hast done more than all this. Thou hast broken into the sanctuary of the Lord, laid violent hands upon a Father of the Church, and defiled the house of God with blood and rapine, like a sacrilegious robber. Such are thy crimes. Now hear the terms I offer, as a merciful Prince and a Christian Prelate, setting aside all personal offence. Renounce thy command, unbind thy prisoners, restore thy spoil, distribute what else thou has of goods to relieve those whom thou has made orphans and widows. Array thyself in sackcloth and ashes, and go barefooted on pilgrimage to Rome, and we will ourselves be intercessors for thee with the Imperial Chamber at Ratisbon for thy life, with our Holy Father the Pope for thy miserable soul."

While Louis of Bourbon proposed these terms, in a tone as decided as if he still occupied his throne, and as if the usurper knelt a suppliant at his feet, the tyrant slowly raised himself in his chair, amazement giving way gradually to rage, until, as the Bishop ceased, he looked to Nikkel Blok, and raised his finger, without speaking a word. The ruffian struck, as if he had been doing his office in the common shambles, and the murdered Bishop sank, without a groan, at the foot of his own episcopal throne. The Liegeois, who were not prepared for so horrible a catastrophe, and who had expected to hear the conference end in some terms of accommodation, started up unanimously, with shouts of vengeance.

But William de la Marck raised his tremendous voice above the tumult: "Up, ye Boar's brood! Let these Flemish hogs see your tusks!" Every one of his followers started up at the command. Every arm was uplifted, but no one struck; for the victims were too much surprised for resistance, and it was probably the object of De la Marck only to impose terror on his civic confederates. But the courage of Quentin Durward gave a new turn to the scene. Imitating the action of the followers of De la Marck, he sprang on Carl Eberson, the son of their leader, and held his dirk at the boy's throat, while he exclaimed, "Is that your game? then here I play my part."

"Hold! hold!" exclaimed De la Marck, "it is a jest—a jest. Think you I would injure my good friends of the city of Liege?— Soldiers, unloose your holds; sit down; take away the carrion" (giving the Bishop's corpse a thrust with his foot) "which hath caused this strife among friends, and let us drown unkindness in a fresh carouse."

All unloosened their holds, and Quentin Durward took advantage of the moment. "Hear me," he said, "William de la Marck, and you, burghers and citizens of Liege."

"Who art thou, in the fiend's name," said the astonished De la Marck, "who art come to take hostages from us in our own lair?"

"I am a servant of King Louis of France," said Quentin boldly, "an Archer of the Scottish Guard, as my language and dress may tell you, here to behold and report your proceedings; and I see with wonder, they are those of heathens, rather than Christians. The hosts of Burgundy will be instantly in motion against you all; and if you wish assistance from France, you must conduct yourselves in a different manner.—For you, men of Liege, I advise your instant return to your own city; and if there is any obstruction offered to your departure, I denounce those by whom it is so offered foes to my master, his most gracious Majesty of France."

"France and Liege!" cried the followers of Pavillon, and several other citizens, whose courage began to rise at Quentin's bold language. "France and Liege, and long live the gallant Archer!"

William de la Marck grasped his dagger as if about to launch it at the heart of the audacious speaker; but glancing around, he read something in the looks of his soldiers, which even *he* was obliged to respect. De la Marck saw he would not be supported, even by his own band, in any further act of immediate violence, and relaxing, he declared that "he had not the least design against his good friends of Liege, all of whom were at liberty to depart from Schonwaldt at their pleasure."

The young Scot returned his thanks, and they were suffered to leave the castle without opposition; and glad was Quentin when he turned his back on those formidable walls. For the first time since they had entered that dreadful hall Quentin ventured to ask the young Countess how she did. "Well, well," she answered, in feverish haste, "but let us not lose an instant in words." She endeavoured to mend her pace as she spoke, but must have fallen from exhaustion had not Durward supported her. The young

Scot raised his precious charge in his arms with tenderness, and while she encircled his neck with one arm, he would not have wished one of the risks of the night unencountered, since such had been the conclusion.

The honest Burgomaster was, in his turn, supported by his faithful counsellor Peter, and thus, in breathless haste, they reached the river where Peter at length procured a boat for the use of the company, and with it an opportunity of some repose, equally welcome to Isabelle, who continued to lie almost motionless in the arms of her preserver, and to the worthy Burgomaster.

When the boat stopped at the bottom of his garden, and Pavillon had got himself assisted on shore by Peter, their kind host called loudly for Trudchen, who presently appeared. She was charged to pay the utmost attention to the care of the beautiful and half-fainting stranger; and Trudchen discharged the hospitable duty with the affection of a sister. Quentin, on his side, was ushered by the mother of the family to the neat and pleasant apartment in which he was to spend the night.

The young Scot slept until late on the day following, when his worthy host entered the apartment, with looks of care on his brow. He seated himself by his guest's bedside, and began a long discourse upon the domestic duties of married life. Quentin listened with some anxiety, and hastened to probe the matter more closely, "by hoping their arrival had been attended with no inconvenience to the good lady of the household."

"Inconvenience!—no," answered the Burgomaster. "No woman on earth so hospitable—only 'tis pity her temper is something particular."

"Our residence here is disagreeable to her?" said the Scot, starting out of bed, and beginning to dress himself hastily. "Were I but sure Lady Isabelle were fit for travel after the horrors of the last night, we would not increase the offence by remaining here an instant longer."

"Nay," said Pavillon, "that is just what the young lady herself said to Mother Mabel; and truly I wish you saw the colour that came to her face as she said it—a milkmaid that has skated five miles to market against the frost-wind is a lily compared to it—I do not wonder Mother Mabel may be a little jealous, poor dear soul."

"Has Lady Isabelle then left her apartment?" said the youth.

"Yes," replied Pavillon, "and she expects your approach with much impatience, to determine which way you shall go—since you are both determined on going. But I trust you will tarry breakfast?"

"Why did you not tell me this sooner?" said Durward impatiently.

"Softly," said the Syndic. "I have a word to say: Trudchen wants you to take some other disguise, for there is word in the town that the Ladies of Croye travel the country in Pilgrim's dresses, attended by a Scottish Archer. It is said one of them was brought into Schonwaldt last night by a Bohemian after we had left it; and it was said still further that this same Bohemian had assured De la Marck that you were charged with no message to the good people of Liege, and that you had stolen away the young Countess, and travelled with her as her paramour. All this news hath come from Schonwaldt this morning; and though our own opinion is that De la Marck has been a thought too rough both with the Bishop and with ourselves, yet he is our only leader against the Duke of Burgundy."

"Your daughter advises well," said Quentin Durward. "We must part in disguise instantly. We may, I trust, rely upon you for the necessary secrecy, and for the means of escape?"

"With all my heart," said the honest citizen who was not much satisfied with the dignity of his own conduct: "I cannot but remember that I owed you my life last night. Nay, now you are ready, come this way—you shall see how far I can trust you." The Syndic led him to his own counting-room and offered Quentin two hundred guilders. Quentin accepted the sum, and by doing so took a great weight from the mind of Pavillon, who considered it as an atonement for his breach of hospitality.

Having carefully locked his treasure-chamber, the wealthy Fleming next conveyed his guest to the parlour where he found the Countess attired in the fashion of a Flemish maiden of the middling class. She extended her hand to him, and when he had reverently kissed it she said to him, "Seignior Quentin, we must leave our friends here, unless I would bring on them the misery which has pursued me ever since my father's death. You must change your dress and go with me, unless you also are tired of befriending a being so unfortunate."

"I tired of being your attendant!—To the end of the earth will I guard you! But can you, after the terrors of last night——"

"Do not recall them to my memory," answered the Countess. "I remember but the confusion of a horrid dream. Has the excellent Bishop escaped?"

"I trust he is in freedom," said Quentin, making a sign to Pavillon to be silent.

"We will consider," said Isabelle, and after a moment's pause she added, "A convent would be my choice, but I fear it would prove a weak defence against those who pursue me."

"Hem!" said the Syndic, "I could not well recommend a convent within the district of Liege. The Boar of Ardennes payeth little regard to nunneries, and the like."

"Get yourself in readiness hastily, Seignior Durward," said Isabelle, "since to your faith I must needs commit myself." No sooner had the Syndic and Quentin left the room, than Isabelle began to ask of Trudchen, who attended her, various questions concerning the roads.

"Take courage, lady," said Trudchen, "tell your beads and throw yourself on the care of Heaven. There is one in whom I have some interest," she added, blushing deeply. "Say nothing to my father, but I have ordered my bachelor, Hans Glover, to wait for you at the eastern gate and never to see my face more unless he brings word that he has guided you safe from the territory." To kiss her tenderly was the only way in which the young Countess could express her thanks to the kind-hearted city-maiden, who returned the embrace affectionately, and added, with a smile, "Nay, if two maidens and their devoted bachelors cannot succeed in a disguise and an escape, the world is changed from what I am told it was wont to be."

At that point Quentin entered attired in Peter's holiday suit. Two stout horses had been provided by the activity of Mother Mabel, who really desired the Countess and her attendant no harm, provided that her own family were clear of the dangers which might attend upon harbouring them. She beheld them mount and go off with great satisfaction, after telling them that they would find their way to the east gate by keeping their eye on Peter, who was to walk in that direction as their guide.

The travellers gained the eastern gate of the city, passed the guards and took leave of Peter Geislaer with a brief exchange of good wishes. Immediately afterwards they were joined by a stout young man riding a good grey horse, who made himself known as Hans Glover, the bachelor of Trudchen Pavillon. Saluting them respectfully, he asked of the Countess in Flemish on which road she desired to be conducted?

"Guide me," said she, "towards the nearest town on the frontiers of Brabant."

"You have then settled the object of your journey?" said Quentin, approaching his horse to that of Isabelle, and speaking French, which their guide did not understand.

"Surely," replied the young lady. "My resolution is taken to return to my native country, and to throw myself on the mercy of the Duke of Burgundy. It was mistaken, though well-meant advice, which induced me ever to withdraw from his protection, and place myself under that of the crafty and false Louis of France."

"And you resolve to become the bride, then, of the Count of Campo-basso, the unworthy favourite of Charles?" asked Quentin, struggling to assume an indifferent tone.

"No, Durward, no," said the Lady Isabelle, sitting up erect in her saddle, "to that hated condition all Burgundy's power shall not sink a daughter of the House of Croye. Burgundy may seize on my lands, he may imprison my person in a convent; but that is the worst I have to expect; and worse than that I will endure ere I give my hand to Campo-basso."

"The worst!" said Quentin; "and what worse can there be than plunder and imprisonment? Oh, think, while you have God's free air around you. Why not rather betake yourself to your own strong castle? Why not call around you the vassals of your father, and make treaty with Burgundy, rather than surrender yourself to him?"

"Alas!" said the Countess, "that scheme, the suggestion of the crafty Louis, has become impracticable since it was betrayed to Burgundy by the double traitor Zamet Maugrabin. My kinsman was then imprisoned, and my houses garrisoned. Any attempt of mine would but expose my dependants to the vengeance of Duke Charles. No, I will submit myself to my Sovereign as a dutiful vassal, the rather that I trust my kinswoman, Countess Hameline, who first counselled my flight, has already taken this wise and honourable step! But know you aught of her?"

Her question, urged in a tone of the most anxious inquiry, obliged Quentin to give some account of what he knew of the Countess's fate. "Oh, my unhappy kinswoman," said Countess Isabelle, "and the wretch Marthon, who enjoyed so much of her confidence, and deserved it so little—it was she that introduced to my aunt the wretched Zamet and Hayraddin Maugrabin, who, by their pretended knowledge in soothsaying, obtained a great ascendency over her mind. I doubt not that, from the beginning, we had been surrounded by these snares by Louis of France, in order to determine us to take refuge at his Court."

In mutual confidence, and forgetting the singularity of their own situation, as well as the perils of the road, the travellers pursued their journey for several hours, only stopping to refresh their horses at a retired hamlet to which they were conducted by Hans Glover. The artificial distinction which divided the two lovers seemed dissolved by the circumstances in which they were placed. They *spoke* not indeed of love, but the thoughts of it were on both sides unavoidable; and thus they were placed in that relation to each other in which sentiments of mutual regard are rather understood than announced, and which often form the most delightful hours of human existence.

It was two hours after noon when the travellers were alarmed by the report of the guide, who, with horror in his countenance, said that they were pursued by a party of De la Marck's Black Troopers. On looking back, and discovering along the road which they had traversed a cloud of dust advancing, with two of the headmost troopers riding furiously in front of it, Quentin addressed his companion, "Dearest Isabelle, I have no weapon left save my sword; but since I cannot fight for you, I will fly with you. Could we gain yonder wood that is before us ere they come up, we may easily find means to escape."

"So be it, my only friend," said Isabelle, pressing her horse to the gallop. The honest Fleming continued to attend them, all three riding towards the shelter of the wood as fast as their jaded horses could go, until a body of men-at-arms under a knight's pennon was discovered advancing from cover to intercept their flight. "They have bright armour," said Isabelle, "they must be Burgundians. Be they who they will, we must yield to them rather than to the lawless miscreants who pursue us." A moment after she exclaimed, "I know the banner—it is the Count of Crève-coeur, a noble Burgundian—to him I will surrender myself."

Quentin Durward sighed; but what other alternative remained? They soon joined the band of Crèvecoeur, and the Countess demanded to speak to the leader: "Noble Count, Isabelle of Croye, the daughter of your old companion in arms, Count Reinold of Croye, renders herself, and asks protection from your valour for her and hers."

"Thou shalt have it, fair kinswoman, were it against a host—always excepting my liege Lord of Burgundy. But there is little time to talk.—By Saint George of Burgundy, the knaves have the insolence to advance against the banner of Crèvecoeur! Lay your spears in the rest. Crèvecoeur to the rescue!" Crying his war-cry, and followed by his men-at-arms, he galloped forward to charge the Black Troopers, and put them to the rout in five minutes. The Count of Crèvecoeur, wiping his bloody sword upon his horse's mane ere he sheathed it, came back to the verge of the forest, where Isabelle had remained a spectator of the combat. "This is a rough welcome to your home, my pretty cousin," said the Count, "but wandering princesses must expect such adventures."

"My Lord Count," said Lady Isabelle, "without further preface, let me know if I am a prisoner, and where you are to conduct me."

"My duty, and it is a sad one," answered the Count, "will be ended when I have conducted you to the Duke's Court at Peronne."

"Cousin of Crèvecoeur," said Countess Isabelle, "let me, in yielding myself prisoner, stipulate at least for the safety of those who have befriended me in my misfortunes. Permit this good fellow, my trusty guide, to go back unharmed to his native town of Liege."

"He shall have his liberty," said Crèvecoeur, after looking sharply at Glover's honest breadth of countenance.

"Remember me to the kind Trudchen," said the Countess to her guide, and added, taking a string of pearls from under her veil, "Pray her to wear this in remembrance of her unhappy friend." Honest Glover took the string of pearls, and kissed her fair hand.

"Any further bequests to make, my fair cousin? It is time we were on our way," said the Count.

"Only," said the Countess, making an effort to speak, "that you will be favourable to this—this young gentleman."

"Umph!" said Crèvecoeur, casting the same penetrating glance on Quentin which he had bestowed on Glover, but apparently with a much less satisfactory result. "And pray, cousin, what has this—this *very* young gentleman done, to deserve such intercession at your hands?"

"He has saved my life and honour," said the Countess, reddening with shame and resentment.

"The young gentleman may wait on us, if his quality permit, and I will see he has no injury," said Crèvecoeur.

"My Lord Count," said Durward, unable to keep silence any longer, "lest you should talk of a stranger in slighter terms than you might afterwards think becoming, I take leave to tell you that I am Quentin Durward, an Archer of the Scottish Body-guard, in which, as you well know, none but gentlemen and men of honour are enrolled."

"I thank you for your information, and I kiss your hands, Seignior Archer," said Crèvecoeur, in the same tone of raillery. "Have the goodness to ride with me to the front of the party."

"My lord," said Quentin in a temperate but firm tone of voice, "may I request you to tell me if I am at liberty, or am to account myself your prisoner?"

"A shrewd question," replied the Count, "which, at present, I can only answer by another—Are France and Burgundy, think you, at peace or war with each other?"

"That," replied the Scot, "you, my lord, should certainly know better than I."

"Why, I, who have been at Peronne with the Duke all this week," said the Count, "cannot resolve this riddle any more than you; and yet, Sir Squire, upon the solution of that question depends the said point, whether you are prisoner or free man; and, for the present, I must hold you as the former. How long have you been about the person of the Lady Isabelle of Croye?"

"Count of Crèvecoeur," said Quentin Durward, "I have acted as escort to the Lady Isabelle since she left France to retire into Flanders."

"Ho! ho!" said the Count, "and that is to say, since she fled from Plessis-les-Tours? You, an Archer of the Scottish Guard, accompanied her, of course, by the express orders of King Louis?"

However little Quentin thought himself indebted to the King of France, he did not conceive himself at liberty to betray any trust which Louis had seemed to repose in him, and therefore replied to Count Crèvecoeur's inference, "that it was sufficient for him to have the authority of his superior officer for what he had done, and he inquired no further."

"It is quite sufficient," said the Count. "It will be difficult for King Louis to continue to aver so boldly that he knew not of the Ladies of Croye having escaped from France, since they were escorted by one of his own Life-guard.—And whither, Sir Archer, was your retreat directed?"

"To Liege, my lord," answered the Scot, "where the ladies desired to be placed under the protection of the late Bishop."

"The *late* Bishop!" exclaimed the Count of Crèvecoeur, "is Louis of Bourbon dead? Not a word of his illness had reached the Duke. Of what did he die?"

"He sleeps in a bloody grave, my lord—that is, if his murderers have conferred one on his remains."

"Murdered!" exclaimed Crèvecoeur again, "young man, it is impossible!"

"I saw the deed done with my own eyes."

"Saw it! and made not in to help the good Prelate!" exclaimed the Count, "or to raise the Castle against his murderers?"

"To be brief, my lord," said Durward, "ere this act was done, the Castle was stormed by the bloodthirsty William de la Marck with the help of the insurgent Liegeois."

"Liege in insurrection!" said Crèvecoeur. "Schonwaldt taken! The Bishop murdered! Messenger of sorrow, speak—knew you of this assault—of this murder?"

"I know no more of these villainies than you, my lord," said Quentin. "What could I do?—they were hundreds, and I but one. My only care was to rescue the Countess Isabelle, and in that I was happily successful. As it was, my abhorrence was spoken loud enough to prevent other horrors."

"I believe thee, youth," said the Count. "But alas! for the kind and generous Prelate, to be murdered on the hearth where he so often entertained the stranger with Christian charity and princely bounty. I know not Charles of Burgundy, if vengeance be not as sudden and severe as this villainy has been unexampled in atrocity."

131

Quentin saw the grief he manifested was augmented by the bitter recollection of past friendship with the sufferer and was silent accordingly. But the Count returned again and again to the subject—questioned him on every particular of the surprise of Schonwaldt, and the Bishop's death; and then suddenly, as if he had recollected something which had escaped his memory, demanded what had become of Lady Hameline, and why she was not with her kinswoman? "Not," he added contemptuously, "that I consider her absence as at all a loss to Countess Isabelle."

In some dread of ridicule, Durward, though with pain, confined his reply to a confused account of the Lady Hameline having made her escape from Schonwaldt before the attack took place. He added to his embarrassed detail that he had heard a vague report of the Lady Hameline having since fallen into the hands of William de la Marck.

"I trust in Saint Lambert that he will marry her," said Crèvecoeur, "as, indeed, he is likely enough to do, for the sake of her money-bags." The Count then proceeded to ask so many questions concerning the mode in which both ladies had conducted themselves on the journey, the degree of intimacy to which they admitted Quentin himself, and other trying particulars, that, vexed, ashamed and angry, the youth was scarce able to conceal his embarrassment from the keen-sighted soldier and courtier. "Umph—I see it as I conjectured, on one side at least; I trust the other party has kept her senses better. Come, Sir Squire, spur on while I fall back to discourse with Lady Isabelle.—Yet stay, young gallant—one word ere you go. Forget it all, young soldier," he said, tapping him on the shoulder, "remember yonder lady only as the honoured Countess of Croye—forget her as a wandering and adventurous damsel."

"My Lord Count, when I require advice of you, I will ask it," Quentin replied indignantly.

"Heyday!" said the Count; "I must expect a challenge to the lists!"

"You speak as if that were an impossibility," said Quentin.

"When I broke a lance with the Duke of Orleans it was against a breast in which flowed better blood than that of Crèvecoeur, and when I measured swords with Dunois I engaged a better warrior."

"If thou speak'st truth, thou hast had singular luck," said Crèvecoeur, laughing. "Thou canst not move me to anger, though thou mayest to mirth. Believe me, thou art by no means the equal of those of whom thou hast been either the casual opponent, or more casual companion."

He reined back his horse to join the Countess, while Quentin rode on, muttering to himself, "Cold-blooded, insolent coxcomb!"

In the evening they reached the town of Charleroi, and Crèvecoeur consigned Countess Isabelle, in a state of great exhaustion, to the care of the Abbess of the Cistercian convent, a noble lady in whose prudence and kindness he could repose confidence. Crèvecoeur himself only stopped to require the governor of a small Burgundian garrison who occupied the place to mount a guard of honour upon the convent during the residence of the Countess Isabelle—ostensibly to secure her safety but perhaps secretly to prevent her attempting to escape. The Count was determined himself to be the first to carry the formidable news of the insurrection and the murder of the Bishop to Duke Charles. Having procured fresh horses for himself and suite, he mounted with the resolution of continuing his journey to Peronne without stopping for repose, and he informed Quentin Durward that he must attend him.

Quentin, during the earlier part of the night journey, had to combat with that bitter heart-ache which is felt when youth parts, and probably for ever, with her he loves. At length, after the cold hour of midnight was past, in spite alike of love and sorrow, the extreme fatigue which Quentin had undergone for two days began to have an effect on him. When at length they reached the town of Landrecy, the Count, in compassion to the youth, allowed his retinue a halt of four hours for rest and refreshment.

Deep were Quentin's slumbers, until they were broken by the sound of the Count's trumpet. Confidence in himself and his fortunes returned with his reviving spirits, and with the rising sun. In this manly mood of bearing his misfortune, Quentin felt himself more able to receive and reply to the jests of the Count of Crèvecoeur. The young Scot accommodated himself good-humouredly to the Count's raillery, and the change of his tone and manner obviously made a more favourable impression on the Count. Thus travelling on with more harmony than on the preceding day, the party came at last within two miles of the famous town of Peronne, near which the Duke of Burgundy's army lay encamped, ready to invade France; and, in opposition to which, Louis XI had himself assembled a strong force for the purpose of bringing to reason his overpowerful vassal.

8. The Unbidden Guest

PERONNE was accounted one of the strongest fortresses in France. The Count of Crèvecoeur, his retinue, and his prisoner, were approaching the fortress about the third hour after noon; when, riding through the forest, they were met by two men of rank, engaged in the amusement of hawking. But on perceiving Crèvecoeur, they came galloping towards him.

"News, Count of Crèvecoeur!" they cried both together. The Count saluted them both courteously—the famous Knight of Hainault, Philip des Comines, at this time one of the most esteemed counsellors of Duke Charles the Bold, and his companion, the Baron d'Hymbercourt. "Crèvecoeur—listen, and wonder—King Louis is at Peronne!" said Comines.

"What!" said the Count, in astonishment, "has the Duke retreated without a battle?"

"No," said D'Hymbercourt, "the banners of Burgundy have not gone back a foot; and still King Louis is here."

"Then Edward of England must have come over the seas with his bowmen," said Crèvecoeur.

"Not so," said Comines. "Hear the extraordinary truth. You know when you left us that the conference between the commissioners of France and Burgundy was broken up, without apparent chance of reconciliation?"

"True; and we dreamt of nothing but war," said Crèvecoeur.

"Only one day later," said Comines, "the Duke had in council protested so furiously against further delay that it was resolved to send a defiance to the King, and march forward instantly into France, when lo! the French herald Mont-joie rode into our camp. We thought that Louis had been beforehand with our defiance. But a council being speedily assembled, what was our wonder when the herald informed us that Louis, King of France, was scarce an hour's riding behind, intending to visit Charles, Duke of Burgundy, with a small retinue, in order that their differences might be settled at a personal interview!"

"You surprise me, Messires," said Crèvecoeur, "and yet when I was last at Plessis-les-Tours, the all-trusted Cardinal Balue, offended with his master, did hint to me that he could so work upon Louis that the Duke might have terms of peace of his own making. But I never suspected that so old a fox as Louis could have been induced to come into the trap. What said the Duke?"

"Spoke brief and bold, as usual," replied Comines. "'If my royal kinsman comes hither in singleness of heart, he shall be royally welcome. If it is meant by this appearance of confidence to circumvent me till he execute some of his politic schemes, by Saint George of Burgundy, let him look to it!' And so he ordered us all to horse to receive so extraordinary a guest."

"How was he accompanied?" asked Crèvecoeur.

"By only two score of the Scottish Guard, and a few gentlemen of his household—among whom his astrologer, Galeotti, made the gayest figure," answered D'Hymbercourt.

"That fellow," said Crèvecoeur, "holds some dependence on Cardinal Balue—I should not be surprised that he has had his share in determining the King to this step of doubtful policy. Any nobility of higher rank?"

"There are Monsieur of Orleans and Dunois," replied Comines.

"I will have a draught with Dunois," said Crèvecoeur, "wag the world as it will. But we heard that both he and the Duke had fallen into disgrace, and were in prison."

"They were both under arrest in the Castle of Loches, that delightful place of retirement for the French nobility," said D'Hymbercourt, "but Louis released them in order to bring them with him—perhaps because he cared not to leave Orleans behind. For his other attendants, faith, I think the Hangman Marshall and Oliver, his barber, may be the most considerable."

"And where is he lodged?" said Crèvecoeur.

"Nay, that," replied Comines, "is the most marvellous of all. Louis himself craved to be quartered in the Castle of Peronne and *there* he hath his abode accordingly."

"Why, God ha' mercy!" exclaimed Crèvecoeur, "this is not only venturing into the lion's den, but thrusting his head into his very jaws. Now, gentlemen, ride close by my rein," he continued, "and when I tell you what has chanced in the bishopric of Liege, I think you will be of opinion that King Louis might as safely have undertaken a pilgrimage to the infernal regions as this ill-timed visit to Peronne." And the party of nobles rode on to the meadows adjoining the town, now whitened with the tents of the Duke of Burgundy's army of fifteen thousand men.

Now princes are required, by the respect which is due to their own dignity, to regulate their expressions to each other by a severe etiquette which precludes all violent display of passion. This ceremony was a severe penalty to Charles of Burgundy, the most impatient prince of his time. Attended by his great officers, he went in gallant cavalcade to receive Louis XI. His retinue blazed with gold and silver, for the wealth of the Court of Burgundy was for the time the most magnificent in Europe. The courtiers attending Louis, on the contrary, were few in number and comparatively mean in appearance, and the exterior of the King himself, in a threadbare cloak, rendered the contrast yet more striking; and as the Duke, richly attired with the coronet and mantle of state, threw himself from his noble charger, and, kneeling on one knee, offered to hold the stirrup while Louis dismounted from his little ambling palfrey, the effect was almost grotesque. The greeting between the two potentates was, of course, full of affected kindness and compliment. But the temper of the Duke rendered it much more difficult for him to preserve the necessary appearances, while in the King, every species of dissimulation seemed so much a part of his nature that those best acquainted with him could not have distinguished what was feigned from what was real.

The King was no doubt sensible from the Duke's constrained manner that the game he had to play was delicate. But repentance was too late, and all that remained for him was that inimitable dexterity of management which the King understood equally with any man that ever lived. The King blamed himself for not having sooner taken the decisive step of convincing his good kinsman by such a mark of confidence as he was now bestowing, that the angry passages which had occurred between them were nothing in his remembrance, when weighed against the kindness which received him when an exile from France.

"Your Majesty," said the Duke, compelling himself to make some reply, "acknowledged that slight obligation in terms which overpaid all the display which Burgundy could make to show due sense of the honour you had done its Sovereign."

"I remember the words you mean, fair cousin," said the King, smiling, "I think they were, that in guerdon of the benefit of that time, I, poor wanderer, had nothing to offer, save the persons of myself, of my wife, and of my child. Well, I think I have in- differently well redeemed my pledge."

"I mean not to dispute what your Majesty is pleased to aver," said the Duke, "but——"

"But you ask," said the King, interrupting him, "how my actions have accorded with my words. Marry thus: the body of

my infant child Joachim rests in Burgundian earth—my own person I have this morning placed unreservedly in your power. And, for that of my wife—truly, cousin, I think, considering the period of time which has passed you will scarce insist on my keeping my word in that particular, but if you insist on my promise being fulfilled to the letter, she shall presently await your pleasure." Angry as the Duke of Burgundy was at the barefaced attempt of the King to assume towards him a tone of friendship and intimacy, he could not help laughing at the monarch's whimsical reply. Having laughed longer and louder than was fitting the occasion, he answered in the same tone, bluntly declining the honour of the Queen's company, but stating his willingness to accept that of the King's eldest daughter whose beauty was celebrated.

"I am happy, fair cousin," said the King, "that your gracious pleasure has not fixed on my younger daughter Joan. I should otherwise have had spear-breaking between you and my cousin of Orleans."

"Nay, my royal sovereign," said Duke Charles, "the Duke of Orleans shall have no interruption from me in the path which he has chosen. The cause in which I couch my lance against Orleans must be fair and straight." Louis was far from taking amiss this brutal allusion to the deformity of the Princess Joan. On the contrary, he was rather pleased to find that the Duke was content to be amused with broad jests in which he was himself a proficient, and which (according to the modern phrase) spared much senti-mental hypocrisy. And so that want of kinder feelings between them was supplied by the tone of good fellowship which exists between two boon companions—a tone natural to the Duke's frank and gross character, and to Louis's caustic humour.

Both Princes were happily able to preserve during the banquet at Peronne the same kind of conversation on which they met on neutral ground. Yet Louis was alarmed to observe that the Duke had around him several of those French nobles in situations of great trust and power whom his own injustice had driven into exile; and it was to secure himself from the possible effects of their resentment and revenge that he requested to be lodged in the Citadel of Peronne rather than in the town itself. This was readily granted by Duke Charles. But when the King asked whether the Scottish Archers of his Guard might not maintain the custody of the Castle of Peronne during his residence there, Charles replied: "Saint Martin! No, my liege. My castle and town are yours, and my men are yours; so it is indifferent whether my men-at-arms or the Scottish Archers guard either the outer gate or defences of the castle."

At length a day closed which must have been wearisome to Louis, and full of constraint to the Duke. The latter retired into his own apartment after he had taken a formal leave of the King for the night, and Louis was escorted to the lodgings he had chosen in the Citadel by the Duke's chamberlains, and received at the entrance by a strong guard of men-at-arms.

"No further than the base-court, my noble lords and gentle-men!" said Louis, "I can permit your attendance no further—you have done me enough of grace. I am something fatigued, my lords; I trust to enjoy your society better tomorrow. And yours too, Seignior Philip of Comines, I am told you are the annalist of the time. We that desire to have a name in history, must speak you fair, for men say your pen hath a sharp point when you will. Good-night, my lords and gentles, to all and each of you."

The Lords of Burgundy retired much pleased with the grace of Louis's manner, and the King was left with only one or two of his personal followers under the archway of the base-court of the Castle, looking on the huge tower, or principal Keep, of the place. (This tall, dark, massive building, was seen clearly by the same moon which was lighting Quentin Durward between Charleroi and Peronne.) "I am not to be lodged *there!*" the King said, with a shudder.

"No," replied the grey-headed Steward, who attended upon him unbonneted. "God forbid! Anciently it was used as a state prison, and there are many tales of deeds which have been done in it, your Majesty." Louis asked no further questions; no man was more bound than he to respect the secrets of a prison-house.

At the door of the apartments destined for his use stood a small token party of the Scottish Guard, permitted in compliment to the King. The faithful Lord Crawford was at their head. "My honest Crawford," said the King, "where hast thou been today? I saw you not at the banquet."

"I declined it, my liege," said Crawford, "times are changed with me. I have few men to command and the more need to keep the knaves in fitting condition. Whether this business be like to end in feasting or fighting, God and your Majesty know better than old John of Crawford.—The word for the night, if your Majesty pleases?"

"Let it be Burgundy, in honour of our host and of a liquor you love, Crawford."

"I will quarrel with neither Duke nor drink so called," said Crawford, "provided always that both be sound. A good night to your Majesty!"

"A good night, my trusty Scot," said the King, and passed on to his apartments. At the door of his bedroom Le Balafré was placed sentinal. "Follow me hither," said the King, as he passed into the apartment. "Have you heard from your nephew of late? Stand back, my masters," he added, addressing the gentlemen of his chamber, "for this concerneth no ears but mine."

"Surely, please your Majesty," said Balafré, "I have seen this very evening the groom Charlot whom my kinsman despatched from the Bishop's Castle where he hath lodged the Ladies of Croye in safety."

"Now our Lady of Heaven be praised!" said the King. "Art thou sure of it?"

"As sure as I can be of anything," said Le Balafré, "the fellow, I think, hath letters for your Majesty from the Ladies of Croye."

"Haste to get them," said the King. "Now our Lady of Embrun be praised! and silver shall be the screen that surrounds her high altar!" Louis, in this fit of gratitude and devotion, doffed, as usual, his hat, selected from the figures with which it was garnished that which represented his favourite image of the Virgin, placed it on a table, and, kneeling down, repeated the vow reverently.

The groom, being the first messenger whom Durward had despatched from Schonwaldt, was now introduced with his letters. They were addressed to the King by the Ladies of Croye, and barely thanked him in cold terms for his courtesy while at his Court, and, something more warmly, for having permitted them to retire and sent them in safety from his dominions; expressions at which Louis laughed very heartily, instead of resenting them. He then demanded of Charlot whether they had not sustained some attack upon the road? Charlot, a stupid fellow, gave a confused account of the affray in which his companion, the Gascon, had been killed, but knew of no other. Again Louis demanded of him the route which the party had taken to Liege, and seemed much interested when he was informed that they had, upon approaching Namur, kept the more direct road to Liege upon the left bank of the Maes, instead of the right bank as recommended in their route. The King then ordered the man a small present, and dismissed him.

On his departure, Louis threw himself into a chair, and appearing much exhausted, dismissed the rest of his attendants, excepting Oliver, who was at length tempted to say, "*Tête-dieu*, Sire, you seem as if you had lost a battle; and yet I, who was near your Majesty during this whole day, never knew you fight a field so gallantly."

"Well, Oliver," said King Louis, looking up, "rejoice with me that my plans in Flanders have not taken effect, whether as concerning those two rambling Princesses of Croye, or in Liege— you understand me?"

"In faith, I do not, Sire," replied Oliver. "It is impossible for me to congratulate your Majesty on the failure of your favourite schemes unless you tell me some reason for the change in your own wishes."

"Nay," answered the King, "there is no change, in a general

view. But, *Pasques-dieu*, my friend, I have this day learned more of Duke Charles than I before knew. When he was Count de Charalois, and I the banished Dauphin of France, we drank and hunted together—and many a wild adventure we had. And in those days I had a decided advantage over him—like that which a strong spirit naturally assumes over a weak one. But he has since changed: I was compelled to glide as gently away from each offensive topic as if I touched red-hot iron. I did but hint at the possibility of those erratic Countesses of Croye ere they attained Liege (for thither I frankly confessed that, to the best of my belief, they were gone), falling into the hands of some wild snapper upon the frontiers, and you would have thought I had spoken of sacrilege. I would have held my head's safety very insecure, if, in that moment, accounts had been brought of the success of thy friend, William with the Beard, in his honest scheme of bettering himself by marriage. However, Oliver, lucky the man who has her not; for hang, draw, and quarter, were the most gentle words which my cousin spoke of him who should wed the young Countess, his vassal, without his most ducal permission."

"And he is, doubtless, as jealous of any disturbances in the good town of Liege?" asked the favourite.

"More so," replied the King, "but my bustling friends Rouslaer and Pavillon have orders to be quiet as a mouse until this happy meeting between my cousin and me is over. No game is to be despaired of until it is lost, and if nothing occurs to stir the rage of this vindictive madman, Burgundy, I am sure of victory. And this my own art foresaw—fortified by that of Galeotti: that the expedition of yonder Scottish Archer should end happily for me— and such has been the issue, though in a manner different from what I expected. Well, Oliver, we will to bed—our resolution has been made and executed; there is nothing to be done but to play manfully the game on which we have entered."

9. Explosion

O N the following morning after the King's arrival, there was a general muster of the troops of the Duke of Burgundy, which were numerous and excellently appointed. It must have added to Louis's mortification that he recognized as part of this host many banners of French nobility. True to his character, however, Louis seemed to take little notice of these malcontents, while, in fact, he was revolving in his mind the various means by which it might be possible to detach them from the banners of Burgundy and bring them back to his own.

During a boar-hunt in the forest, while the Duke, eager always upon the immediate object, whether business or pleasure, gave himself up to the ardour of the chase, Louis found the means of speaking secretly and separately to many of those who were reported to have most interest with Charles. The notice of so great and so wise a King was in itself a mighty bribe; promises did much, and direct gifts did still more; not, as he represented, to alienate their faithful services from their noble master, but that they might lend their aid in preserving peace between France and Burgundy—an end so excellent in itself, and so obviously tending to the welfare of both countries, and of the reigning Princes of either. Such an opportunity of personally conciliating, or, if the reader pleases, corrupting, the ministers of Charles, was perhaps what the King had proposed to himself as a principal object of his visit even if his art should fail to cajole the Duke himself. The King had been long paving the way by his ministers for an establishment of an interest in the Court of Burgundy, but Louis's own personal exertions did more to accomplish that object in a few hours than his agents had effected in years of negotiation.

The Court upon this occasion dined in the forest when the hour of noon arrived, as was common in those great hunting-parties; an arrangement particularly agreeable to the Duke, desirous as he was to abridge that deferential solemnity with which he was otherwise under the necessity of receiving King Louis. But although it was possible to avoid much ceremony by having the dinner upon the green turf with all the freedom of a woodland meal, it was necessary that the evening repast should for that very reason be held with more than usual solemnity.

Upon returning to Peronne, King Louis found a banquet prepared with a profusion of splendour and magnificence. At the head of the long board, which groaned under plate of gold and silver filled with the most exquisite dainties, sat the Duke, and on his right hand, upon a seat more elevated than his own was placed his royal guest. Behind him stood on one side the son of the Duke of Gueldres, who officiated as his grand carver—on the other, Le Glorieux, his jester, very richly dressed. Louis neglected not to take notice of the favourite buffoon of the Duke, and to applaud his repartees; which he did the rather, that he saw that the folly of Le Glorieux covered more than the usual quantity of shrewd and caustic observation proper to his class. To this personage Charles, and Louis, in imitation of his host, often addressed themselves during the entertainment. "Whose seats be those that are vacant?" said Charles to the jester.

"One of those at least should be mine, Charles," replied Le Glorieux.

"Why so, knave?" said Charles.

"Because they belong to the Sieurs D'Hymbercourt and Des Comines, who are gone so far to fly their falcons that they have forgot their supper."

"Well, fools or wise men," said the Duke, "here come the defaulters." As he spoke, Comines and D'Hymbercourt entered the room, and, after having made their reverence to the two Princes, assumed in silence the seats which were left vacant for them. "What ho! sirs," exclaimed the Duke, "your sport has been either very good or very bad to lead you so far and so late. Sir Philip des Comines, you are dejected—By Saint George! D'Hymbercourt looks as sad as thou dost.—How now, sirs? By my honour, you seem as if you were come to a funeral, not a festival." While the Duke spoke, the eyes of the company were all directed towards D'Hymbercourt and Des Comines, and the embarrassment and dejection of their countenances seemed so remarkable that the mirth of the company was gradually hushed. "What means this silence, Messires?" said the Duke.

"My gracious lord," said Des Comines, "as we were about to return hither from the forest we met the Count of Crèvecoeur."

"How!" said the Duke, "already returned from Brabant?—but he found all well there, doubtless?"

"The Count himself will presently give your Grace an account of his news," said D'Hymbercourt, "which we have heard but imperfectly."

"Body of me, where is the Count?" said the Duke.

"He changes his dress, to wait upon your Highness," answered D'Hymbercourt.

"His dress!" exclaimed the impatient Prince, "what care I for his dress? I think you have conspired with him to drive me mad!"

"Or rather, to be plain," said Des Comines, "he wishes to communicate his news at a private audience."

"My Lord King," said Charles, "this is ever the way our counsellors serve us—some one bid Crèvecoeur come to us directly! He comes from the frontiers of Liege and *we*, at least, have no secrets in that quarter."

All perceived that the Duke had drunk so much wine as to increase the obstinacy of his disposition; they knew the impetuosity of his temper too well to venture on further interference and sat in anxious expectation. Louis alone maintained perfect composure and continued his conversation alternately with the grand carver and the jester. At length Crèvecoeur entered, and was saluted by the hurried question of his master, "What news from Liege and Brabant, Sir Count?"

"My liege," answered the Count, in a firm, but melancholy tone, "the news I bring you is fitter for the council than the feast."

"Out, with it, man," said the Duke, "I can guess it—the Liegeois are again in mutiny."

"They are, my lord," said Crèvecoeur, very gravely.

"It could not be in better time, for we may at present have the advice of our own Suzerain," said the Duke, bowing to King Louis, with eyes which spoke the most bitter, though suppressed resentment, "to teach us how such mutineers should be dealt with.—Hast thou more news? Out with it, and then answer for yourself why you went not to assist the Bishop."

"My lord, the further tidings are heavy for me to tell, and will be afflicting to you to hear. No aid of mine, or of living chivalry, could have availed the excellent Prelate. William de la Marck, united with the insurgent Liegeois, has taken his Castle of Schonwaldt, and murdered him in his own hall."

"*Murdered him!*" repeated the Duke, in a deep and low tone, "thou hast been imposed upon, Crèvecoeur, by some wild report —it is impossible!"

"Alas! my lord!" said the Count, "I have it from an eye-witness, an archer of the King of France's Scottish Guard, who was in the hall when the murder was committed by William de la Marck's order."

"And who was doubtless aiding and abetting in the horrible

sacrilege!" exclaimed the Duke, starting up in fury. "Bar the doors of this hall, gentlemen—let no stranger stir from his seat, upon pain of instant death!—Gentlemen of my chamber, draw your swords." And turning upon Louis, he advanced his own hand slowly and deliberately to the hilt of his weapon, while the King only said, "These news, fair cousin, have staggered your reason."

"No!" replied the Duke, in a terrible tone, "but they have awakened a just resentment, which I have too long suffered to be stifled by trivial considerations of circumstance and place. Murderer of thy brother! Rebel against thy parent! Tyrant over thy subjects! Treacherous ally! Perjured King! Thou art in my power, and I thank God for it."

"Rather thank my folly," said the King.

The Duke still held his hand on the hilt of his sword, but refrained to draw his weapon or strike a foe who offered no sort of resistance which could provoke violence. Meanwhile, wild confusion spread itself through the hall. The doors were now guarded by order of the Duke; but several of the French nobles, few as they were in number, started from their seats, and prepared for the defence of their Sovereign. Louis had spoken not a word either to Orleans or Dunois since they were liberated from restraint at the Castle of Loches, but, nevertheless, the voice of Dunois was first heard above the tumult addressing the Duke of Burgundy. "Sir Duke, you have forgotten that you are a vassal of France, and that we, your guests, are Frenchmen. If you lift a hand against our Monarch, credit me, we shall feast as high with the blood of Burgundy as we have done with its wine."

Lord Crawford, with an agility no one would have expected at his years, forced his way through all opposition and threw himself boldly between the King and the Duke. His cloak was wrapped about his left arm, while he unsheathed his sword with his right. "I have fought for his father and his grandsire," was all he said, "and, by Saint Andrew, end the matter as it will, I will not fail him at this pinch."

The Duke of Burgundy still remained with his hand on his

sword, and seemed in the act of giving the signal for a general onset which must necessarily have ended in the massacre of the weaker party, when Crèvecoeur rushed forward, and exclaimed, "My Lord of Burgundy, beware what you do! This is *your* hall— do not spill the blood of your guest on your hearth. For the sake of your house's honour, do not attempt to revenge one horrid murder by another yet worse!"

"He is right," said Louis, whose coolness forsook him not in that dreadful moment. "My cousin Orleans—kind Dunois—and you, my trusty Crawford—bring not on ruin and bloodshed by taking offence too hastily. Our cousin the Duke is chafed at the tidings of the death of a loving friend, the venerable Bishop of Liege, whose slaughter we lament as he does. Ancient, and, un-happily, recent subjects of jealousy, lead him to suspect us of having abetted a crime which we abhor. Should our host murder us on this spot—us, his King and his kinsman, under a false im-pression of our being accessory to this unhappy accident, our fate will be little lightened, but, on the contrary, greatly aggravated, by your stirring—therefore, stand back. I command you to do so, and your oath obliges you to obey."

The Duke stood with his eyes fixed on the ground for a con-siderable space, and then said, with bitter irony, "Crèvecoeur, you say well; and it concerns our honour, that our obligations to this great King, our honoured guest, be not so hastily adjusted, as in our anger we had at first proposed. We will so act, that all Europe shall acknowledge the justice of our proceedings.—Gentlemen of France, you must render up your arms to my officers! Your master has broken the truce, and has no title to take further benefit of it."

"Not one of us," said Dunois, "will resign our weapon unless we are assured of our King's safety."

"Nor will a man of the Scottish Guard," exclaimed Crawford, "lay down his arms, save at the command of the King of France."

"Brave Dunois," said Louis, "and you, my trusty Crawford, your zeal will do me injury instead of benefit. Give up your swords—the noble Burgundians who accept such honourable pledges will protect both you and me. Give up your swords— it is I who command you." It was thus that, in this dreadful emergency, Louis showed the prompt clearness of judgment which alone could have saved his life. He was aware that until actual blows were exchanged, he should have the assistance of most of the nobles present to moderate the fury of their Prince; but that were a *mêlée* once commenced, he himself and his few adherents must be instantly murdered. At the same time, his worst enemies confessed that his demeanour had in it nothing either of meanness or cowardice. He shunned to aggravate the wrath of the Duke; but he did not seem to fear it, and continued to look on him with calm attention.

Crawford, at the King's command, threw his sword to Crèvecoeur, saying, "Take it! and the devil give you joy of it."

"Louis of Valois," said the Duke, "you must regard yourself as my prisoner, until you are cleared of having abetted sacrilege and murder. Have him to the Castle. Let him have six gentlemen to attend him such as he shall choose.—My Lord Crawford, your guard must leave the Castle, and shall be honourably quartered elsewhere. Up with every drawbridge, and down with every portcullis!" He started from the table in moody haste, darted a glance of mortal enmity at the King, and rushed out of the apartment.

"Sirs," said the King, looking with dignity around him, "grief for the death of his ally hath made your Prince frantic."

At this moment was heard in the streets the sound of drums beating to call out the soldiery. "We are," said Crèvecoeur, who acted as the Marshal of the Duke's household, "subjects of Burgundy, and must do our duty as such. I myself must be your Majesty's chamberlain, and bring you to your apartments in other guise than would be my desire, remembering the hospitality of Plessis. You have only to choose your attendants, whom the Duke's commands limit to six."

"Then," said the King, looking around him, "I desire the

attendance of Oliver le Dain, a private of my Life-Guard, called Balafré, who may be unarmed if you will, Tristan l'Hermite, with two of his people, and my trusty philosopher, Martius Galeotti."

"Your Majesty's will shall be complied with in all points," said the Count de Crèvecoeur. Under a strong guard, yet forgetting no semblance of respect, the Count conducted the King towards his new apartment. Forty men-at-arms, carrying alternately naked swords and blazing torches, served as the escort of King Louis from the town-hall of Peronne to the Castle's dark and gloomy strength. The glare of the torches outfacing the pale moon, their red smoky light gave a darker shade to that huge dungeon called Earl Herbert's Tower. It was the same that Louis had viewed with misgiving the preceding evening, and of which he was now doomed to become an inhabitant.

The Steward, hastily summoned, turned the ponderous key which opened the reluctant gate of the huge Gothic Keep, and six men entered with torches and showed the way through a narrow, winding passage to what had been the great hall of the dungeon. Two or three bats and other birds of evil presage flew against the lights, while the Steward formally apologized to the King that the State-hall had not been put in order, such was the hurry of the notice sent to him; and adding that, in truth, the apartment had not been in use since the time of King Charles the Simple.

"King Charles the Simple!" echoed Louis, "I know the history of the Tower now. He was here murdered by his treacherous vassal, Herbert, Earl of Vermandois—so say our annals. *Here*, then, my predecessor was slain?"

"Not here, not exactly here, and please your Majesty," said the old Steward, stepping with eager haste to show the curiosities of the place. "Not *here*, but in the side-chamber a little onward, which opens from your Majesty's bedchamber." He opened a wicket at the upper end of the hall which led into a bedchamber. Some hasty preparations had been here made for the King's accommodation. "We will get beds in the hall for the rest of your attendants," said the garrulous old man, "but we have had such brief notice, if it please your Majesty. And if it please your Majesty to look upon this little wicket behind the arras, it opens into the little old cabinet in the thickness of the wall where Charles was slain; and there is a secret passage from below, which admitted the men who were to deal with him. And your Majesty, whose eyesight I hope is better than mine, may see the blood still on the oak-floor, though it was done five hundred years ago."

While he thus spoke, he kept fumbling to open the postern of which he spoke, until the King said, "Forbear, old man— forbear but a little while, when thou mayst have a newer tale to tell, and fresher blood to show.—My Lord of Crèvecoeur, what say you?"

"I can but answer, Sire, that these two interior apartments are as much at your Majesty's disposal as those in your own Castle at Plessis, and that Crèvecoeur, a name never blackened by treachery or assassination, has guard of their exterior defences."

"Your honour is sufficient warrant," said the King. "But what will your Duke do with me, Crèvecoeur? He cannot hope to keep me long a prisoner."

"Sire," said the Count, "my master is noble in his disposition, and made incapable, even by the very strength of his passions, of any underhand practices. And it will be the wish of every coun-sellor around him—excepting perhaps one—that he should be-have in this matter with mildness, generosity, and justice."

"How happy were I, noble Crèvecoeur," said Louis, "had it been my lot to have such as thou art among my counsellors!"

"It had in that case been your Majesty's study to have got rid of them as fast as you could," said Le Glorieux.

"Aha! Sir Wisdom," said Louis, turning round, and instantly changing the pathetic tone in which he had addressed Crèvecoeur, and adopting with facility one which had a turn of gaiety in it, "Hast *thou* followed us hither?"

"Ay, sir," answered Le Glorieux, "Wisdom must follow in motley, where Folly leads the way in purple."

"Wouldst thou change conditions with me?" asked Louis.

"Not I," quoth Le Glorieux.

"Why, wherefore so? Methinks I could be well enough contented, as princes go, to have thee for my king."

"Ay, Sire," replied Le Glorieux, "but the question is, whether, judging of your Majesty's wit from its having lodged you here, I should not have cause to be ashamed of having so dull a fool."

"Peace, sirrah!" said the Count of Crèvecoeur, "your tongue runs too fast."

"Let it take its course," said the King; "I know of no such fair subject of raillery as the follies of those who should know better. Here, my sagacious friend, take this purse of gold and do me so much favour as to send me my astrologer, Martius Galeotti."

"I will, without fail, my Liege," answered the jester, "and I know well I shall find him where the best wine is sold."

"Let me pray for free entrance for this learned person through your guards, Seignior de Crèvecoeur," said Louis.

"For his entrance, unquestionably," answered the Count, "but it grieves me to add that my instructions do not authorize me to permit any one to quit your Majesty's apartments—I wish your Majesty good night." And the Count of Crèvecoeur took his leave.

"Go into the hall," said Louis to Oliver and Tristan, "but do not lie down to sleep. Hold yourselves in readiness, for there is still something to be done tonight." They retired to the hall accordingly and the whole party sat in silent dejection.

Meanwhile, their master underwent, in the retirement of his secret chamber, agonies that might have atoned for some of those which had been imposed by his command. "Charles the Simple!— what will posterity call the Eleventh Louis? Louis the Fool!—To think these hot-headed Liegeois, and the Wild Boar of Ardennes, would remain quiet—to suppose that I could use reason to any good purpose with Charles of Burgundy—Fool, and double idiot that I was! But the villain Martius Galeotti shall not escape— he has been at the bottom of this, he and the detestable Balue. If I ever get out of this danger, I will tear from his head the Cardinal's cap, though I pull the scalp with it! But the other traitor is in my hands—I am yet king enough—have yet an empire roomy enough—for the punishment of the word-mongering, star-gazing impostor who has at once made a prisoner and a dupe of me!"

The King thrust his head out at the door of the hall, and summoned Le Balafré into his apartment. "My good soldier," he said, "thou hast served me long, and hast had little promotion. We are here in a case where I may either live or die; but I would not willingly die an ungrateful man, or leave either a friend or an enemy unrecompensed. Now, I have a friend to be rewarded, that is thyself—an enemy to be punished according to his deserts, and that is the base, treacherous villain, Martius Galeotti, who by his falsehoods has trained me hither into the power of my mortal enemy."

"I will challenge him on that quarrel, sire, since they say he is a fighting blade, though he looks somewhat unwieldy," said Le Balafré.

"I commend your bravery and your devotion to my service," said the King. "But it is not our pleasure to risk thy life, Balafré. This traitor comes hither, summoned by our command. We would have thee, so soon as thou canst find occasion, close up with him, and smite him under the fifth rib—dost thou understand me?"

"Truly I do," answered Le Balafré, "but if he be a traitor, let him die a traitor's death—I will not meddle with it. Your Majesty has your Provost, and two of his Marshal's men without, who are more fit for dealing with him than a Scottish gentleman of my family and standing in the service."

"You say well," said the King, "but, at least, it belongs to thy duty to prevent interruption, and to guard the execution of my most just sentence."

"I will do so against all Peronne," said Le Balafré. "Your Majesty need not doubt my fealty."

"Let no one intrude—that is all I require of you. Go hence, and send the Provost-Marshal to me," said the King. Balafré left the apartment accordingly, and a minute afterwards Tristan l'Hermite entered from the hall. "Welcome, gossip," said the King, "what thinkest thou of our situation?"

"As of men sentenced to death," said the Provost-Marshal, "unless there come a reprieve from the Duke."

"Reprieved or not, he that decoyed us into this snare shall go to the next world to take up lodgings for us," said the King, with a ferocious smile. "Tristan, thou must stand by me to the end."

"I will, my liege," said Tristan, "I will do my duty within these walls, or elsewhere; and while I live, your Majesty's breath shall pour as potential a note of condemnation, and your sentence be as literally executed, as when you sat on your own throne."

"It is even what I expected of thee," said Louis, "but hast thou good assistance? The traitor is strong and able-bodied, and will doubtless be clamorous for aid—the Scot will do nought but keep the door."

"I have Trois-Eschelles and Petit-André with me," said Tristan, "men so expert in their office, that out of three men, they would hang up one ere his two companions were aware.—But what is to be our present subject, an it please your Majesty?"

"The condemned person is Martius Galeotti.—You start, but it is even as I say. The villain hath trained us all hither by false and treacherous representations, that he might put us into the hands of the Duke of Burgundy without defence," said the King.

"But not without vengeance!" said Tristan.

"I know thy trusty spirit," said the King. "But away, and prepare for the victim." Louis charged the Provost-Marshal to have everything ready for the execution of his commands the moment the Astrologer left his apartment; "for," said the King, "I will see the villain once more, just to observe how he bears himself towards the master whom he has led into the toils. Begone, Tristan—thou wert not wont to be so slow when business was to be done."

"Now, please your Majesty to give me a sign, just when you part with Galeotti for the night, whether the business goes on or no. I have known your Majesty once or twice change your mind, and blame me for over despatch," said the Provost-Marshal.

"Thou suspicious creature," answered King Louis, "I tell thee I will *not* change my mind; but to silence thy remonstrances, observe, if I say to the knave at parting, 'There is a Heaven above us!' then let the business go on; but if I say, 'Go in peace,' you will understand that my purpose is altered."

"And the body," said the Provost, "how shall we dispose of it?"

"Let me see an instant," said the King, "the windows of the hall are too narrow; but that projecting oriel is wide enough. We will over with him into the Somme, and put a paper on his breast, with the legend, 'Let the justice of the King pass toll-free.' The Duke's officers may seize it for duties if they dare." The Provost-Marshal left the apartment of Louis, and summoned his two assistants to council in the great hall.

With infinite dexterity and even a sort of professional delight, the worthy executioners of the Provost's mandates adapted their rope and pulley for putting in force the sentence which had been uttered against Galeotti by the captive Monarch—seeming to rejoice that that last action was to be one so consistent with their past life, and Tristan l'Hermite sat eyeing their proceedings with a species of satisfaction.

10. Uncertainty

THE jester, Le Glorieux, found Martius Galeotti in the best tavern in Peronne, sitting with a female in Moorish garb, who, as Le Glorieux approached, rose to depart. "This," she said, "is news on which you may rely with absolute certainty," and with that disappeared among the crowd of guests.

"Cousin Philosopher," said the jester, "one fool being gone, here I come another, to guide you to the apartments of Louis of France."

"How if I refuse to come, when summoned at so late an hour and by such a messenger?" said Galeotti.

"In that case we will consult your ease, and carry you," said Le Glorieux. "Here are half a score of stout Burgundian yeomen at the door, with whom Crèvecoeur has furnished me. For know, that my friend Charles of Burgundy and I have not taken away our kinsman Louis's crown—though reduced to the size of a spangle, it is still pure gold. In plain terms, he is still paramount over his own people, and Most Christian King of the old dining-hall in the Castle of Peronne, to which you, as his liege subject, are presently obliged to repair."

"I attend you, sir," said Martius Galeotti, and accompanied Le Glorieux accordingly.

"Ay, sir," said the Fool, as they went towards the Castle, "you do well—only my mother always told me to go warily near an old rat in a trap, for he was never so much disposed to bite." This hint of the jester was not lost on Galeotti, and he saw something which seemed to confirm it in Tristan's manner, as he marshalled him to the King's bed-chamber. A close observer of what passed on earth, as well as among the heavenly bodies, the Astrologer caught sight of the pulley and rope and summoned together his subtlety to evade the impending danger. Thus resolved, he presented himself before Louis, undismayed at the Monarch's anger.

"Every good planet be gracious to your Majesty!" said Galeotti, with an inclination almost Oriental in manner.

"Art thou not ashamed, Martius Galeotti, to see me here, and a prisoner, when you recollect by what assurances I was lured hither?" said the King.

"And art *thou* not ashamed, Sire?" replied the philosopher. "Didst thou propose to become participant of those mysteries which raise men above the passions and sorrows of life and dost thou shrink from the first pressure of adversity, frightened out of the course by shadowy and unreal evils?"

"Shadowy and unreal!" exclaimed the King. "Is this dungeon unreal? The weapons of the guards of my detested enemy Burgundy, which you may hear clash at the gate, are those shadows? What, traitor, *are* real evils, if imprisonment, dethronement, and danger of life, are not so?"

"Ignorance—ignorance, my brother, and prejudice," answered the sage, with great firmness, "are the only real evils."

"Go sir, and think not to escape condign punishment," said the King bitterly.

"I leave you not to your fate," replied Martius, "until I have vindicated my reputation."

159

"Speak on," said Louis, "thine impudence cannot make me change my purposes. Yet as I may never again pass judgment as a King, I will not censure thee unheard. Speak, then, confess thy falsehood. You foretold yonder Scot should accomplish his enterprise fortunately for my interest. Here thy craft deceived thee—thou wert weak enough to make a specific prediction which has proved directly false."

"Which will prove most firm and true," answered the Astrologer boldly. "I desire no greater triumph of art over ignorance than that prediction and its accomplishment will afford. I told thee he would be faithful in any honourable commission. Hath he not been so? I told thee he would scruple to aid any evil enterprise—hath it not proved so? If you doubt it, go ask the Bohemian, Hayraddin Maugrabin. I told thee that the planets under which he set forth augured danger—and hath not his path been beset by danger? I told thee that it augured advantage to the sender—and of that thou wilt soon have the benefit."

"This is too insolent," said the King. "Hence!—think not my wrongs shall be unavenged. *There is a Heaven above us!*" Galeotti turned to depart. "Yet stop," said Louis. "Let me hear your answer to one question: Can thy pretended skill ascertain the hour of thine own death?"

"Only by referring to the fate of another," said Galeotti.

"I understand not thine answer," said Louis.

"Know then, O King," said Martius, "that this only I can tell with certainty concerning mine own death, that it shall take place exactly twenty-four hours before that of your Majesty."

"Ha! say'st thou?" said Louis, his countenance altering. "Hold—wait one moment. Saidst thou *my* death should follow *thine* so closely?"

"Within the space of twenty-four hours," repeated Galeotti firmly. "I wish Your Majesty good rest."

"Hold," said the King, taking him by the arm, and leading him to the door, where he pronounced as he opened it, in a loud voice, "Tomorrow we'll talk more of this. Go in peace, my

learned father." He repeated these words three times; and still afraid the Provost-Marshal might mistake his purpose, he led the Astrologer into the hall, and made a private signal to the Provost-Marshal to enjoin a suspension of all proceedings against the Astrologer. Thus did the possession of some secret information joined to readiness of wit save Galeotti from the most imminent danger; and thus was Louis, the most sagacious as well as the most vindictive amongst the monarchs of the period, cheated of his revenge by the influence of superstition.

When the first light of dawn penetrated the ancient Gothic chamber in the Tower, the King summoned Oliver to his presence, and charged him to prosecute, so soon as he should be permitted to stir abroad, the various modes by which he had previously endeavoured to form friends at the Court of Burgundy. And never was that wily minister more struck with the clearness of the King's intellect, and his intimate knowledge of all the springs which influence human actions, than he was during that memorable consultation.

About two hours afterwards, Oliver accordingly obtained permission from the Count of Crèvecoeur to go out and execute the commissions which his master had entrusted him with; and Louis, sending for the Astrologer, in whom he seemed to have renewed his faith, held with him a long consultation, the issue of which appeared to give him more confidence, so that he received the morning compliments of Crèvecoeur with a calmness at which the Burgundian Lord could not help wondering, the rather that he had already heard that the Duke had passed several hours in a state of mind which seemed to render the King's safety very precarious. For if the night passed by Louis was anxious, that spent by the Duke of Burgundy, who had at no time the same mastery over his passions, was still more disturbed. Distracted by sorrow, by the desire of revenge, and by the sense of honour which forbade him to exercise it upon Louis in his present condition, the Duke's mind resembled a volcano in eruption. He refused to sleep, and spent the night in a succession of the most violent bursts of grief for the murdered Bishop, and still more incoherent oaths of vengeance. At one time he expressed his determination to send for the Duke of Normandy, the brother of the King, with whom Louis was on the worst terms, in order to compel the captive monarch to surrender the Crown, and in that event, the prison of the French monarch would probably have been a brief road to his grave.

Another day and night passed in the same stormy and fitful deliberations; the Duke scarcely ate or drank, never changed his dress, and altogether demeaned himself like one in whom rage might terminate in insanity. By degrees he became more composed, and began to hold, from time to time, consultations with his ministers, in which much was proposed, but nothing resolved on. But when Charles had exhausted his fury, he sat like one who broods over some desperate deed to which he is as yet unable to work up his resolution. And unquestionably it would have needed little more than a hint from any of his counsellors to have pushed the Duke to some desperate action. But the nobles of Burgundy were almost unanimously inclined to recommend moderate measures.

On the third day, the Count of Campo-basso brought his Italian wit to assist the counsels of Charles; and well was it for Louis that he had not arrived when the Duke was in his first fury. Immediately on his arrival, a meeting of the Duke's counsellors was convened; and Campo-basso gave his opinion that the Duke should crush his mortal enemy now that chance had placed his fate at his disposal. Des Comines, who saw the Duke's eye sparkle at a proposal which his own violence of temper had already repeatedly suggested, hastened to state the possibility that Louis might be able to clear himself of the charge; and that if an act of violence were perpetrated on the King, the English might avail themselves of the civil discord which must needs ensue to renew those dreadful wars which had only, and with difficulty, been terminated by the union of France and Burgundy against the common enemy. Finally he confessed that he did not mean to urge the free dismissal of Louis; but only that the Duke should avail himself of his present condition to establish an equitable treaty between the countries, with security on the King's part, by which more permanent advantages could be obtained, and in a manner more honourable for Burgundy than by an action which would stain her with a breach of faith and hospitality.

The Duke listened to these arguments with looks fixed to the ground. But when Crèvecoeur proceeded to say that he did not believe Louis either knew of, or was accessory to, the atrocious act of violence committed at Schonwaldt, Charles raised his head, and darting a fierce look at his counsellor, exclaimed, "Have you too, Crèvecoeur, heard the gold of France clink? Dare any one say that Louis is not the fomenter of these feuds in Flanders?"

"My gracious lord," said Crèvecoeur, "my hand has been more conversant with steel than with gold; and so far am I from holding that Louis is free from the charge of having caused the disturbances in Flanders that it is not long since, in the face of his whole Court, I charged him with that breach of faith, and offered him defiance in your name. But although his intrigues have been doubtless the original cause of these commotions, I am so far from believing that he authorized the death of the Archbishop that I believe one of his emissaries publicly protested against it; and I could produce the man, were it your Grace's pleasure to see him."

"It *is* our pleasure," said the Duke. "Saint George! can you doubt that we desire to act justly? We will see France ourself. If he shall be found guiltless of this murder, the atonement for other crimes may be more easy. If he hath been guilty, who shall say that a life of penitence in some retired monastery were not a most deserved and merciful doom? Let your witness attend—we will to the Castle at noon. Break up the council. I will but change my dress, and wait on *my most gracious Sovereign*." With bitter emphasis on the last expression, the Duke arose and strode out of the room.

"Louis's safety, and, what is worse, the honour of Burgundy, depend on the cast of the dice," said D'Hymbercourt to Crèvecoeur and to Des Comines. "Haste thee to the Castle, Des Comines. Explain to Louis what storm is approaching—he will best know how to pilot himself. I trust this life-guardsman will say nothing which can aggravate; for who knows what may have been the secret commission with which he was charged?"

"The young man," said Crèvecoeur, "seemed bold, yet prudent and wary. I trust he will be equally so in the Duke's presence. I must go and seek him, and also the young Countess of Croye."

"The Countess!—you told us you had left her at Saint Bridget's Nunnery?"

"Aÿ, but I was obliged to send her here," said the Count, "by the Duke's orders."

The information that the young Countess was in the hands of Charles added fresh thorns to Louis's reflections. He was conscious that, by explaining the intrigues by which he had induced the Lady Hameline and her to resort to Peronne, she might supply that evidence which he had removed by the execution of Zamet Maugrabin. Louis discoursed on these matters with anxiety to the Sieur Des Comines, whose acute political talents suited the King's temper. Des Comines was naturally gratified with the approbation of the most sagacious Prince in Europe. "I would," continued Louis, "that I had such a servant. I had not then been in this unfortunate situation; which, nevertheless, I should hardly regret, could I but discover any means of securing the services of so experienced a statist." Des Comines said, that all his faculties, such as they were, were at the service of his Most Christian Majesty, saving always his allegiance to his rightful lord, Duke Charles of Burgundy.

"And am I one who would seduce you from that allegiance?" said Louis pathetically. "No, Philip Des Comines—continue to serve Charles of Burgundy; and you will best serve him, by bringing round a fair accommodation with Louis of France. In doing thus, you will serve us both, and one, at least, will be grateful. I am told your appointments in this Court hardly match those of the Grand Falconer. France has wide lands—her King has much gold. Allow me, my friend, to rectify this scandalous inequality. The means are not distant—permit me to use them." The King produced a weighty bag of money; but Des Comines, more delicate in his sentiments than most courtiers of that time, declined the proffer. "Wisdom is to be desired more than fine gold!" exclaimed the King, "and believe me, I trust in thy kindness, Philip, more than I do in the purchased assistance of many who have received my gifts. I pray you—what does your Duke expect of me?"

"I am the bearer of no propositions, my lord," said Des Comines. "The Duke will soon explain his own pleasure; but some things occur to me as proposals for which your Majesty ought to hold yourself prepared. As, for example, that you should disown the Liegeois and William de la Marck."

"As willingly as I disclaim Hell and Satan," said Louis.

"Ample security will be required, by hostages or occupation of fortresses, that France shall in future abstain from stirring up rebellion among the Flemings."

"It is something new," answered the King, "that a vassal should demand pledges from his Sovereign: but let that pass too."

"My lord," said Des Comines, "what remains to be mentioned, is a thing indeed in great measure within the Duke's own power, though he means to invite your Majesty's accession to it, for in truth it touches you nearly. Your Majesty's cousin, the illustrious Duke of Orleans——"

"Ha!" exclaimed the King, but Des Comines proceeded without heeding the interruption. "—Having conferred his affections on the young Countess Isabelle de Croye, the Duke expects your Majesty will, on your part, yield your assent to the marriage and unite with him in endowing the noble couple with such an appanage, as, joined to the Countess's estates, may form a fit establishment for a child of France."

"Never, never!" said the King, "Orleans shall not break his plighted faith to my daughter, or marry another while she lives! Des Comines, consider the great loss—the utter destruction such a marriage will bring upon my kingdom. Recollect, I have but one feeble boy, and this Orleans is the next heir—consider that the Church hath consented to his union with Joan, which unites so happily the interests of both branches of my family—and think too that this union has been the favourite scheme of my whole life—that I have fought for it, schemed for it, prayed for it—and sinned for it. Philip des Comines, I will not forego it!"

"Your Majesty may command my best advice and service," replied Des Comines. "The things which I have suggested for your Majesty's consideration, harsh as they sound in your ear, are but substitutes for still more violent proposals brought forward in the Duke's councils by such as are more hostile to your Majesty. And I need scarce remind your Majesty that the more direct and violent suggestions find readiest acceptance with our master, who loves brief and dangerous measures better than those that are safe, but at the same time circuitous. He will, on the same impulse, prefer the gratification of his will to the increase of his substantial power."

"Most true," replied the King, "a fool will ever grasp rather at the appearance than the reality of authority. All this I know to be true of Charles of Burgundy. But, my dear friend Des Comines, what do you infer from these premises?"

"Simply this, my lord," answered the Burgundian, "that your Majesty, by satisfying the Duke in these particulars on which he has pitched his ideas of honour, and the gratification of his revenge, may evade many of the other unpalatable propositions."

"I understand you, Sir Philip," said the King. "But to which of those happy propositions is your Duke so much wedded that contradiction will make him unreasonable?"

"Your Majesty may make the lightest of his demands the most important, simply by opposing it," said Des Comines. "Nevertheless, my lord, thus far I can say, that every shadow of treaty will be broken off, if your Majesty renounce not William de la Marck and the Liegeois."

"I have already said that I will disown them," said the King.

"More than mere disavowal of their cause will be expected of your Majesty by Duke Charles; for know, that he will demand your Majesty's assistance to put the insurrection down, and your royal presence to witness the punishment which he destines for the rebels," replied the historian.

"That may scarce consist with our honour, Des Comines," said the King.

"To refuse it will scarcely consist with your Majesty's safety," replied Des Comines.

"But, Sir Philip, I will speak plainly," answered the King, "might not these rogues of Liege hold out their town against Duke Charles?"

"With the help of the thousand archers of France whom your Majesty promised them, they might have done something, but——"

"Whom I promised them!" said the King. "Alas! good Sir Philip! you much wrong me in saying so."

"—But without whom," continued Des Comines, "as your Majesty will not *now* likely find it convenient to supply them, what chance will the burghers have of making good their town, in whose walls the large breaches made by Charles after the battle of St. Tron are still unrepaired?"

"The improvident idiots!" said the King. "If they have thus neglected their own safety, they deserve not my protection. Pass on—I will make no quarrel for their sake."

"The next point, I fear, will sit closer to your Majesty's heart," said Des Comines.

"Ah!" replied the King, "you mean that infernal marriage! I will not consent to the breach of the contract between my daughter Joan and my cousin of Orleans—it would be wresting the sceptre of France from me and my posterity.—Besides, it is inhuman to require me, with my own hand, to destroy at once my own scheme of policy, and the happiness of a pair brought up for each other."

"Are they then so much attached?" said Des Comines.

168

"One of them at least is," said the King, "and the one for whom I am bound to be most anxious. But you smile, Sir Philip—you are no believer in the force of love."

"Nay," said Des Comines, "if it please you, Sire, I was about to ask whether it would reconcile you to your acquiescing in the proposed marriage between the Duke of Orleans and Isabelle de Croye, were I to satisfy you that the Countess's inclinations are so much fixed on another that it is likely it will never be a match?"

King Louis sighed. "Alas!" he said. "*Her* inclination, indeed!—Why, to speak truth, supposing that Orleans detested my daughter Joan, he must needs have married her; so you may conjecture how little chance there is of this damsel being able to refuse him under a similar compulsion, and he a Child of France besides. Ah, no, Philip!—little fear of her standing obstinate against the suit of such a lover."

"Your Majesty may undervalue the courage of this young lady. She comes of a race determinately wilful; and I have picked out of Crèvecoeur that she has formed a romantic attachment to a young squire, who, to say truth, rendered her many services on the road."

"Ha!" said the King, "an archer of my Guards, by name Quentin Durward?"

"The same, I think," said Des Comines. "He was made prisoner along with the Countess, travelling almost alone together."

"Now Saint Julian be praised!" said the King, "and all honour to the learned Galeotti! If the maiden be so attached to him as to make her refractory to the will of Burgundy, this Quentin hath indeed been rarely useful to me.—And now, Philip, have you given me the full map of your master's mind?"

"I have possessed you, Sire, of those particulars on which he is at present most disposed to insist. But were more distinct evidence of your Majesty's practices with the Liegeois and William de la Marck to occur unexpectedly, the issue might be terrible. There are strange news from that country—they say La Marck hath married Hameline the elder Countess of Croye. There is a report also," continued Des Comines, "that an envoy from La Marck is approaching Peronne—I trust that he has no letters to show on your Majesty's part?"

"Letters to a Wild Boar!" asked the King. "No, no, Sir Philip, I was no such fool as to cast pearls before swine. I always employed such vagabonds as messengers to the brute that their evidence would not be received in a trial for robbing a hen-roost."

"I can only recommend," said Des Comines, taking his leave, "that your Majesty should avoid using any argument with the Duke which may better become your dignity than your present condition."

"My dignity," said the King, "seldom grows troublesome to me while there are deeper interests to think of.—And now, my friend, must thou be gone? Well, Sir Philip, if Louis of Valois lives, thou hast a friend in the Court of France."

"Meantime, Sire, be prepared, for the Duke will presently confer with you," said the historian. Louis looked after Philip when he left the apartment, and burst into a bitter laugh. "And he thinks himself virtuous because he took no bribe, but contented himself with flattery and promises.—Well, now for nobler game, and to face this leviathan Charles!"

11. Interview and Investigation

On the morning which preceded the meeting of the two Princes in the Castle of Peronne, Oliver le Dain did his master the service of a skilful agent, making interest for Louis in every quarter with presents and promises; so that when the Duke's anger should blaze forth, all around should be interested to smother, and not to increase, the conflagration. By favour of the Count de Crèvecoeur Oliver obtained an interview between Lord Crawford, accompanied by Le Balafré, and Quentin Durward, who, since he had arrived at Peronne, had been detained in honourable confinement. Private affairs were assigned as the cause of requesting this meeting; but it is probable that Crèvecoeur was not sorry to afford an opportunity to Crawford to give some hints to the young archer which might prove useful to his master. The meeting between the countrymen was cordial, and even affecting.

"Thou art a singular youth," said Crawford, "and have had meikle good fortune."

"All comes of his gaining an archer's place at such early years," said La Balafré.

"I fear," said Quentin, "it is my purpose to resign the service of the Archer-guard."

Le Balafré was struck almost mute with astonishment: "Resign from the Scottish Archers!—Such a thing was never dreamt of."

"Hush! Ludovic," said Crawford, "this youngster's journey hath given him some pretty tales to tell about King Louis; and he is turning Burgundian that he may make his own little profit by telling them to Duke Charles."

"Know, my lord," answered Quentin, "that I am no tale-bearer; nor shall either question or torture draw out of me a word to King Louis's prejudice, which may have come to my knowledge while I was in his service.—So far my oath of duty keeps me silent. But I will not remain in that service, in which, besides the peril of fair battle with mine enemies, I am to be exposed to the dangers of ambush on the part of my friends."

"Nay, if he objects to lying in ambush," said the slow-witted Le Balafré, "I am afraid, my lord, all is over with him! It wounds me to the very quick to think my sister's son should fear an ambushment."

"Hold your peace, Ludovic," answered Lord Crawford. "I believe I understand this gear better than you. Young man," he continued, "I partly guess your meaning. You have met foul play on the road where you travelled by the King's command, and you think you have reason to charge him as the author of it?"

"Whether his Majesty be innocent or guilty in the matter I leave to God and his own conscience. The King received me when I was a wandering stranger; I will never load him in his adversity with accusations which may indeed be unjust, since I heard them only from the vilest mouths," answered Quentin.

"My dear boy—my own lad!" said Crawford. "—And now tell me, Quentin, hath the King any advice of this brave, Christian, and manly resolution of yours? For he has need, in his strait, to know what he has to reckon upon."

"I can hardly tell," answered Quentin, "but I assured his learned astrologer, Martius Galeotti, of my resolution to be silent on all that could injure the King with the Duke of Burgundy."

"Ay!" answered Lord Crawford, "Oliver did indeed tell me that Galeotti prophesied most stoutly concerning the line of conduct you were to hold; and I am glad to find he did so on better authority than the stars. My blessing with you, my lad; there will be good blows going presently in the eye of day, and no ambush."

"And my blessing too, nephew," said Ludovic Lesly, "for, since you have satisfied our most noble captain, I also am satisfied, as in duty bound."

"Stay, my lord," said Quentin, and led Lord Crawford a little apart from his uncle. "I must not forget to mention that there is a person besides who, having learned from me these circumstances which it is essential to King Louis's safety should at present remain concealed, may not think the same obligation of secrecy which attaches to me as the King's soldier, is at all binding on her."

"Oh *her!*" replied Crawford. "Nay, if there be a woman in the secret, the Lord ha' mercy, for we are on the rocks again!"

"Do not suppose so, my lord," replied Durward, "but use your interest with the Count de Crèvecoeur to permit me an interview with the Countess Isabelle of Croye, who is the party possessed of my secret, and I doubt not that I can persuade her to be as silent as I shall myself remain concerning whatever may incense the Duke against King Louis."

The old soldier shook his head and said, "There is something in all this, which, by my honour, I do not understand. The Countess Isabelle of Croye—and thou, a raw Scottish lad, so certain of carrying thy point with her? Thou art either strangely confident, my young friend, or else you have used your time well upon the journey. But, by the Cross of Saint Andrew! I will move Crèvecoeur in thy behalf; and, as he truly fears the Duke Charles may be provoked against the King to the extremity of falling foul, I think it likely he may grant thy request, though by my honour it is a comical one!" So saying, and shrugging his shoulders, the old Lord left the apartment, followed by Ludovic Lesly.

In a few minutes Crawford returned, but without his attendant Le Balafré. "Countryman," said he, "you will never lose fair lady for faint heart! Crèvecoeur swallowed your proposal as he would have done a cup of vinegar, and swore to me roundly that were less than the honour of princes and the peace of kingdoms at stake, you should never see so much as the print of the Countess Isabelle's foot on the clay. A Countess!—But come along—your interview with her must be brief."

Vexed at beholding in what an absurd light his passion was viewed by every person of experience, Durward followed Lord Crawford in silence to the Ursuline convent in which the Countess was lodged. In the parlour he found the Count de Crèvecoeur. "So, young gallant," said the latter sternly, "you must see the fair companion of your romantic expedition once more, it seems?"

"Yes, my Lord Count," answered Quentin firmly, "and what is more, I must see her alone."

"That shall never be," said the Count de Crèvecoeur. "Lord Crawford, I make you judge. This young lady, the daughter of my old friend, and the richest heiress in Burgundy, has confessed a sort of a—in short, she is a fool, and your man-at-arms here a presumptuous coxcomb. They shall not meet alone."

"Then will I not speak a single word to the Countess in your presence," said Quentin, much delighted. "You have told me much that I did not dare, presumptuous as I may be, even to hope."

"Ay, truly said, my friend," said Crawford, "you have been imprudent in your communications; and, since you refer to me, and there is a good stout grating across the parlour, I would advise you to trust to it, and let them do the worst with their tongues. What, man! the life of a King is at stake and many thousands besides."

So saying, he dragged off Crèvecoeur, who followed very reluctantly. A moment after, Countess Isabelle entered on the other side of the grate, and no sooner saw Quentin alone in the parlour, than she stopped short: "Yet why should I be ungrateful," she said, "because others are unjustly suspicious?—My friend, my only faithful and constant friend!" As she spoke, she extended her hand to him through the grate, nay, suffered him to retain it, until he had covered it with kisses. She only said, "Durward, were we ever to meet again, I would not permit this folly." The Countess extricated her hand at length, and stepping a pace back, asked Durward what boon he had to ask of her?—"For that you have a request to make, I have learned from the old Scottish Lord, who came here with my cousin of Crèvecoeur. Tell me what it is you have to ask of me."

"Forgiveness to one," replied Quentin, "who, for his own selfish views, hath conducted himself as your enemy."

"I trust I forgive all my enemies," answered Isabelle, "but oh, Durward! through what scenes have your courage and presence of mind protected me! Yonder bloody hall—the good Bishop— I knew not till yesterday half the horrors I had unconsciously witnessed!"

"Do not think on them," said Quentin, who saw the transient colour which had come to her cheek during their conference, fading into the most deadly paleness. "Do not look back, but look steadily forward, as they needs must who walk a perilous road. King Louis deserved nothing better at your hand than to be proclaimed the wily politician he really is. But to tax him as the author of a plan to throw you into the hands of De la Marck will at this moment produce perhaps the King's death or dethrone-ment, and, at all events, the most bloody war between France and Burgundy."

"These evils shall not arrive for my sake, if they can be pre-vented," said Countess Isabelle. "Yet how is this to be? When I am called before my Sovereign, the Duke of Burgundy, I must either stand silent, or speak the truth."

"Let your evidence concerning Louis be confined to what you yourself positively know to be true," said Durward, "and when you mention what others have reported, no matter how credibly, let it be as hearsay only."

"I think I understand you," said the Countess Isabelle, when the convent-bell tolled. "That," said the Countess, "is a signal that we must part—part forever! But do not forget me, Durward; I will never forget you." She could speak no more, but again extended her hand, which was again pressed to his lips; and I know not how it was that, in endeavouring to withdraw her hand, the Countess came so close to the grating that Quentin was encouraged to press the adieu on her lips. Crèvecoeur and Crawford, who had been from some loop-hole eye-witnesses of what was passing, rushed into the apartment, the first in a towering passion, the latter laughing and holding the Count back.

"To your chamber, young mistress!" exclaimed the Count to Isabelle, who retired in all haste, "which should be exchanged for a cell and bread and water. And you, sir, shall learn the penalty of your audacity——"

"Enough said," said the old Lord, "and you Quentin, I command you, be silent, and begone to your quarters.—There is no room for so much scorn, Sir Count. That I must say now that he is out of hearing. Quentin Durward is as much a gentleman as the King, only, as the Spaniard says, not so rich. He is as noble as myself, and I am chief of my name. Tush! man, you must not speak to us of penalties."

"Well, my lord," said Crèvecoeur, "I meant you no disrespect; and for these young people, I am satisfied to overlook the past, since I will take care they never meet again."

"Hark! they toll the summons to the Castle—an awful meeting, of which God only can foretell the issue," said Crawford.

"My lord," said the Burgundian, "obey the orders of your royal master and give no pretext for violence by taking hasty offence, and you will find that the day will pass over more smoothly than you perhaps conjecture."

At the first toll of the bell which was to summon the nobles of Burgundy to council, with the few French peers who could

be present, Duke Charles, followed by a part of his train, armed with battle-axes, entered the Hall of Herbert's Tower, in the Castle of Peronne. King Louis, who had expected the visit, arose and made two steps towards the Duke, and then remained standing with an air of dignity, which he knew very well how to assume when he judged it necessary. It was evident that the Duke was scarce able to control his feelings of resentment and thirst for revenge, though he compelled himself to use the outward acts of courtesy. "I come," said the Duke, "to pray your Majesty to attend a high council, if such be your pleasure——"

"Nay, fair cousin," said the King, "never strain courtesy so far as to entreat what you may boldly command—to council, since such is your Grace's pleasure." Marshalled by Toison d'Or, chief of the heralds of Burgundy, the Princes left the Tower, and crossed the castle-yard and entered the Council-hall. Two chairs of state were erected under the same canopy, that for the King being raised two steps higher than the one which the Duke was to occupy.

Duke Charles, having bowed slightly to the royal chair, bluntly opened the sitting with the following words: "My good vassals and councillors, it is not unknown to you what disturbances have arisen in our territories by the scandalous flight of the Countesses of Croye to take refuge with a foreign power, thereby renouncing their fealty to us; and in another more dreadful instance, by the sacrilegious murder of our beloved brother the Bishop of Liege, and the rebellion of that treacherous city. We have been informed that these sad events may be traced to the interference of a mighty neighbour, for whom Burgundy could have expected nothing but friendship. If this should prove truth," said the Duke, setting his teeth, "what consideration shall withhold us—the means being in our power—from taking such measures, as shall effectually, at the very source, close up the main spring from which these evils have yearly flowed on us?"

The King addressed the council in his turn with some courage: "Since a King must plead his cause as an accused person, he cannot desire more distinguished judges than the flower of chivalry. Nobles of France and Burgundy, I might truly appeal to the circumstances in which I now stand, as being in themselves a complete contradiction of our fair cousin's accusation; for is it to be supposed that I should have thrown myself unreservedly into the power of the Duke of Burgundy while I was practising treachery against him? I have no doubt that, amongst the perpetrators of those horrible treasons at Schonwaldt, villains have been busy with my name—but am I to be answerable, who have given them no right to use it? If two silly women sought refuge at my Court, does it follow that they did so by my direction? Since chivalry forbade my sending them back prisoners to Burgundy, I placed them in the hands of the venerable father in God, whose situation, exalted condition in the Church, and, alas! whose numerous virtues, qualified him to be the mediator betwixt them and their liege lord. I say, moreover, that no particle of evidence can be brought to support the charges which have induced my brother to alter his friendly looks towards one who came to him in full confidence of friendship—have caused him to turn his festive hall into a court of justice, and his hospitable apartments into a prison."

"My lord," said Charles, breaking in so soon as the King paused, "for what is to follow, let it depend on the event of this solemn inquiry. Bring hither Countess Isabelle of Croye!" As the young lady was introduced, supported on one side by the Countess of Crèvecoeur, and on the other by the Abbess of the Ursuline convent, Charles exclaimed, with his usual harshness of voice and manner, "So! sweet Princess—what think you of the fair work you have made between two great Princes and two mighty countries that have been like to go to war for you?" The Duke burst out into a laugh. "Give a seat to yonder simple girl," he said, "to whom, so far from feeling enmity, I design the highest honour.—Sit down, mistress, and tell us at your leisure what fiend possessed you to fly from your native country." With much pain, Isabelle confessed that, being absolutely determined against a match proposed to her by the Duke of Burgundy, she had indulged the hope of obtaining protection of the Court of France. "And under protection of the French Monarch," said Charles. "Of that, doubtless, you were well assured?"

"I did indeed so think myself assured," said Countess Isabelle, "otherwise I had not taken a step so decided." Here Charles looked upon Louis with a smile of bitterness. "But my information concerning King Louis's intentions towards us," continued the Countess, "was derived from my unhappy aunt, Lady Hameline, and her opinions were formed upon the assertions of persons whom I have since discovered to be the vilest traitors." She then stated what she had since learned of the treachery of Marthon and Hayraddin Maugrabin, and added, that she "entertained no doubt that the elder Maugrabin, called Zamet, the original adviser of their flight, was capable of every species of treachery, as well as of assuming the character of an agent of Louis without authority."

All remained mute after she had finished her narrative, and the Duke of Burgundy bent his fierce dark eyes on the ground: "Yet I would know of King Louis wherefore he maintained these ladies at his Court, had they not gone thither by his invitation?"

"I did not so entertain them, fair cousin," answered the King. "Out of compassion, indeed, I received them in privacy, but I boldly ask this young lady whether my reception of them was cordial, or whether it was not, on the contrary, such as made them express regret that they had made my Court their place of refuge?"

"So much was it otherwise than cordial," answered the Countess, "that it induced me to doubt how far it was possible that your Majesty should have actually given the invitation of which we had been assured by those who called themselves your agents; since it would have been hard to reconcile your Majesty's conduct with that to be expected from a king and a gentleman." The Countess turned to the King as she spoke with a look which was probably intended as a reproach, but Louis, looking round the circle, seemed to make a triumphant appeal of this testimony borne to his innocence.

Burgundy, meanwhile, if in some degree silenced, was far from being satisfied, and said abruptly, "Tell me, King Louis, before this vagrant Helen of Troy set more kings by the ears, were it not well to carve out a fitting match for her?"

King Louis, though conscious what ungrateful proposal was likely to be made next, gave a calm and silent assent to what Charles said; but the Countess herself was restored to courage by the very extremity of her situation. She came forward timidly, yet with an air of dignity, and, kneeling before the Duke's throne, thus addressed him: "My liege Lord, I acknowledge my fault in having withdrawn myself from your dominions without your gracious permission, and will most humbly acquiesce in any penalty you are pleased to impose. I place my lands at your disposal, and pray you only of your own bounty, and for the sake of my father's memory, to allow the last of the line of Croye out of her large estate such moderate maintenance as may find her admission into a convent for the remainder of her life."

"What think you, Sire, of the young person's petition to us?" said the Duke, addressing Louis.

"As of a holy and humble motion," said the King, "which doubtless comes from that grace which ought not to be resisted."

"Arise, Countess Isabelle—we mean better for you than you have devised for yourself," said Charles.

"Alas! my lord," said the Countess, "it is that goodness which I fear still more than your Grace's displeasure, since it compels me——"

"Saint George of Burgundy!" said Duke Charles, "is our will to be thwarted at every turn? Up, I say, minion, and withdraw for the present." At this stern answer, the Countess of Crèvecoeur raised her young friend and conducted her from the hall.

Quentin Durward was now summoned to appear, and presented himself before the King and Duke, again equipped as an Archer of the Scottish Guard; his bearing suited in an uncommon degree his splendid appearance. His extreme youth, too, prepossessed the councillors in his favour, the rather that no one could easily believe that the sagacious Louis would have chosen so very young a person to become the confidant of political intrigues. At the command of the Duke, sanctioned by that of Louis, Quentin commenced an account of his journey with the Ladies of Croye to the neighbourhood of Liege, premising a statement of King Louis's instructions, which were that he should escort them safely to the castle of the Bishop. "And you obeyed my orders accordingly?" said the King.

"I did, Sire," replied the Scot. At the command of Duke Charles he produced the written instructions which he had received for the direction of his journey. "Did you follow these instructions literally, soldier?" said the Duke.

"No, if it please your Grace," replied Quentin. "I kept the left bank of the river as being the nearer and safer road to Liege, because I began to suspect the fidelity of my guide."

"Now mark the questions I have next to ask thee," said the Duke. "Reply truly to them, and fear nothing from the resentment of any one. But if you palter in your answers, I will have thee hung alive in an iron chain from the steeple of the market-house, where you shalt wish for death for many an hour ere he come to relieve you!" A deep silence ensued. At length the Duke demanded to know of Durward who his guide was, by whom supplied, and wherefore he had been led to suspect him? The first of these questions Quentin Durward answered by naming Hayraddin Maugrabin, the Bohemian; the second, that the guide had been recommended by Tristan l'Hermite; and in reply to the third point, he mentioned what had happened in the Franciscan convent near Namur; how the Bohemian had been expelled from the holy house; and how he had dogged him to a rendezvous with one of William de la Marck's lanzknechts, where he overheard a plan for surprising the ladies who were under his protection.

"Now, hark thee," said the Duke, "and once more remember thy life depends on it, did these villains mention their having King Louis's authority for their scheme of surprising the escort, and carrying away the ladies?"

"If such infamous fellows had said so," replied Quentin, "I know not how I should have believed them, having the word of the King himself to place in opposition to theirs." Louis, who had listened hitherto with most earnest attention, could not help drawing his breath deeply when he heard Durward's answer, in the manner of one from whom a heavy weight has been removed. The Duke again looked disconcerted and moody; and, returning to the charge, questioned Quentin still more closely whether he did not understand, from these men's private conversation, that the plots which they meditated had King Louis's sanction?

"I repeat, that I heard nothing which could authorize me to say so," answered the young man, who, though internally convinced of the King's accession to the treachery of Hayraddin, yet held it contrary to his allegiance to bring forward his own suspicions on the subject.

"Thou art a faithful messenger," said the Duke, with a sneer.

"I understand you not, my lord," said Quentin Durward. "All I know is that my master King Louis sent me to protect these ladies, and that I did so accordingly, to the extent of my ability. I understood the instructions of the King to be honourable, and I executed them honourably; had they been of a different tenor, they would not have suited one of my name or nation."

"But hark thee, Archer," said Charles, "what instructions were those which made thee, as some sad fugitives from Schonwaldt have informed us, parade the streets of Liege at the head of those mutineers who afterwards cruelly murdered their temporal Prince and spiritual Father? And what harangue was it which thou didst make after that murder was committed, in which you took upon you, as agent for Louis, to assume authority among the villains who had just perpetrated so great a crime?"

"My lord," said Quentin, "there are many who could testify that I assumed not the character of an envoy of France in the town of Liege, but had it fixed upon me by the clamours of the people themselves. This I told those in the service of the Bishop when I had made my escape from the city, and recommended their attention to the security of the Castle, which might have prevented the horror of the succeeding night. I had no commission of any kind from the King of France respecting the people of Liege, far less instructions to instigate them to mutiny. It is, no doubt, true, that I did, in the extremity of danger, avail myself of the influence which my imputed character gave me, to save the Countess Isabelle, to protect my own life, and, so far as I could, to rein in the humour for slaughter, which had already broken out in so dreadful an instance."

"And therein my young companion and prisoner," said Crèvecoeur, unable any more to remain silent, "acted with spirit and good sense; and his doing so cannot be justly imputed as blame to King Louis." There was a murmur of assent among the nobility which sounded joyfully in the ears of King Louis, whilst it gave no little offence to Charles. Des Comines, who foresaw danger, prevented it by announcing a herald from the city of Liege.

"A herald from weavers and nailers?" exclaimed the Duke, "but admit him instantly."

12. The Herald

THERE was great curiosity in the assembly to see the herald whom the insurgent Liegeois had ventured to send to so haughty a Prince as the Duke of Burgundy, while in such high indignation against them. For it must be remembered that, at this period, heralds were only despatched from sovereign princes to each other upon solemn occasions; and to heraldry the pride of Duke Charles attached great importance. The herald who was now introduced into the presence of the monarchs was dressed in a coat embroidered with the arms of his master; but the Boar's head, in the opinion of the skilful, was more showy than accurate in blazonry. The rest of his dress was overcharged with lace, embroidery, and ornament of every kind, and there was something in the man's appearance which seemed to imply a mixture of fear and effrontery. The manner in which he paid his respects also showed a grotesque awkwardness not usual among those who were accustomed to be received in the presence of princes. "Who art thou, in the devil's name?" was the greeting with which Charles the Bold received this singular envoy.

"I am Rouge Sanglier," answered the herald, "the officer-at-arms of William de la Marck, by the grace of God, and the election of the Chapter, Prince Bishop of Liege. And, in right of his wife, the Honourable Countess Hameline, Count of Croye. And I let you, Charles of Burgundy and Earl of Flanders, know that my master proposes to exercise at once the office of Prince Bishop, and maintain the rights of Count of Croye."

The Duke of Burgundy, to the astonishment of all present, made no answer but kept his eyes bent on the ground, as if unwilling to betray the passion which gleamed in them. The envoy, therefore, proceeded unabashed in his message. "In the name, therefore, of the Prince Bishop of Liege, and Count of Croye, I am to require you, Duke Charles, to desist from those encroachments you have made on the free and imperial city of Liege, by connivance with the late Louis of Bourbon, unworthy Bishop thereof. Also to rebuild the breaches in its walls, and restore the fortifications which you tyrannically dismantled—and to acknowledge my master, William de la Marck, as Prince Bishop, lawfully elected."

"Have you finished?" said the Duke.

"One word more," answered Rouge Sanglier, "from my noble and venerable lord aforesaid, respecting his trusty ally, the Most Christian King——"

"Ha!" exclaimed the Duke, starting.

"—Which most Christian King's royal person it is rumoured that you, Charles of Burgundy, have placed under restraint, contrary to your duty as a vassal of the Crown of France. For which reason, my venerable master, by my mouth, charges you to put his Royal ally forthwith at freedom, or to receive the defiance which I am authorized to pronounce to you."

"Now, by Saint George of Burgundy," said the Duke—but ere he could proceed further, Louis arose, and struck in with so much dignity and authority that Charles could not interrupt him.

"Under your favour, fair cousin of Burgundy," said the King, "we ourselves crave priority in replying to this insolent fellow. Sirrah herald, or whatever thou art, carry back notice to the perjured outlaw and murderer, William de la Marck, that the King of France will be presently before Liege for the purpose of punishing the sacrilegious murderer of his late beloved kinsman, Louis of Bourbon; and that he proposes to gibbet de la Marck alive, for the insolence of terming himself his ally, and putting his royal name into the mouth of one of his own base messengers."

"Add whatever else on my part," said Charles, "which it may not misbecome a prince to send to a common thief, and murderer. And begone!—Yet stay. Never herald went from the Court of Burgundy without having cause to cry, Largesse! Let him be scourged till the bones are laid bare!"

"Nay, but if it please your Grace," said D'Hymbercourt, "he is a herald, and so far privileged."

"I see by that fellow's blazoning he is a mere impostor," replied the Duke. "Let Toison d'Or step forward, and question him in your presence." In spite of his natural effrontery, the envoy of the Wild Boar of Ardennes now became pale. "Show him a coat, and let him blazon it his own way," said the Duke, "if he fails, I promise him his back shall be all the colours of heraldry."

"Here," said the herald of Burgundy, taking from his pouch a piece of parchment, "is a scroll which I will pray my brother to decipher in fitting language." Le Glorieux had by this time bustled himself close up to the two heralds. "I will help thee, good fellow," said he to Rouge Sanglier, as he looked hopelessly upon the scroll. "This, my lords, represents the cat looking out of the dairy-window." This sally occasioned a laugh. "And," added Le Glorieux, "if the cat resemble Burgundy, she has the right side of the grating nowadays."

"True, good fellow," said Louis, laughing, while the rest of the presence, and even Charles himself, seemed disconcerted at so broad a jest, "I owe thee a piece of gold for turning what looked like earnest into the merry game which I trust it will end in."

"Silence, Le Glorieux," said the Duke, "and you, Toison d'Or, stand back. Bring that rascal forward, some of you.—Speak, villain, art thou herald or not?"

"Only for this occasion!" acknowledged the detected official.

"No-one with brains a whit better than those of a wild boar would have thought of passing such a trick upon the accomplished Court of Burgundy," said Louis.

"Send him who will," said the Duke fiercely, "he shall return on their hands in poor case. Here!—drag him to the marketplace! Slash him with dog-whips!—upon the Rouge Sanglier!—Haloo, haloo!" Four or five large hounds caught the well-known notes with which the Duke concluded, and began to yell and bay as if the boar were just roused from his lair.

"By the rood!" said King Louis, observant to catch the vein of his dangerous cousin, "since the ass has put on the boar's hide, I would set the dogs on him to tear him out of it!"

"Right!" exclaimed Duke Charles, the fancy exactly chiming in with his humour at the moment, "it shall be done! Uncouple the hounds! We will course him from the door of the Castle to the east gate."

"I trust your Grace will treat me as a beast of chase," said the fellow, putting the best face he could upon the matter, "and allow me fair law?"

"Thou art but vermin," said the Duke, "and entitled to no law; nevertheless thou shalt have sixty yards in advance, were it but for the sake of thy unparalleled impudence. Away, sirs!—we will see this sport." And the council breaking up tumultuously, all hurried to enjoy the humane pastime which King Louis had suggested.

Rouge Sanglier showed excellent sport; for, winged with terror, and having half a score of fierce boar-hounds hard at his haunches, he flew like the very wind, and had he not been encumbered with his herald's coat he might fairly have escaped dog-free. None of the spectators was so delighted with the sport as King Louis, who, partly from political considerations, and partly as being naturally pleased with the sight of human suffering when ludicrously exhibited, laughed till the tears ran from his eyes, and in his ecstasies of rapture, caught hold of the Duke's ermine cloak, as if to support himself; whilst the Duke, no less delighted, flung his arm around the King's shoulder. At length the speed of the pseudo-herald could save him no longer from the fangs of his pursuers; they seized him and pulled him down, but the Duke called out, "Take them off him!—He hath shown so good a course that we will not have him despatched."

Several officers accordingly busied themselves in taking off the dogs, and while the Duke was too much engaged with what passed before him to mind what was said behind him, Oliver le Dain, gliding behind King Louis, whispered into his ear, "He is the Bohemian, Hayraddin Maugrabin. It were not well he should come to speech of the Duke."

"He must die," answered Louis, in the same tone, "dead men tell no tales."

One instant afterwards, Tristan l'Hermite, to whom Oliver had given the hint, stepped forward before the King and the Duke, and said, in his blunt manner, "So please your Majesty and your Grace, this piece of game is mine, and I claim him—the fleur-de-lis is branded on his shoulder, as all men may see. He is a known villain, and hath slain the King's subjects, robbed churches——"

"Enough, enough," said Duke Charles. "What will your Majesty do with him?"

"If he is left to my disposal," said the King, "I will at least give him one lesson in the science of heraldry in which he is so ignorant —only explain to him practically, the meaning of a cross, with a noose dangling proper."

"Not as to be by him borne, but as to bear him. Let him take the degrees under your gossip Tristan—he is a deep professor in such mysteries." Thus answered the Duke, with a burst of discordant laughter at his own wit, which was so cordially chorussed by Louis, that his rival could not help looking kindly at him, while he said: "Ah, Louis! would to God thou wert as faithful a monarch as thou art a merry companion! I cannot but think often on the jovial time we used to spend together."

"You may bring it back when you will," said Louis. "I will grant you as fair terms as for very shame's sake you ought to ask in my present condition, without making yourself the fable of Christendom; and I will swear to observe them upon the holy relic which I bear about my person, being a fragment of the true cross."·

"Well, cousin," answered the Duke, "for once, without finesse and doubling, will you make good your promise, and go with me to punish this murdering La Marck and the Liegeois?"

"I will march against them," said Louis, "with the Oriflamme displayed."

"Nay, nay," said the Duke, "that is more than is needful, or maybe advisable. The presence of your Scottish Guard, and two hundred choice lances, will serve to show that you are a free agent. A large army might——"

"Make me so in effect, you would say, my fair cousin?" said the King. "Well, you shall dictate the numbers of my attendants."

"And to put this fair cause of mischief out of the way, you will agree to the Countess Isabelle of Croye wedding with the Duke of Orleans?"

"Were I to say I did this willingly," said the King, "no one would believe me; therefore do you, my fair cousin, judge of the extent of my wish to oblige you, when I say, most reluctantly, that the parties consenting, and a dispensation from the Pope being obtained, my own objections shall be no bar to this match which you propose."

"All besides can be easily settled by our ministers," said the Duke, "and we are once more cousins and friends."

"May Heaven be praised!" said Louis.—"Oliver," he added apart to the favourite, "Hark thee—tell Tristan to be speedy in dealing with yonder runagate Bohemian."

Whilst the principal parties concerned had so far made up their differences, one of the agents concerned in their intrigues was bitterly experiencing the truth of the political maxim that if the great have frequent need of base tools, they make amends to society by abandoning them to their fate so soon as they find them no longer useful. This was Hayraddin Maugrabin, whom the King's Provost-Marshal placed in the hands of his two trusty men, Trois-Eschelles and Petit-André, to be despatched without loss of time. One on either side of him, and followed by guards and a rabble, he was marched off to the forest, where they proposed to knit him up the first sufficient tree. They were not long in finding an oak, as Petit-André facetiously expressed it, fit to bear such an acorn; and placing the wretched criminal on a bank under guard, they began their preparations.

At that moment, Hayraddin encountered the eyes of Quentin Durward, who had followed with the crowd, thinking he recognized the countenance of his faithless guide in that of the detected impostor. When the executioners informed him that all was ready, Hayraddin, with much calmness, asked a single boon at their hands. "Anything, my son, consistent with our office," said Trois-Eschelles. "As you seem resolved to die like a man— why, though our orders are to be prompt, I care not if I indulge you ten minutes longer."

"I only pray to speak a few minutes with yonder Archer of the Scottish Guard," said the Bohemian. The executioners hesitated a moment; but Trois-Eschelles recollecting that Quentin Durward was believed to stand high in the favour of their master, King Louis, they resolved to permit the interview. When Quentin, at their summons, approached the condemned criminal, he could not but be shocked at his appearance, however justly his doom might have been deserved. The remnants of his heraldic finery, rent to tatters by the fangs of the dogs, gave him a ludicrous and wretched appearance. Yet, strong in passive courage, he seemed to bid defiance to the death he was about to die. "I must speak with him in privacy," said the criminal.

"That may hardly consist with our office," said Petit-André, "we know you for a slippery eel of old."

"I am tied with your horse-girths, hand and foot," said the criminal. "You may keep guard around me, though out of ear-shot—the Archer is your own King's servant. And if I give you ten guilders——"

"Let them be forthcoming, my little crack-rope."

"Pay the blood-hounds their fee," said Hayraddin to Durward. "I was plundered of every stiver when they took me—it shall avail thee much." Quentin paid the executioners their guerdon, and, like men of promise, they retreated out of hearing—keeping, however, a careful eye on the criminal. "I have a boon to ask," said Hayraddin, "but first I will buy it of you; for your tribe, with all their professions of charity, give nought for nought."

"I could well nigh say thy gifts perish with thee," answered Quentin, "but that thou art on the very verge of eternity. Ask thy boon—reserve thy bounty. It can do me no good—I remember enough of your good offices of old."

"Why, I loved you," said Hayraddin, "for the matter that chanced on the banks of the Cher; and I would have helped you to a wealthy dame."

"Talk not so idly, unhappy man," said Quentin, "yonder officers become impatient."

"Well, know then," said Hayraddin, "I came hither in this accursed disguise, moved by a great reward from De la Marck, and hoping a mightier one from King Louis for an important secret."

"It was a fearful risk," said Durward.

"It was paid for as such, and such it hath proved," answered the Bohemian. "Hear my secret: William de la Marck has assembled a strong force within the city of Liege, and augments it daily by means of the old priest's treasures. But he proposes not to hazard a battle with the chivalry of Burgundy, and still less to stand a siege in the dismantled town. This he will do—he will suffer the hot-brained Charles to sit down before the place without opposition; and in the night, make a sally upon the besieging army with his whole force. Many he will have in French armour, who will cry France, Saint Louis, and Denis Montjoye, as if there were a strong body of French auxiliaries in the city. This cannot choose but strike utter confusion among the Burgundians; and if King Louis, with his guards, shall second his efforts, the Boar of Ardennes nothing doubts the discomfiture of the whole Burgundian army. There is my secret, and I bequeath it to you. Sell the intelligence to King Louis, or to Duke Charles, I care not!"

"It is indeed an important secret," said Quentin, instantly comprehending how easily the national jealousy might be awakened in a camp consisting partly of French, partly of Burgundians.

"Ay, so it is," answered Hayraddin, "and now you have it, you would fain begone, and leave me without granting the boon for which I have paid beforehand."

"Tell me thy request," said Quentin. "I will grant it if it be in my power."

"Nay, it is no mighty demand—it is only in behalf of poor Klepper, my palfrey, the only living thing that may miss me. A due mile south, you will find him feeding by a deserted collier's hut; call him by name and he will come to you. Take him, and make much of him—I do not say for his master's sake, but because I have placed at your disposal the event of a mighty war. He will never fail you at need; had I cleared the gates of Peronne, and got as far as where I left him, I had not been in this case. Will you be kind to Klepper?"

"I swear to you that I will," answered Quentin.

"Then fare thee well!" said the criminal. "Yet stay—I would not willingly die in discourtesy, forgetting a lady's commission. This billet is from the very gracious and extremely silly Lady of the Wild Boar of Ardennes, to her black-eyed niece—I see by your look I have chosen a willing messenger. And one word more—I forgot to say, that in the stuffing of my saddle you will find a rich purse of gold pieces, for the sake of which I put my life on the venture which has cost me so dear. Take them, and replace a hundredfold the guilders you have bestowed on these bloody slaves—I make you mine heir."

"I will bestow them in good works, and masses for the benefit of thy soul," said Quentin.

"Name not that word," said Hayraddin. "There is—there can be—no such thing!"

"Unhappy—most unhappy being!" said Quentin. "What canst thou expect, dying in such opinions, and impenitent?"

"To be resolved into the elements," said the hardened atheist, pressing his fettered arms against his bosom. "In this faith have I lived, and I will die in it! Hence! Begone!—disturb me no further!"

Deeply impressed with the horrors of his condition, Quentin Durward saw that it was vain to hope to awaken him to a sense of his fearful state. He bid him, therefore, farewell, bent his course towards the forest, and easily found where Klepper was feeding. The creature came at his call, but long ere he returned to Peronne, the Bohemian had gone where the vanity of his dreadful creed was to be put to the final issue.

13. Diplomacy

WHEN Quentin Durward reached Peronne, a council was sitting. King Louis was engaged in consulting the Duke upon the troops by whom, as auxiliary to the Duke of Burgundy, he was to be attended in their joint expedition against Liege. He plainly saw the wish of Charles was to call into his camp such Frenchmen as, from their small number and high quality, might be considered rather as hostages than as auxiliaries; but, observant of Crève-coeur's advice, he assented as readily to whatever the Duke proposed as if it had arisen from the free impulse of his own mind.

The King failed not, however, to indulge his vindictive temper against Balue, whose counsels had led him to repose such exuberant trust in the Duke of Burgundy. Tristan, who bore the summons for moving up his auxiliary forces, had the further commission to carry the Cardinal to the Castle of Loches and there shut him up in one of those iron cages, which he himself is said to have invented. "Let him make proof of his own devices," said the King. "And see the troops are brought up instantly."

Perhaps, by this prompt acquiescence, Louis hoped to evade the more unpleasing condition with which the Duke had clogged their reconciliation. But no sooner were the necessary expresses despatched to summon up his forces than Louis was called upon by his host to give public consent to the espousals of the Duke of Orleans and Isabelle of Croye. The King complied with a heavy sigh: "The whole shall be as you, my cousin, will; if you can bring it about with consent of the parties themselves," said Louis.

"Fear not that," said the Duke; and accordingly, the Duke of Orleans and the Countess of Croye, the latter attended by the Countess of Crèvecoeur and the Abbess of the Ursulines, were summoned to the presence of the Princes, and heard from the mouth of Charles of Burgundy that the union of their hands was designed by the wisdom of both Princes to confirm the perpetual alliance which in future should take place betwixt France and Burgundy. The Duke of Orleans threw himself on his knees, and kissed—and, for once, with sincerity—the hand which the King, with averted countenance, extended to him. Charles next turned to the young Countess, and bluntly announced the proposed match to her, as a matter which neither admitted delay nor hesitation.

"My Lord Duke and Sovereign," said Isabelle, summoning up all her courage, "I observe your Grace's commands, and submit to them."

"Enough, enough," said the Duke, interrupting her, "we will arrange the rest."

The young Countess saw the necessity of decision. "Your Grace mistakes my meaning," she said. "My submission only respected those estates which your Grace's ancestors gave to mine, and which I resign to the House of Burgundy, if my Sovereign thinks my disobedience in this matter renders me unworthy to hold them."

"Ha! Saint George!" said the Duke, stamping furiously on the ground, "does the fool know in what presence she is—and to whom she speaks?"

"My lord," she replied, still undismayed, "I am before my Suzerain, and, I trust, a just one. If you deprive me of my lands, you take away all that your ancestors' generosity gave, and you break the only bonds which attach us. You gave not this poor and persecuted form, still less the spirit which animates me—and these it is my purpose to dedicate to Heaven in the convent of the Ursulines, under the guidance of this Holy Mother Abbess."

"Will the Holy Mother receive you without a dowry?" he said, in a voice of scorn.

"If she doth her convent, in the first instance, so much wrong," said Lady Isabelle, "I trust there is charity enough among the noble friends of my house, to make up some support for the orphan of Croye."

"It is false!" said the Duke. "It is a base pretext to cover some secret and unworthy passion. My Lord of Orleans, she shall be yours, if I drag her to the altar with my own hands!"

"If I were permitted," said Orleans, on whose facile mind Isabelle's beauty had made a deep impression, "some time to endeavour to place my pretensions before the Countess in a more favourable light——"

"My lord," said Isabelle, with firmness, "it were to no purpose —my mind is made up to decline this alliance, though far above my deserts."

"Monseigneur d'Orleans, she shall learn within this hour that obedience becomes matter of necessity," said the Duke.

"Not in my behalf, Sire," answered the Prince, who felt that he could not, with any show of honour, avail himself of the Duke's obstinate disposition. "To have been once openly and positively refused is enough for a son of France. He cannot prosecute his addresses further."

The Duke darted one furious glance at Louis, and reading in his countenance, in spite of his utmost efforts to suppress his feelings, a look of secret triumph, he became outrageous: "She shall to the penitentiary, to herd with those whose lives have rendered them her rivals in effrontery!"

There was a general murmur. "My Lord Duke," said the Count of Crèvecoeur, "if the Countess hath done amiss, let her be punished—but in the manner that becomes her rank, and ours, who stand connected with her house by blood and alliance."

The Duke paused a moment, and looked full at his councillor; prudence, however, prevailed over fury, for he saw the sentiment was general in his council and he probably felt ashamed of his own dishonourable proposal. "You are right, Crèvecoeur," he said, "and I spoke hastily. Her fate shall be determined according to the rules of chivalry. Her flight to Liege hath given the signal for the Bishop's murder. He that best avenges that deed and brings us the head of the Wild Boar of Ardennes shall claim her hand of us; and if she denies his right, we can at least grant him her estates, leaving it to his generosity to allow her what means he will to retire into a convent."

"Nay!" said the Countess, "think I am the daughter of Count Reinold. Would you hold me out as a prize to the best sword-player?"

"Your ancestress," said the Duke, "was won at a tourney— you shall be fought for in real *mêlée*. Only thus far, for Count Reinold's sake, the successful prizer shall be a gentleman, of unimpeached birth, and unstained bearings. Ha! Messires," he added, turning to the nobles present, "this at least is, I think, in conformity with the rules of chivalry?" Isabelle's remonstrances were drowned in a general and jubilant assent.

"Are we, to whom fate has given dames already," said Crèvecoeur, "to be bystanders at this fair game?"

"Strike boldly in, Crèvecoeur," said the Duke, "win her, and bestow her where thou wilt—on Count Stephen, your nephew, if you like."

"Gramercy, my lord!" said Crèvecoeur, "I will do my best in the battle; and, should I be fortunate enough to be the foremost, Stephen shall try his eloquence against that of the Lady Abbess."

"I trust," said Dunois, "that the chivalry of France are not excluded from this fair contest?"

"Heaven forbid! brave Dunois," answered the Duke. "But it will be necessary that the Count of Croye must become a subject of Burgundy."

"Enough," said Dunois, "I will live and die French. But yet, though I should lose the lands, I will strike a blow for the lady."

Le Balafré dared not speak aloud in such a presence, but he muttered to himself—"Now it was said the fortune of our house was to be won by marriage."

"No one thinks of me," said Le Glorieux, "who am sure to carry off the prize from all of you."

"Right, my sapient friend," said Louis, "when a woman is in the case, the greatest fool is ever the first in favour." While the princes and their nobles thus jested over her fate, the Abbess endeavoured in vain to console Isabelle, who had withdrawn with the ladies from the council-presence. The Countess of Crèvecoeur whispered more temporal consolation, that perhaps the successful competitor might prove one who should find such favour in her eyes as to reconcile her to obedience.

Few days had passed ere Louis had received, with a smile of gratified vengeance, the intelligence that his favourite, the Cardinal Balue, was groaning within a cage of iron, so disposed as scarce to permit him to enjoy repose in any posture; and of which, be it said in passing, he remained the unpitied tenant for nearly twelve years. The auxiliary forces which the Duke had required Louis to bring up had also appeared; and, although he was sensible to the indignity of serving with his noblest peers under the banners of his own vassal, and against the people whose cause he had abetted, he did not allow these circumstances to embarrass him, trusting that a future day would bring him amends. "For chance," said he to Oliver, "may indeed gain one hit, but it is patience and wisdom which win the game at last." With such sentiments, upon a beautiful day in the latter end of harvest, the King mounted his horse; and, surrounded by his guards and his chivalry, King Louis sallied from under the Gothic gateway of Peronne, to join the Burgundian army which commenced its march against Liege.

Most of the ladies of distinction who were in the place attended, dressed in their best array, upon the battlements to see the gallant show of the warriors setting forth on the expedition. Thither had the Countess Crèvecoeur brought the Countess Isabelle; the peremptory order of Charles had been that she who was to bestow the palm in the tourney should be visible to the knights who were about to enter the lists. As they thronged out from under the arch, each knight put his courser to his mettle, and assumed his most valiant seat in the saddle as he passed for a moment under the view of the fair bevy of damsels, who encouraged their valour by their smiles, and the waving of kerchiefs.

The Archer-Guard drew a general applause from the gallantry and splendour of their appearance. And there was one among these strangers who ventured on a demonstration of acquaintance with the Lady Isabelle which had not been attempted even by the most noble of the French nobility. It was Quentin Durward, who, as he passed, presented to the Countess of Croye, on the point of his lance, the letter of her aunt. "Now, by my honour," said the Count of Crèvecoeur, "that is over insolent in an unworthy adventurer!"

"Do not call him so, Crèvecoeur," said Dunois. "I have good reason to bear testimony to his gallantry—and in behalf of that lady, too."

"You make words of nothing," said Isabelle, blushing with shame, and partly with resentment, "it is a letter from my unfortunate aunt. She writes cheerfully, though her situation must be dreadful."

"Let us hear what says the Boar's bride," said Crèvecoeur. The Countess Isabelle read the letter, in which her aunt seemed determined to make the best of a bad bargain, and to console herself for the haste and indecorum of her nuptials, by the happiness of being wedded to one of the bravest men of the age, who had just acquired a princedom by his valour. She implored her niece not to judge of her William (as she called him) by the report of others, but to wait till she knew him personally; and the whole concluded with the request that Isabelle would endeavour her escape from the tyrant of Burgundy, and come to her loving kinswoman's Court of Liege.

Here the Countess Isabelle stopped, and the Count of Crèvecoeur broke out, "Why, this device smells rank as the toasted cheese in a rat-trap!"

The Countess of Crèvecoeur gravely rebuked her husband for his violence. "Lady Hameline," she said, "must have been deceived by de la Marck with a show of courtesy."

"He show courtesy!" said the Count, "I acquit him of all such dissimulation. But you women are all alike—fair words carry it—and, I dare say, here is my pretty cousin impatient to join her aunt in this fool's paradise."

"So far from being capable of such folly," said Isabelle, "I am doubly desirous of vengeance on the murderers of the excellent Bishop, because it will, at the same time, free my aunt from the villain's power."

"Ah! there indeed spoke the voice of Croye!" exclaimed the Count; and no more was said concerning the letter. But while Isabelle read her aunt's epistle to her friends, it must be observed that she did not think it necessary to recite a certain *postscript*, in which Countess Hameline gave an account of her occupations, and informed her niece that she had laid aside for the present a surcoat which she was working for her husband bearing the arms of Croye and La Marck, because her William had determined, for purposes of policy, in the first action to have others dressed in his coat-armour, and himself to assume the arms of Orleans, with a bar sinister—in other words, those of Dunois. There was also a slip of paper in another hand, the contents of which the Countess did not think it necessary to mention, being simply these words: "If you hear not of me soon, and that by the trumpet of Fame, conclude me dead, but not unworthy."

A thought, hitherto repelled as wildly incredible, now glanced with double keenness through Isabelle's soul. As female wit seldom fails in the contrivance of means, she so ordered it that ere the troops were fully on march, Quentin Durward received from an unknown hand the billet of Lady Hameline, marked with three crosses opposite the post-script, and having these words subjoined: "He who feared not the arms of Orleans when on the breast of their gallant owner, cannot dread them when displayed on that of a tyrant and murderer." A thousand times was this kissed by the young Scot! for it possessed him with a secret unknown to others, by which to distinguish him whose death could alone give him hope. But Durward saw the necessity of acting otherwise respecting the information communicated by Hayraddin, since the proposed sally of De la Marck, unless heedfully guarded against, might prove the destruction of the besieging army. After pondering the matter, he resolved that he would communicate the intelligence personally, and to both the Princes while together; perhaps because he felt that to mention so well-contrived a scheme to Louis whilst in private, might be too strong a temptation to the wavering probity of that Monarch, and lead him to assist, rather than repel the intended sally.

Meanwhile the march continued, and the confederates soon entered the territories of Liege. Here the conduct of the Burgundian soldiers greatly prejudiced the cause of Charles, but the French observed the strictest discipline; a contrast which increased the suspicions of Charles, who could not help remarking that the troops of Louis demeaned themselves as if they were rather friends to the Liegeois, than allies of Burgundy. At length, without experiencing any serious opposition, the army arrived before the city of Liege. The Castle of Schonwaldt they found had been totally destroyed, and learned that De la Marck, whose only talents were of a military cast, had withdrawn his whole forces into the city, and was determined to avoid the encounter of the chivalry of France and Burgundy in the open field.

A small country villa of some wealthy citizen of Liege was secured and cleared of other occupants for the accommodation of the Duke and his immediate attendants; and the authority of D'Hymbercourt and Crèvecoeur established a guard in the vicinity of about forty men-at-arms, who lighted a large fire. A little to the left of this villa lay another pleasure-house. In this the King of France established his own headquarters, and a part of his Scottish Guard were placed in the court. The remainder of the French men-at-arms were quartered closely together and in good order, with alarm-posts stationed, in case of their having to sustain an attack. Dunois and Crawford, assisted by several old officers and soldiers, amongst whom Le Balafré was conspicuous for his diligence, contrived, by breaking down walls, making openings through hedges, filling up ditches, and the like, to facilitate the communication of the troops with each other, and the orderly combination of the whole in case of necessity.

Meanwhile, the King judged it proper to go without further ceremony to the quarters of the Duke of Burgundy. His presence occasioned a sort of council of war to be held, of which Charles might not otherwise have dreamed. It was then that Quentin Durward prayed earnestly to be admitted, as having something of importance to deliver to the two Princes. Great was the astonishment of Louis when he heard him calmly relate the purpose of William de la Marck to make a sally upon the camp of the besiegers, under the dress and banners of the French. Louis would probably have been much better pleased to have had such important news communicated in private; but as the whole story had been publicly told in the presence of the Duke of Burgundy, he only observed, "that, whether true or false, such a report concerned them most materially."

"Not a whit!" said the Duke carelessly. "Had there been such a purpose as this young man announces, it had not been communicated to me by an Archer of the Scottish Guard."

"However that may be," answered Louis, "I pray you, fair cousin, you and your captains, to attend, that to prevent the unpleasing consequences of such an attack, should it be made unexpectedly. I will cause my soldiers to wear white scarfs over their armour—Dunois, see it given out on the instant—that is," he added, "if our brother and general approves it."

"I see no objection," replied the Duke, "if the chivalry of France are willing to run the risk of having the name of Knights of the Smock sleeve bestowed on them in future."

"It would be a right well adapted title, friend Charles," said Le Glorieux, "considering that a woman is the reward of the most valiant."

"Well spoken, Sagacity," said Louis. "Cousin, good-night, I will go arm me.—By the way, what if I win the Countess with mine own hand?"

"Your Majesty," said the Duke, in an altered tone of voice, "must then become a true Fleming."

"I cannot," answered Louis, in a tone of the most sincere confidence, "be more so than I am already, could I but bring you, my dear cousin, to believe it." And Louis returned to his own quarters. "Go, Oliver," he said; "tell no man to unarm himself; and let them shoot, in case of necessity, as sharply on those who cry *France* and *St. Denis!* as if they cried Hell and Satan! I will myself sleep in my armour. *Pasques-dieu!* This Scot," he added, "is such a mixture of shrewdness and simplicity, that I know not what to make of him. Let Crawford place Quentin Durward on the extreme point of our line of sentinels, next to the city. Let him have the first benefit of the sally he has announced to us—if his luck bear him out, it is the better for him. But take especial care of Martius Galeotti, and see he remain in the rear, in a place of the most absolute safety. See to these things, Oliver, and good night."

14. Siege and Battle

A DEAD silence soon reigned over the great host before Liege. Overcome by the fatigues of the day, the soldiers crowded under such shelter as they could find under walls and hedges, there to wait for morning—a morning some of them were never to behold. A dead sleep fell on almost all; but not so with Quentin Durward. The knowledge that he alone was possessed of the means of distinguishing La Marck in the contest, the thought that his fortune had brought him to a perilous crisis indeed, but one where there was still a chance of his coming off triumphant, banished every desire to sleep.

Posted by the King's order on the extreme point between the French quarters and the town, he sharpened his ears to catch the slightest sound which might announce any commotion in the beleaguered city. But its clocks had successively knelled three hours after midnight, and all continued silent. At length, and just when Quentin began to think the attack would be deferred till daybreak, he thought he heard in the city a humming murmur. As the noise rose louder, he fell back as silently as possible, and called his uncle, who commanded the small body of Archers. All were on their feet in a moment and in less than a second, Lord Crawford was at their head, and, despatching an archer to alarm the King and his household, drew back his little party behind their watchfire, that they might not be seen by its light, for they still heard distinctly the heavy tread of a large body of men approaching the suburb. "The lazy Burgundians are asleep on their post," whispered Crawford, "make for the suburb, Cunningham, and awaken the stupid oxen."

"Keep well to the rear as you go," said Durward, "there is a strong body between us and the suburb."

"Well said, Quentin," said Crawford, "thou art a soldier beyond thy years, but I would I had some knowledge where they are!"

"I will creep forward, my lord," said Quentin, "and endeavour to bring you information."

"Do so, my bonny lad; thou hast sharp ears and eyes."

Quentin, with his harquebuss ready prepared, stole forward, through ground which he had reconnoitred carefully the preceding evening, until he was not only certain that he was in the neighbourhood of a large body of men standing fast between the King's quarters and the suburbs, but also that there was a small advance party very close to him. They seemed to whisper together, as if uncertain what to do next. At last, the steps of two or three, detached from that smaller party, approached him so near as twice a pike's length. Seeing it impossible to retreat undiscovered, Quentin called out aloud "Who goes there?" and was answered by "Li-ege- no" (added he who spoke, correcting himself), "France!"—Quentin instantly fired his harquebuss—a man groaned and fell, and he himself, under fire which ran in a disorderly manner along the column and showed it to be very numerous, hastened back to the main guard.

"Admirably done, my brave boy!" said Crawford. "Now,

gallants, draw in within the courtyard—they are too many to mell with in the open field." They drew within the garden accordingly, where they found all in great order, and the King prepared to mount his horse. "Whither away, Sire?" said Crawford, "you are safest here with your own people."

"Not so," said Louis, "I must instantly to the Duke. He must be convinced of our good faith at this critical moment, or we shall have both Liegeois and Burgundians upon us at once." And springing on his horse, he bade Dunois command the French troops outside the house, and Crawford the Archer-Guard and other household troops. Having commanded them to bring up the artillery, he rode off with a small escort to the Duke's quarters.

The delay which permitted these arrangements to be carried into effect was owing to Quentin's having fortunately shot the proprietor of the house, who acted as guide to the column which was to attack it, and whose attack, had it been made instantly, might have had a chance of being successful.

Durward, who, by the King's order, attended him to the Duke's, found the latter in a state of fury; for, besides the combat which had now taken place in the suburb upon the left of their whole army—besides the attack upon the King's quarters, which was fiercely maintained in the centre—a third column of Liegeois had filed out and had fallen upon the right flank of the Burgundian army, who, alarmed at their war-cries of *Vive la France*! which mingled with those of *Liege* and *Sanglier*, and at the idea thus inspired of treachery by the French, made a very desultory and imperfect resistance. The Duke, foaming and swearing, and cursing his liege Lord and all that belonged to him, called out to shoot with bow and gun on all that was French.

The arrival of the King, attended only by Le Balafré and Quentin, and half a score of Archers, restored confidence between France and Burgundy. D'Hymbercourt, Crèvecoeur, and others of the Burgundian leaders, whose names were then the praise and dread of war, rushed into the conflict; and, as some commanders hastened to bring up more distant troops, others threw themselves into the tumult, and while the Duke toiled in the front, hacking and hewing like an ordinary man-at-arms, brought their men by degrees into discipline, and dismayed the assailants by the use of their artillery. The conduct of Louis on the other hand, was that of a calm and collected leader who neither sought nor avoided danger, and the Burgundians readily obeyed the orders which he issued.

The scene was now become horrible; on the left the suburb, after a fierce contest, was now in flames, and on the centre, the French troops, though pressed by immense odds, kept up a close and constant fire. On the right, the battle swayed backwards and forwards with varied success, and the strife continued with unremitting fury for three mortal hours, which at length brought the dawn. The enemy, at this period, seemed to be slackening their efforts upon the right.

"Go," said the King, to Le Balafré and Quentin, "Tell Dunois to cut in between those thick-headed Liegeois on the right and the city, from which they are supplied with recruits."

The uncle and nephew galloped off to Dunois and Crawford, who, tired of their defensive war, joyfully obeyed the summons, and, filing out at the head of a gallant body of about two hundred French gentlemen, marched across the field till they gained the flank of the large body of Liegeois, by whom the right of the Burgundians had been so fiercely assailed. The increasing daylight discovered that the enemy were continuing to pour out from the city, perhaps to bring safely off the forces who were already engaged.

"By Heaven!" said old Crawford to Dunois, "were I not certain it is *thou* that art riding by my side, I would say I saw thee among yonder banditti marshalling them with thy mace."

"I will presently punish him for his insolence," said Dunois. "Yonder caitiff has *my* bearings on his shield and crest."

"In the name of all that is noble, my lord, leave the vengeance to me!" said Quentin.

"To *thee* indeed, young man?" said Dunois. "No—these things brook no substitution." Then turning on his saddle, he called out to those around him, "Gentlemen of France, form your line, level your lances against yonder swine of Liege, that masquerade in our ancient coats of arms."

The men-at-arms answered with a loud shout of "A Dunois!—Orleans to the rescue!" And, with their leader in the centre, they charged the enemy infantry at full gallop, who, setting the butt of their lances against their feet; the front rank kneeling, the second stooping, and those behind presenting their spears over their heads, offered such resistance to the rapid charge of the men-at-arms as the hedgehog presents to his enemy. Few were able to make way through that iron wall; but of those few was Dunois, who, giving spur to his horse, broke his way into the middle of the phalanx, and made towards the object of his animosity. What was his surprise to find Quentin still fighting by his side— desperate courage and the determination to do or die having kept the youth abreast with the best knight in Europe; for such was Dunois reported, and truly reported, at the period.

Suddenly Dunois, observing the boar's-head and tusks—the usual bearing of De la Marck—in another part of the conflict, called out to Quentin, "Thou art worthy to avenge the arms of Orleans! I leave thee the task. Balafré, support your nephew; let none dare to interfere with Dunois' boar-hunt!"

That Quentin Durward joyfully acquiesced in this division of labour cannot be doubted, and each pressed forward upon his separate object. But at this moment the column which De la Marck had proposed to support, when his own course was arrested by the charge of Dunois, had lost all the advantages they had gained during the night; while the Burgundians, with returning day, had begun to show the qualities which belong to superior discipline. The great mass of Liegeois were compelled to retreat, and at length to fly; and, falling back towards the city-walls, at last poured into the undefended breach through which they had sallied.

Quentin made more than human exertions to overtake the special object of his pursuit, who was still in his sight, striving to renew the battle, and bravely supported by a chosen party of lanzknechts. Le Balafré, and several of his comrades, attached themselves to Quentin, marvelling at the extraordinary gallantry displayed by so young a soldier. At the breach, De la Marck succeeded in effecting a momentary stand. He had a mace of iron in his hand, covered with blood, before which everything seemed to go down. But Quentin sprang from his horse and ascended the ruins of the breach to measure swords with the Boar of Ardennes. The latter turned towards Durward with mace uplifted; and they were on the point of encounter, when a dreadful shout of triumph announced that the besiegers were entering the city at another point, in the rear of those who defended the breach.

De la Marck, at those appalling sounds, abandoned the breach, and endeavoured to effect his retreat. His immediate followers formed a body of well-disciplined men, who, never having given quarter, were resolved now not to ask it, and who, in that hour of despair, threw themselves into such firm order that their front occupied the whole breadth of the street, through which they slowly retired, checking the pursuers, many of whom began to seek a safer occupation by breaking into the houses for plunder. It is therefore probable that De la Marck might have effected his escape, his disguise concealing him from those who promised themselves to win honour upon his head, but for the staunch pursuit of Quentin, his uncle Le Balafré, and some of his comrades. At every pause which was made by the lanzknechts, a furious combat took place between them and the Archers, but De la Marck, whose present object was to retreat, seemed to evade the young Scot's purpose of bringing him to single combat. The confusion was general in every direction. The shrieks of women, the yelling of the terrified inhabitants, now subjected to the extremity of military licence, sounded horribly shrill amid the shouts of battle—the voice of misery and despair contending with that of fury and violence.

It was just when De la Marck, retiring through this infernal scene, had passed the door of a small chapel that the shouts of "Burgundy! Burgundy!" apprised him that a part of the besiegers were entering the further end of the street, which was narrow, and that his retreat was cut off.

"Comrade," he said, "take all the men with you. Charge yonder fellows and break through if you can—with me it is over. I am man enough, now that I am brought to bay, to send some of these vagabond Scots to hell before me." His lieutenant obeyed; about six of De la Marck's men remained to perish with their master, and fronted the Archers, who were not many more in number.

"Sanglier! Sanglier! Hola! gentlemen of Scotland," said the ruffian but undaunted chief, waving his mace, "who longs to gain a coronet—who strikes at the Boar of Ardennes?—You, young man, have, methinks, a hankering; but you must win ere you wear it."

Quentin had but time to bid his comrades, as they were gentlemen, to stand back, when De la Marck sprang upon him with a bound, aiming at the same time a blow with his mace, and giving his stroke full advantage of the descent of his leap; but, light of foot and quick of eye, Quentin leaped aside, and disappointed an aim which would have been fatal had it taken effect. They then closed, their comrades on either side remaining spectators, for Le Balafré roared out for fair play.

Although the blows of the despairing robber fell like those of the hammer on the anvil, yet the quick motions, the dexterous swordsmanship, of the young Archer, enabled him to escape, and to requite them with the point of his less noisy, though more fatal weapon; and that so often that the huge strength of his antagonist began to give way to fatigue, while the ground on which he stood became a puddle of blood. Yet, still unabated in courage, the Wild Boar fought on with as much mental energy as at first, and Quentin's victory seemed distant, when a female voice behind him called him by his name, ejaculating, "Help! help! for the sake of the blessed Virgin!"

Quentin turned his head, and with a single glance beheld Trudchen Pavillon, her mantle stripped from her shoulders, dragged forcibly along by a French soldier; one of several, who, breaking into the chapel close by, had seized as their prey on the terrified females who had taken refuge there. "Wait for me but one moment," exclaimed Quentin to De la Marck, and sprang to extricate his benefactress from a situation of which he conjectured all the dangers.

"I wait no man's pleasure," said De la Marck, flourishing his mace, and beginning to retreat—glad, no doubt, of being free of so formidable an assailant.

"You shall wait mine, though, by your leave," said Balafré: "I will not have my nephew baulked." So saying, he instantly assaulted De la Marck with his two-handed sword.

Quentin found, in the meanwhile, that the rescue of Trudchen was a task more difficult than could be finished in one moment. Her captor, supported by his comrades, refused to relinquish his prize; and whilst Durward, aided by one or two of his countrymen, endeavoured to compel him to do so, the former beheld the chance of fortune and happiness glide out of his reach; so that when he stood at length in the street with the liberated Trudchen, there was no one near them. Totally forgetting the defenceless situation of his companion, he was about to spring away in pursuit of the Boar of Ardennes, when, clinging to him in her despair, she exclaimed, "Leave me not here! As you are a gentleman, protect me to my father's house, which once sheltered you and the Lady Isabelle!—For her sake leave me not!" Her call was agonizing, but it was irresistible; and bidding adieu, with unutterable bitterness of feeling, to all the gay hopes which had carried him through that bloody day, Quentin, like an unwilling spirit, who obeys a talisman which he cannot resist, protected Trudchen to Pavillon's house, and arrived in time to defend that and the Syndic himself against the fury of the licentious soldiery.

Meantime, the King and the Duke of Burgundy entered the city on horseback through one of the breaches. The Princes

213

despatched orders to stop the sack of the city, and proceeded towards the great church, in order to hold a sort of military council after they had heard High Mass.

Busied like other officers in collecting those under his command, Lord Crawford met Le Balafré sauntering composedly towards the river, holding in his hand, by the gory locks, a human head. "How now, Ludovic!" said his commander, "what are you doing with that carrion?"

"It is all that is left of a bit of work which my nephew nearly finished, and I put the last hand to," said Le Balafré, "a good fellow that I despatched yonder, and who prayed me to throw his head into the river."

"And are you going to throw that head into the Maes?" said Crawford, looking at it more attentively.

"Ay, truly am I," said Ludovic Lesly. "If you refuse a dying man his boon, you are likely to be haunted by his ghost, and I love to sleep sound at nights."

"You must take your chance of the ghaist, man," said Crawford, "for, by my soul, there is more lies on that dead poll than you think for. Not a word more—come along with me."

When High Mass had been said in the Cathedral and the terrified town restored to some degree of order, Louis and Charles, with their peers around, proceeded to hear the claims of those who had any to make for services performed during the battle. Those which respected the County of Croye and its fair mistress were first received, and, to the disappointment of sundry claimants who had thought themselves sure of the rich prize, there seemed doubt and mystery to involve their several pretensions. Crèvecoeur showed a boar's hide such as De la Marck usually wore; Dunois produced a cloven shield, with his armorial bearings; and there were others who claimed the merit of having despatched the murderer of the Bishop, producing similar tokens. There was much noise and contest among the competitors, and Charles, regretting the rash promise which had placed the hand and wealth of his fair vassal on such a hazard, was in hopes he might find means of evading these conflicting claims, when Crawford pressed forward into the circle, dragging Le Balafré after him and crying: "No one, save he who slew the Boar, can show the tusks!" So saying, he flung on the floor the bloody head, easily known as that of De la Marck, by the singular conformation of the jaws, which, in reality, had a certain resemblance to those of the animal whose name he bore, and which was instantly recognised by all who had seen him.

"Crawford," said Louis, while Charles sat silent, in gloomy and displeased surprise, "I trust it is one of my faithful Scots who has won this prize?"

"It is Ludovic Lesly, Sire, whom we call Le Balafré," replied the old soldier.

"But is he noble?" said the Duke, "otherwise our promise is void."

"He is a cross ungainly piece of wood enough," said Crawford, looking at the tall, awkward, embarrassed figure of the Archer, "but I will warrant him a branch of the tree of Rothes for all that— and they are as noble as any house in France or Burgundy."

"There is then no help for it," said the Duke, "and the fairest and richest heiress in Burgundy must be the wife of a mercenary soldier, or die secluded in a convent—and she the only child of our faithful Reinold de Croye! I have been too rash."

"Hold," said Lord Crawford, "it may be better than your Grace conjectures. Hear what this cavalier has to say.—Speak out, man," he added, apart to Le Balafré. But that blunt soldier was awkward and bashful before so splendid an assembly. "May it please your Majesty, and your Grace," said Crawford, "I must speak for my old comrade. You shall understand that he has had it prophesied to him by a Seer in his own land, that the fortune of his house is to be made by marriage; but loving the wine-house better than a lady's summer-parlour, and having some barrack tastes and likings which would make greatness in his own person rather an encumbrance to him, he hath acted by my advice, and resigns the pretensions acquired by slaying De la Marck to him by whom the Wild Boar was actually brought to bay, who is his nephew."

"I will vouch for that youth's services and prudence," said King Louis, overjoyed to see that fate had thrown so gallant a prize to one over whom he had some influence. "Without his vigilance, we had been ruined—It was he who made us aware of the night-sally."

"I then," said Charles, "owe him some reparation for doubting his veracity."

"And I can attest his gallantry as a man-at-arms," said Dunois.

"But," interrupted Crèvecoeur, "though the uncle be of the Scottish nobility, that makes not the nephew necessarily so."

"He is of the House of Durward," said Crawford, "descended from Allan Durward, who was High Steward of Scotland."

"Nay, if it be young Durward," said Crèvecoeur, "I say no more. Fortune has declared herself on his side too plainly for me to struggle further with her humoursome ladyship."

"We have yet to inquire," said Charles thoughtfully, "what the fair lady's sentiments may be towards this fortunate adventurer."

"By the mass!" said Crèvecoeur, "I have but too much reason to believe your Grace will find her more amenable to authority than on former occasions.—But why should I grudge this youth his preferment? since, after all, it is sense, firmness, and gallantry, which have put him in possession of WEALTH, RANK, AND BEAUTY!"